The Callaway men are about to capture a few more hearts! Annette Broadrick's irresistible heroes are coming home again. Are you ready for them?

Praise for Annette Broadrick

"Annette Broadrick's glorious love stories always sparkle with irresistible joy and grace."
—Melinda Helfer, *Romantic Times*

MARRIAGE TEXAS STYLE!
"Enjoy this unusual tale of love found and allowed to mature as well as danger finally discovered and a villain overcome."
—*Heartland Critiques*

TEMPTATION TEXAS STYLE!
"Ms. Broadrick provides lots of warm fuzzies for romance devotees in this delightful outing."
—*Romantic Times*

ANNETTE BROADRICK

is a native of Texas, currently residing in the hill country of central Texas. Fascinated by the complexities found in all relationships, she continues to write about life and love, joy and fulfillment, and the bountiful gifts that are bestowed upon us as we travel along life's path.

SONS OF TEXAS

COWBOYS AND WEDDING BELLS

ANNETTE BROADRICK

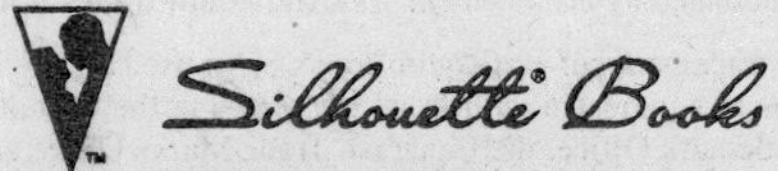

Published by Silhouette Books
America's Publisher of Contemporary Romance

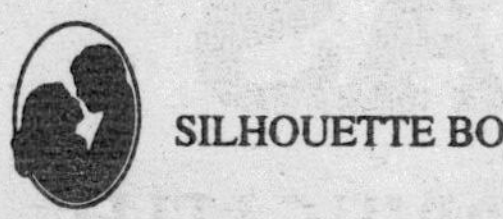

SILHOUETTE BOOKS

ISBN 0-373-20157-5

by Request

SONS OF TEXAS: COWBOYS AND WEDDING BELLS

This edition published by arrangement with Harlequin Books S.A.

Printed in U.S.A.

CONTENTS

MARRIAGE TEXAS STYLE! 9

TEMPTATION TEXAS STYLE! 193

Dear Reader,

I had no idea when I first started writing about the Callaways of Texas that they would become so much a part of my life. Although I wasn't raised on a ranch, I always enjoyed visiting them and watching the work that goes into making a ranch successful.

The fictitious Callaways go back for several generations in southwest Texas. They fought to keep the land in the family, working it, sacrificing their lives to it. Being a Callaway carried its own responsibility—the name stood for something in that part of the land. Over the years, the name grew to mean something all over Texas.

Each succeeding generation had a great deal to live up to, and some found that easier to do than others.

Sons of Texas: Love and Courtship! featured Cole's and Cameron's stories. In this collection we have an uncle—Cody—only ten years older than his nephew—Tony. Each of these men had his own struggles with being a part of the Callaway clan.

Cody rebelled. He didn't want any part of the grueling responsibilities that weighed down his two older brothers. So he took another direction that eventually led him back to his roots.

Funny how that seems to happen to all of us, sooner or later.

Tony, on the other hand, didn't know anything about his Callaway heritage until he was a teenager, which caused him a great deal of pain, turmoil and a need to redefine who he thought he was. He also had to decide how he wanted to relate to the others bearing that name.

It's almost amusing to watch these men—these sons of Texas—as they fight to claim their own independence. We have us a couple of mavericks here, who don't care to be corralled, roped or broken to reins of any kind.

I hope you enjoy their stories. I hope you enjoy watching them come to terms with who they are and how they adjust to everything that happens to them.

Most of all, I hope that you fall in love with the men of the Callaway clan—Cole, Cameron, Cody and Tony—as completely as I have over the years.

Enjoy.

Annette Broadrick

MARRIAGE TEXAS STYLE!

CALLAWAY FAMILY TREE

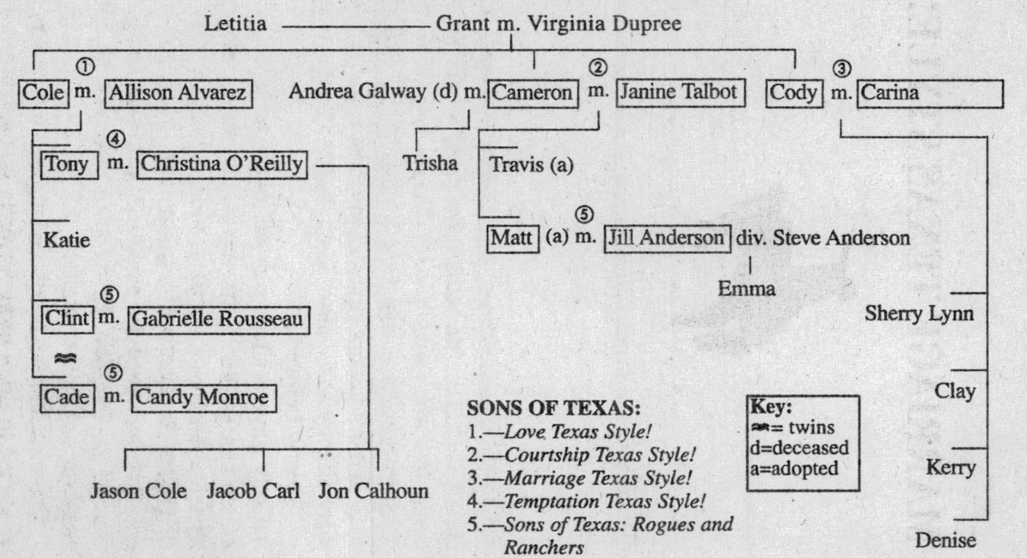

SONS OF TEXAS:

1.—*Love Texas Style!*

2.—*Courtship Texas Style!*

3.—*Marriage Texas Style!*

4.—*Temptation Texas Style!*

5.—*Sons of Texas: Rogues and Ranchers*

Key:
≈ = twins
d=deceased
a=adopted

Prologue

Cody Callaway slipped inside the rear door of the crowded church. He wasn't surprised to see that the event had the pews packed tightly. After a quick glance around the room, he leaned against the back wall and folded his arms. The bride and the groom were already at the altar. The minister began to speak.

"Dearly beloved..."

Cody gave a silent sigh of relief. At least he had gotten here in time for the actual ceremony. Absently, he felt the knot of his tie to make certain it was still in place. He was not a suit-and-tie man. He could count on one hand the number of times he had gotten dressed up like this. He kept his gaze on the couple standing before the minister.

Funerals and weddings. Strange how a person was supposed to dress more formally at such times. He'd been to his share of funerals, unfortunately. A wedding was a much more pleasant reason to dig out his respectable clothes.

He searched the wedding party and recognized most of the faces. His oldest brother, Cole, stood by the groom, obviously filling the position of best man for his brother Cameron.

Cole's wife, Allison, was one of the attendants for the bride.

In one of the first few rows he saw his Aunt Letitia, dabbing at her eyes. Was it possible the woman had a heart beneath that stiff exterior? His gaze swept over the attendants, then darted back to one face in particular. His twenty-year-old nephew, Tony, stood there, almost as tall as his father, Cole. My God, wasn't the kid ever going to stop growing?

The sonorous voice of the minister continued.

His family. Cody struggled to handle the emotion that welled up inside him. He had almost missed a very important occasion in the history of his family—his brother Cameron's wedding. As much as he resented the media's intense interest in anything and everything the Callaways did, if news of the wedding hadn't been splashed all over the newspapers when he crossed into McAllen, Texas, from Mexico that morning he would never have known about the event until it was too late to attend.

Even so, he had almost missed it. He had driven like a bat out of hell to reach the Circle C Ranch—the family's headquarters—only to discover that his aunt and most of the ranch help had already left. He had searched for and found the suit that he had worn at Cole's wedding...when was that? Five years ago...six?

He had seen very little of his family during the past

few years; he had seen nothing of them in the past six months. He knew that he would hear plenty on that subject after the wedding. He smiled to himself. There was something pleasurable in being able to predict his family's reactions. He would feel that he was truly back home once the family began cataloging his many irritating traits...such as disappearing without a trace for months at a time.

He watched Cameron slip a ring on his bride's finger. Janine looked radiant standing there beside his tall brother, Cody thought. Cody had met her last spring, as he recalled, the same weekend that Cameron had met her. Even then, he had seen the sparks fly between the two of them. He shouldn't have been surprised at the outcome.

Movement near the bride caught his eye, and Cody saw Cameron's six-year-old daughter fussing with her ruffled dress. He was comforted by the thought that Trisha now had a mother. From the adoring glances she continued to give her former preschool teacher, Cody guessed she was quite pleased with the situation.

Thank God, Cameron had found a new love. When his wife, Andrea, was killed in the accident that almost took Cameron's life, Cody and Cole had worried that Cameron would never snap out of the despair he had experienced. The accident had been no accident, in Cody's mind. A similar mishap had killed both of his parents many years before. Cody had never believed in coincidences.

Following up on years of old leads had led him to spending most of his time south of the Texas-Mexico border. Without knowing about the wedding, he had returned north to discuss his latest findings with Cole. Thank God, he hadn't postponed the trip another day.

He had missed his family more than he would have thought possible. Orphaned at ten, Cody had learned through necessity to be self-reliant and self-sufficient. Although he had two older brothers and an overbearing aunt, Cody had learned to go his own way for almost twenty years now. He knew that part of his independence had been due to the unholy glee he felt in irritating and thwarting Aunt Letty's need to dominate and control those around her. His independence eventually became a habit...a way of life.

Cody watched as Cameron slipped his arm around Janine and leaned down to kiss her. His tenderness touched Cody as nothing else had in a long time. His brothers had found happiness in relationships that evolved into marriage. Cody could almost envy that closeness, except that he knew he would be stifled in a similar relationship.

What worked for Cole and Cameron would never work for him. He treasured his freedom too much. However, he could celebrate their happiness with his family. For this little while, he could include himself in the Callaway family circle.

The swell of a triumphant wedding march filled the church. The spectators stood and watched the happy couple start up the aisle toward the exit near where Cody stood. He wasn't certain what caught Cameron's eye, but his brother glanced in his direction. The wide grin of recognition and joy at his presence caused a lump to form in Cody's throat. What was it about weddings that tugged at people's emotions? He gave Cameron a thumbs-up sign of approval and a smile.

By the time the wedding party and all the onlookers and well-wishers had emptied out of the church, Cody had been spotted by several members of the family.

"Uncle Cody! Uncle Cody! You came!" Trisha came tearing across the sidewalk and flung herself at him.

He lifted her high into his arms and was rewarded by a life-threatening squeeze around his neck. "You look like a princess, sweetheart," he managed to say when he could get some wind back into his lungs.

She patted her dress. "I know," she admitted with a great deal of satisfaction, causing Cody to laugh.

A deep voice interrupted him. "I'm glad you were able to make it today," Cole said, holding out his hand. Cody ignored the offering and threw his other arm around his brother. "It's good to see you, Cole. I'm glad I could be here." He could see the color flood his brother's face. Cole had always had trouble with public displays of affection. Flashbulbs were going off all around them. Cody grinned, thinking about possible captions that might accompany such a picture.

"I did everything I could to find you," Cole admitted. "You've got a damn good way of disappearing."

Cody nodded. "I didn't mean to stay away so long, Cole. The past six months have been crazy. I've managed to get some information that you'll want to hear, once we have a little privacy." He hitched Trisha higher on his hip for emphasis. Glancing around at the milling people, he said, "Allison looks great. Didn't you mention something about expecting twins the last time we talked?"

Trisha clapped her hands. "Oh, yes, Uncle Cody!

Katie has two little bitty brothers called Clint and Cade. They make funny faces and gurgly sounds, and once I got to hold Clint.''

Cole's grin was filled with pride. ''We left the twins in Austin with their nurse. Allison had all she could handle today with Katie.'' The two men glanced over to where Allison stood visiting with some of the local people, her small daughter bouncing by her side as if she were on a pogo stick.

''How old are they now?'' Cody asked.

''Almost three months. They were a little early but, thank God, they were all right.'' He lifted a brow and drawled, ''You think you could hang around long enough to be introduced to them?''

Cody met his brother's level gaze. ''Not this time, I'm afraid. I've got to head back south in a few hours. I came up to see you, but I didn't expect to find you at a wedding.'' He glanced across the church grounds at Cameron and Janine. ''I'm so glad I managed to get here. Seeing Cameron happy again was worth the effort.''

''How did you hear about the wedding, anyway?''

Cody grinned. ''Can a Callaway do anything in this state without it being reported in some fashion? I happened to pick up a paper when I stopped in McAllen for coffee.''

''So none of my messages reached you?''

Cody shook his head.

''I don't like it, Cody. I'm not trying to pry into your affairs, dammit, but it wouldn't be asking all that much to have some way to contact you in an emergency, now, would it?''

''Shame on you, Uncle Cole. You aren't supposed to cuss,'' Trisha pointed out sternly.

"So I'm told," Cole admitted with a sheepish grin. "I do humbly apologize, Miss Callaway."

"Well, just don't do it again," she replied in her best schoolmarm voice.

Both men laughed at her perfect mimicry of their Aunt Letty.

"Cody!" Allison had spotted him and was hurrying to him, Katie clutched in her arms. Heads turned in his direction and Cody almost winced. He had never cared for the attention being a Callaway drew, even though he had eventually learned to deal with the inevitability of public exposure. He schooled his expression to reveal nothing of his discomfort, lowering Trisha to the sidewalk just in time to catch his petite sister-in-law in his arms. "Oh, Cody!" Tears made her black eyes glisten. "We've been so worried about you! I'm so glad you made it." She gave him a ferocious hug. "Have you met Janine yet?"

He hugged her back. "I met her the same weekend Cameron did, last spring. I'm glad to see they made a match of it. It's good to see him smiling again."

She laughed. "Now you're the last holdout in the family, Cody. We're going to have to find you a wife!"

He shook his head, not having to simulate horror. "No way, Allison. I think it's great Cole and Cameron are married. Cole seems to be singlehandedly populating the region with Callaways." He grinned when she blushed. "I'm just not the marrying kind."

"Well," she replied, cocking her head, "I must admit that a wife would want to see you more than once or twice a year."

Before Cody could reply, he heard Cole mutter under his breath, "Brace yourself, bro. Here comes Aunt

Letty.'' They looked at each other, recognizing their shared response toward the woman marching over to him.

Cody sighed. He would rather be engaged in battle with a gang of Mexican bandits than deal with the woman who had been in charge of him for so many years.

Family. That was what it was all about. You could love 'em, fight with 'em, leave 'em and marry 'em off. Regardless, you stood by them, just as Cole was doing now. He might give his brother hell, but he would defend him whenever anyone else attempted to do the same.

Family. What would he do without them?

Several hours later, Cody and Cole sat in the study located in the Big House at the Circle C Ranch. Cody had to admire the way his brother cleared the way for the two of them to leave the reception early so they could get back to the ranch and talk.

At the moment they were enjoying a couple of belated congratulatory cigars. Their coats and ties had been discarded and a crystal decanter of bourbon sat between them on the desk.

''So what have you got?'' Cole asked.

Cody studied the ash that clung to the end of his very expensive cigar. ''Does the name Enrique Rodriguez mean anything to you?'' he finally asked, looking up at his brother.

''That's a rather common name in this part of the country, Cody. You know that.''

''Yeah, I know. Let's go back to a little family history. When our ancestor, Caleb Callaway, came to Texas, he managed to acquire this ranch from a Spanish don whose family had lived here for several generations."

Cole gave him a sharp look. "The Rodriguez family."

"That's correct."

"Do you think there's some link between the thievery, accidents and anonymous threats we've been experiencing at some of our companies and that ancient history?"

"I believe there's a strong possibility. I've talked with many people in the past few years, in an effort to get to the bottom of all these seemingly unrelated incidents. What has slowly emerged is a psychological profile of a person filled with bitterness, resentment and hatred toward anyone or anything connected with the Callaways. About six months ago, I was given the name Enrique Rodriguez. In finding out more about him, I discovered that he's a direct descendant of the family that originally owned the ranch."

"Good God, Cody. The Callaways acquired this land almost a hundred years ago. How could someone still be holding a grudge?"

"Enrique, or Kiki as his friends call him, seems to hold the Callaway family responsible for every bad thing that ever happened to him since he was born. He was fed all of the family bitterness and resentment along with his mother's milk. Every time we get mentioned in the news, more fuel is added, because his family's fortunes have continued to deteriorate over the years."

"Didn't Caleb win the place in a game of cards?"

"That's the story I always heard."

"Is this Enrique accusing the Callaways of stealing the land?"

"I don't think he's gone quite that far, but then, again, I wouldn't put it past him."

"How old is he?"

"In his forties." Cody leaned forward, resting his elbows on his knees. "I think Enrique may be responsible for the accident that killed Andrea and almost killed Cameron five years ago."

Cole carefully set his glass down. "The accident we never quite believed was an accident," he murmured. "Then we were right in our suspicions."

"From what I've been able to find out from my contacts, the man is capable of the act, and he was seen in the area during that time."

Cole caught the part Cody had hoped to gloss over. "Your contacts," he repeated, in a level tone of voice that didn't fool Cody in the least.

Cody sighed. Even though he had received permission from his immediate superior, he didn't relish telling Cole what he had been doing for the past four years.

So he hedged. "You know how it is. I come into contact with all kinds of people when I'm out roaming the countryside."

"Ah. You must be talking about your well-known reputation—how you've made a career out of being the wild, youngest son—the one who runs with the fastest crowds, drives the flashiest cars, and is seen with the most glamourous women."

The ten-year age difference between them had never seemed so wide to Cody. He understood that gulf much better now that he was an adult. It was more than age—it was the vast difference in their life experiences. Cole had been forced by circumstances to take on tremendous responsibilities by the time he was twenty, forced to mature before he'd had an opportunity to enjoy the life of the oldest son of a privileged family. Cody had never envied Cole his role in the family dynasty. The responsibilities thrust upon Cole would have destroyed a lesser man.

"Is this where you're going to lecture me on my wasted life?" he asked Cole, with a wry grin.

Cole took a sip of his whiskey before replying. "I might, if I believed it."

Cody straightened, staring at the older man. "What's that supposed to mean?"

"I don't know what you're really up to, Cody, but I don't believe this reputation you've gone to such pains to build up. I know you too well. There are too many unexplained absences in your life, between bouts of lavish living and conspicuous consumption. Would you be willing to enlighten me on what's been going on?"

Cody felt like a schoolboy who thought he had been getting away with something, only to discover the teacher had known what he was doing all along. Thankful for the clearance he had received earlier from his boss, he said, "I've been using my reputation to cover my activities along the border."

"Which are?"

"I'm working with the DEA."

Cole froze, his eyes narrowing. "The hell you are. Since when?"

"Almost four years."

"Four years! You mean all this time you've been pretending to— Then all these parties and—"

Cody couldn't recall ever seeing Cole at a loss for

words before. Even though Cole admittedly had suspected something didn't quite ring true about Cody's life-style, obviously he hadn't come close to guessing the truth. Cody savored the moment. He found it reassuring to know that even Cole could be rattled upon occasion. Somehow it made him endearingly human.

"The agency suggested we use my playboy image as a cover. It's been a good one. My name has opened doors to many places that another agent could not have managed."

"No wonder I haven't been able to find you," Cole murmured almost to himself after a few minutes.

"You're right that you need to know where to contact me in case of an emergency. I'll give you a number to call."

"So you're working in Mexico."

"For the most part, yes. I'm working with several agents, some with our government, others are with the Mexican government. I'm doing everything I can to stem the flow of drugs across the border."

"Is this Enrique involved with drug smuggling?"

"I can't tell at this point. My investigation of him has had to be done in my spare time. I was fortunate to find out that he has been seen in the area I'm working. That was an unexpected break."

"So what are you going to do now?"

"I've got to get back. There's a series of meetings I'm to attend that may break the case we've been working on for the last couple of years. However, I wanted to get Enrique's name to you. If something should happen to me, I want you to follow up on my investigation."

"Are things heating up for you?"

"Enough."

"Is what you are doing worth risking your life for?"

"I think so."

Cole slowly stood up and held out his hand. Cody stood and clasped his brother's hand in a firm grip. "If I can help, let me know," Cole said quietly.

"You already have, by just listening. I finally received clearance to tell you what I'm doing. One of the big honchos in D.C. went to school with you and considers you trustworthy."

"Glad to hear it," Cole drawled. He punched Cody's shoulder. "Keep in touch as much as you can, will you?"

"I'll do my best."

Cody walked out of the study, down the wide hallway to the massive front door. He walked out and got into his car without looking back at the only home he'd ever known.

One

The tiny snick of sound made by someone turning the knob on the door would have gone unnoticed, had Cody been asleep. However, the airless primitive room directly over a raucous Mexican cantina did not lend itself to quiet, restful sleep. Cody had decided a couple of hours ago that his choice of a room would never meet the AAA requirements for travel accommodations.

He had been lying there for what seemed to be hours, gazing at the pattern of light on the wall reflected from the gaudy neon sign flickering its liquid-refreshment advertisement outside his window. He had been thinking about his recent visit with his family and questioning his sanity in choosing this particular life-style. He could have been at home in his very comfortable bed, instead of lying there on the lumpy mattress unable to sleep.

When he discovered that there was no lock on the door, he had considered placing the only chair in the room beneath the doorknob. After a moment of deliberation, he had decided against the idea. He had doubted that anyone would be foolish enough to bother him.

Obviously, he had miscalculated.

No doubt whoever was intruding either had the wrong room or was under the erroneous impression he would be easy pickin's for a thief because he was *un americano.*

Cody reached beneath his pillow and slid the pistol hidden there into the palm of his hand. Making no sound, he eased from the narrow bed and in a few silent strides stood directly behind the door.

The cheap bulb in the hallway cast a thin stripe of light on the wooden floor when the door eased open. Cody watched the laser-thin line widen, then suddenly disappear as a body noiselessly stepped into the room.

Before the door closed completely, he got a glimpse of a feminine profile and long hair. In a low growl directly behind the unknown woman, he said, "I don't care what you're selling, sweetheart, I'm not buying. Now get out."

She gasped and whirled around to face him. "Cody?" she whispered urgently.

The flickering light coming through the dirty glass window caught the side of the woman's face as she turned, but even without the sight of her face he would have recognized her by the sound of her voice. Carina Ramirez was the only woman he knew who spoke his name in quite that way, her husky voice invariably accenting the second syllable of his name.

Shock ran through his body, with the realization

that Carina was in his room. His mind whirled with all the reasons why this person could not possibly be here. The young girl would be the last female to enter a man's room at this late hour—or any other hour, for that matter.

The word he muttered was short and unprintable. Despite all logic, Cody had to accept the physical evidence before him. She was actually standing there.

What the hell was she doing there? She had absolutely no business being anywhere around him.

Then he suddenly realized that he was standing there buck naked. Her eyes would soon be adjusting to the light. His friend Alfonso's extremely sheltered little sister was about to receive the shock of her life.

Fury and embarrassment swept over him in equal parts. Thrust into a situation not of his own making, Cody felt the helplessness of not being the one in control. He didn't like the feeling at all.

He reached for his worn jeans and growled, "What in the hell are you doing here, Carina?" He kept his voice low, even though he didn't expect anyone outside the room to be able to hear over the racket of loud music and strident voices coming from downstairs.

He tugged the tight jeans up over his muscled calves and thighs, keeping his back to her in an effort to save them both from further embarrassment.

"Cody, I had to come," she said from behind him, her voice trembling. "I had to w-warn you." Her voice broke on the last words.

He glanced over his shoulder, while he zipped his jeans. Turning to face her, he frowned and asked, "Warn me? What about?"

The light fell across her face for a moment. In the

wash of bright colors dancing over her, he could see her expressive black eyes staring up at him, imploring him to believe her. "Some men, they are coming here. They plan to kill you."

Whatever was going on, Cody knew that Carina fully believed what she was saying. Her wide eyes, trembling lips and tense body eloquently spoke to him.

He took her gently by the arm and led her to the bed. Easing her down to sit beside him, he took her hand in an attempt to comfort her. She was little more than a child, after all. Whatever had pushed her into braving her brother's wrath and risking her reputation had to be taken seriously, regardless of his doubts. Perhaps she had misunderstood what she had heard. After all, why would anyone be plotting against him in her hearing?

She lived with her brother, a wealthy landowner whose hacienda sprawled in the foothills of the Sierra Madres, an hour's drive from Monterrey. Cody and Alfonso had known each other for the four years since Cody began to work on this side of the border. They had become friends.

Surely, no one at the hacienda would have reason to want Cody dead.

He reached out and pushed a wave of hair away from her face. Cody could well understand Alfonso's protectiveness of his young sister. There was no denying Carina's delicate beauty...from the midnight black of her hair, which rippled down her back like a waterfall, to her mysteriously dark eyes, which slanted ever so slightly above her high cheekbones. Even in the poor light, her fair skin glowed like the finest of porcelain.

Alfonso was justifiably proud of his beautiful, young sister and guarded her from the men who visited him, Cody included.

In the four years he had known Alfonso and his sister, Cody had never been alone with her. Looking at her now, he could not ignore the fact that she had grown into an exotic beauty. However, the innocence in her shining eyes reflected how untouched she was by the world around her.

Placing her small hand between his large ones, he searched for and managed to find a soothing tone, before he said, "Tell me about these men, *chula.* Do you know them? Have you seen them before?"

The light from the street lamps betrayed the color in her cheeks at his term of endearment, but her gaze never wavered.

"I was in my room. I had left the doors to my balcony open for air. I hadn't gone to sleep yet when I heard voices coming from the courtyard below. Curious to see who was there, I tiptoed over to the door and peered out. They were directly beneath my bedroom balcony so that I couldn't see them, but I heard some of their conversation quite clearly. The room was dark and they had no way of knowing that I was there." Her voice shook so that he had to concentrate in order to understand her.

He slipped his arm around her and pulled her closer in an effort to comfort her. "Don't be afraid, little one. It's okay, now. Take a couple of deep breaths...that's it. Relax. You managed to find me. Nobody is going to hurt either one of us. Not if I can help it." He ran a soothing hand down her back and hugged her close to his chest. "Can you tell me what these men were saying?"

She pushed back and looked at him with an imploring expression. ''But Cody, we must hurry. I don't know how much time we have before they show up here. They were planning to come tonight.''

He glanced around the room with frustration. He could deal with a couple of men coming after him much easier than he could deal with having Alfonso's sister sitting there trying to save him. If someone *was* plotting to take him out, he had to get her out of there. But he needed more information. Fast.

''Carina,'' he said, placing his hands on her shoulders. ''Listen to me. I need to know what you overheard. Tell me.''

She drew in some air, emitting a soft sob, before she answered. ''I didn't recognize their voices. There were two of them, one with a deep voice. I had difficulty hearing *everything* he said. But I recognized your name and began to listen. They were talking about you being in their way and that it was time to get rid of you.''

A bolt of adrenaline shot through him. Perhaps his work was finally netting some results. He must be getting close to some drug sources who were feeling the pressure, but the last place he had expected to find them was at the home of Alfonso Ramirez.

''Did they say why they had to get rid of me?''

''Only that they didn't trust you. They think you work for the government.'' She sounded puzzled and uncertain.

What had he done to arouse suspicion? Perhaps nothing. All Americans south of the border were watched by those in the drug trade. There was no reason for him to believe that his cover had been blown.

There could also be other explanations to what she had overheard.

"Did they mention any other names that you can recall?"

She was silent for a moment. He assumed she was trying to remember when she finally lifted her head and he saw the agonized expression on her face. "Only one. Alfonso."

"Alfonso! Did you warn him, as well?"

Tears trickled down her cheeks and she shook her head. In a tone so low it was almost inaudible, she whispered, "No. I am afraid that it is Alfonso who told them to get rid of you."

Cody stiffened. This latest shock, coming as it did after a series of them, almost caused him to reel. He and Alfonso had never discussed Cody's reasons for spending so much time in Mexico. They had accepted each other at face value, finding they had a great deal in common. After running a check on Alfonso, Cody had been relieved to find that Alfonso had a clean record and was a very respected businessman who was above suspicion. Over the years, he had begun to trust Alfonso more and more.

How could he have so completely misjudged a person? Had Alfonso been secretly watching and laughing at Cody's naive acceptance of him? Was Alfonso the man whose organization he had been seeking all this time?

The irony of Alfonso's sister coming to warn him was not lost on Cody. The question was, what was he going to do with her now?

"How did you get here, *chula?*" He knew the small village was at least ten miles from the hacienda, much too far for her to have walked. A car leaving the hacienda would have been noticed immediately. Had she placed herself in danger by her foolhardy need to warn him?

"I slipped out of the house as soon as I could after the men left the courtyard. I knew I had to warn you, but I didn't know how. You mentioned at dinner tonight that you were staying here in the village, so I tried to think of a way to reach you without anyone in the household knowing. I didn't know what else to do, so I finally slipped away and ran to the house of Berto, my friend Angelina's brother. When I explained to him that I needed to see you tonight, he agreed to bring me to the village. Because I knew the cantina had the only rooms available for visitors I came up the back steps, looking for you. I peeked into the other two rooms, but they were empty." Her smile was filled with relief when she added, "I was very happy to finally find you."

The thought of what could have happened to her if those other two rooms hadn't been empty, the thought of the many risks she had been taking on his behalf, infuriated him and he exploded with barely suppressed anger.

"For hell's sake, Carina. Couldn't you have just sent me word of what you overheard? You should never have taken the risk of slipping out this late at night. Any number of unspeakable things could have happened to you."

Even the thought of some of them unnerved him.

A silent pause was interrupted by the sound of breaking glass, and boisterous laughter drifted up to them from the cantina below. The music never faltered. They faced each other.

She nodded slightly and said with a quiet dignity,

"Berto offered to give you a message, but I didn't want him to know my suspicions. He thinks I am enamored of you—" her cheeks filled with color "—and I allowed him to believe it. Besides, I didn't think you would accept such a message from a stranger. I knew that I must come myself."

Cody could no longer stay seated. He stood up and began to pace. "All right," he growled, running his hand through his hair. "Fine." He reached the end of the room and turned, pacing toward her. "I can follow your reasoning, even if I'm appalled by the chances you took." He sat down beside her and reached for his boots. While he was pulling them on, he said, "I want you to know that I appreciate what you've done for me." He grabbed his shirt and slid his arms inside the long sleeves. "Now, then, you let me handle the situation from here. Run back downstairs and have your friend Berto take you home. Hopefully, nobody has discovered that you're not tucked into bed sound asleep." He reached out to her and she took his hand, allowing him to pull her to her feet.

He turned away and headed toward the door. He had his hand on the doorknob when she spoke behind him.

"I told Berto not to wait—that I would visit with you and that you would see that I got back home safely."

Cody felt another shock run through him. This was obviously his night for calamity in various shapes and forms. What the hell was he going to do with her? How could she have blithely planned to warn him, then expect him to see to her safety, as well? Slowly he turned to face her, unable to hide his reaction to this latest tidbit of unwelcome information. Before he could find the necessary words to tell her exactly what he thought of her behavior, she nodded toward the door and, in the calmest voice he had heard from her since she first arrived, said, "We can't go that way. It is too dangerous."

Ignoring the fact that she had obviously decided that they were a team working together, he glanced around the room. Other than the two windows overlooking the street, there was only a small opening with a grill cover placed high on the side wall for ventilation. He walked over to the windows and looked out. There was a great deal of activity along the street, despite the late hour. Even if he felt like playing Tarzan to Carina's Jane by swinging out of one of the windows and lowering both of them to the ground, they couldn't possibly escape that way without attracting attention.

He looked back at her, frustrated by her newfound mood of quiet dignity. "What do you suggest we do, then?" he asked irritably.

She pointed to the small ventilation opening.

Cody knew for a fact that a steep ravine ran alongside the building on that side. There was a good twenty-foot drop. "Forget it. We'd break our necks."

"No! Please listen, Cody. Berto and I discussed it when we first arrived. No one would think to watch this side of the building. He found a ladder in the back and we propped it against the wall between the two rooms on this side. Luckily, you weren't in the room on the opposite wall. We would have had to come up with something else."

"And how did you manage to explain to Berto our possible need for a ladder? Does he think this is some kind of an elopement?" Cody could feel himself losing control of some of his frustrated anger and clenched his teeth.

"Not exactly. I just told him that I didn't want to be caught in your room, so we thought about another way out, just in case."

Cody sighed. Save him from overimaginative children. He couldn't allow her to stampede him into doing something silly. Hell, he didn't need to run. He wanted to find out more about these two characters. The only way he could do that would be to hang around and form a welcoming committee of one.

He fished into the pocket of his jeans and brought out his car keys. "Look, *chula,* I don't need an escape route. If someone's looking for me, I want them to find me. I want to know who's after me and exactly what they want."

He walked over and took her hand, placing the keys in her palm and curling her fingers around them. "Here. I want you to take my car and go home. Use some discretion about where you leave it, so I won't be accused of sneaking back to the hacienda for some obscure reason. Maybe we can save your reputation, yet. Perhaps it would be a good idea if you did slip out another way. There's no reason to take any more chances than we need to, at this point."

"Please, Cody. You must leave as well. I don't want anything to happen to you. If you won't come, then I will stay here, too. Between the two of us, maybe we can—"

"Dammit, Carina! You're being ridiculous. What possible use do you think—"

He paused in his tirade, listening. The noise from downstairs still reverberated throughout the building, but he had just heard a protesting squeak of the aging floor outside his doorway, signaling that he was about to receive more company.

He realized that his time had run out. He could stand there and debate the issue with this wisp of a girl, and possibly get both of them killed, or he could go along with her escape plan. Since someone was already outside the door, he had little choice but to accept her alternative route.

Grabbing the chair, he quickly—and with a minimum of sound—wedged the back beneath the doorknob, then took her hand and pulled her across the room. Lifting her above him, he waited while she removed the grill, then scrambled through the opening. He checked to make sure his pistol was in the waistband of his jeans at the small of his back, while she lowered herself out of sight.

Grabbing the sill of the opening he pulled himself up, then through the narrow opening. He had a tougher time getting his larger body through the small area than Carina had. He was forced to place one shoulder through at a time, then pretend to be a contortionist, in order to swing his legs out toward the ladder.

There was barely enough light to create shadows, and Cody felt a momentary relief when his foot brushed against the ladder. He lowered himself, finding a couple of rungs where he could brace himself.

None too soon. He heard the doorknob rattle as he quickly climbed down the ladder.

When he reached the bottom he glanced around, peering into the gloom. He felt a small hand grab his and tug him away from the wall.

The area on this side of the cantina had been allowed to return to nature. The steep slopes and heavy underbrush obviously had discouraged the citizens of the small settlement from cleaning the area out of a civic need to beautify the town's landscape. Cody had cause to feel grateful at that moment for the townspeople's lack of pride, as he and Carina moved through the heavy brush deeper into the ravine and away from the noisy cantina. The brush was vicious to move through, tearing at their clothing, but Cody didn't lessen his pace. Now that his course of action had been set, he was determined to get Carina away from the area until he felt it was safe to circle to where he had hidden his car just outside the town, then get her home.

He continued to follow the twists and turns of the ravine, but the going was slow without light. Carina had prudently dressed in black slacks and sweater, so that only her face was a faint blur in the shadows.

She hadn't made a sound since they had left the room. He was amazed at her bravery. Everything had happened so fast. His brain was still sorting and filing away the information he had received in the past few minutes. He didn't doubt that Carina had heard something definite enough for her to risk dire consequences in her effort to warn him.

He just wished that she had gotten a glimpse of the men. Since she had not recognized their voices, there was a good chance they were not part of the group that had gathered for dinner at the hacienda earlier that evening.

The thought that Alfonso might be behind this threat shook him. Could his instincts have been so wrong about the man? During the years he had worked in this area, he had uncovered several pockets of drug smuggling and seen them stopped. He felt useful and he felt that his time was well spent.

Alfonso Ramirez and his home had offered a haven of sorts, a place for Cody to visit in order to rest and relax. Alfonso had been insistent earlier that night that Cody stay at the hacienda, but Cody had planned to get an early start to Monterrey and hadn't wanted to disturb the household by his early departure.

Had his refusal to stay forced Alfonso into a change of plans? Could his friend be plotting to have him killed? The thought sickened him. He would not have given the matter a moment's consideration if Carina had not felt that he was in danger and that the danger came from Alfonso.

What must that have done to her? Cody continued to be amazed that she had chosen to contact him. He still couldn't fathom her reasons for doing so. Although he had seen her often during the years, and had treated her with the kindly indulgence of an uncle to a young girl, Cody could not recall anything he might have said or done that would justify her possible betrayal of her brother's plans in order to save Cody.

Her courageous actions baffled him.

The one thing he was absolutely sure of was that he had to get her back to the hacienda before she was discovered missing. Whatever else happened, he must protect her from her own impulsive behavior.

When he finally paused for breath, Cody discovered that they were only a few yards from a dirt road. Still holding Carina's hand in a firm clasp, he led her through the remaining underbrush out onto the road.

As though celebrating their escape, the moon came from behind a low-hanging cloud and flooded the surrounding landscape with a silvery radiance that filled Cody with relief. With light and a decent road to follow, he would be able to find his car in no time.

He turned to Carina in time to see a shadow separate itself from a nearby clump of trees and grab Carina.

"What the—?" Cody felt a burst of pain at the back of his head. The fading moonlight was the last thing he remembered.

Two

Carina felt an arm snake around her throat at the same time she saw a shadowy figure strike Cody on the back of his head. She watched in horror as Cody fell in a crumpled heap at her feet. Without conscious thought she struggled to get away from whoever held her in an effort to see if Cody was badly hurt.

Surely they hadn't made good their intent to kill him!

She fought with desperation—kicking, biting and clawing at the arm around her throat. She caused enough damage to her captor that he let out a yell and released her, cursing. Ignoring the two men, she ran to where Cody lay and fell to her knees beside him.

"Cody? Are you all right? Oh, Cody," she whispered feeling the knot already forming at the base of his skull. She pressed her cheek against his, feeling his warmth and hearing his quiet breathing. She closed her eyes in relief, holding him.

One of the men grabbed her by the arm and yanked her to her feet. Carina winced, but refused to acknowledge the pain she felt from his grip. She realized, as she glanced up at the tall, shadowy man, that he was the one who had hit Cody. In Spanish, he began to tell off his companion for not hanging on to her. The man immediately answered with equal spirit in his own defense.

From what she could gather, these two men had been told to watch the ravine as a possible escape route. They had not really expected Cody to get this far. They certainly had not expected to find him with a woman.

The ensuing argument revolved around what to do with her. From listening to them, she discovered that they had explicit instructions not to harm Cody if they should catch him. She found that remark reassuring, although the knot on his head and his unconscious status revealed that at least one of the men had his own interpretation of harm.

Carina could feel her heart pounding in her chest. She couldn't remember another time in her life when she had been so frightened, not even when she had slipped away from the hacienda earlier and had hiked through the darkness to Berto's home. Obviously she had not overreacted to what she had heard. Cody was in grave danger, despite everything she could do.

Were these men part of the same group she had heard plotting? Was it possible there was more than one group looking for him?

Ever since she had heard Alfonso's name mentioned Carina had fought her pain and panic at the possibility that her brother could have ordered the death of their friend.

She still could not grasp what was happening. How could her brother possibly betray his friend? Cody had become a familiar figure in her life. She had been such a child the first time he had come to their home—barely sixteen, she knew that she looked more like twelve at the time. Despite her lack of stature, he had treated her as an adult—with teasing respect and a gentle dignity that had endeared him to her, causing her to look forward to the periodic visits of the tall and very attractive Texan.

When she had overheard those men earlier tonight, she had known immediately that Cody had to be warned. Since she couldn't be certain that Alfonso wasn't part of the conspiracy, she had to find a way to contact Cody, herself.

Now she was a part of whatever was going on. Her warning had not helped him at all.

The men had finally stopped arguing. They took what Carina assumed to be handkerchiefs and tied her hands and feet together, warning her that if she gave them any trouble they would knock her out as well. At least she knew Cody was alive. She would just have to wait and watch for a way to help him.

She cried out in shocked surprise when they covered her eyes. One of the men slapped her, hard, across the mouth, causing her lower lip to bleed. Helplessly she ran her tongue across her lip, feeling the puffiness forming. One of the men picked her up and carried her a brief distance, then placed her on a ridged surface that felt like the flooring of a pickup truck. Jostled by movement beside her she knew that Cody lay nearby. A truck engine started, causing a vibration in the surface beneath her cheek. The painful joltings of the truck bed told Carina they were moving, but she had no idea where they were going, or in what direction.

In an attempt to distract herself during the uncomfortable ride, Carina forced herself to think about more pleasant things. Her thoughts turned to Cody.

She would never forget the first time she saw him. She and her mother had been sitting in the courtyard of the hacienda when her brother had appeared in the doorway with a blond giant of a man who wore a heart-stopping grin on his handsome face.

"I can't believe this, Alfonso," she heard him saying. "Your place is practically a duplicate of the Big House on the Circle C Ranch. Of course, our family has added a couple of additions since the original hacienda, but if I didn't know better, I would think I was stepping into my mother's courtyard. Even the plants and flowers look familiar."

"I would like you to meet my mother and my sister, Carina," Alfonso said, motioning for the man to come toward them.

To Carina, he looked like a sun god, with the light glinting on his blond hair and tanned skin. He had taken her hand in his, and said, "I'm very pleased to meet you, Miss Ramirez." He glanced at Alfonso. "I envy you having a sister, something I've missed in my life." He went on to speak to her mother, and they had chatted, but Carina didn't pay much attention to the words. Instead, she focused on the sound of his deep voice, and watched the play of his smile across his lips.

A few years before she had read a magazine article about the Texas Callaways. The article had displayed several pictures of the three brothers. Even then, her eyes had been drawn to the blondest, the one with the winsome smile. She and her friend Angelina had giggled about how handsome the men were. She had never thought she would be able to meet one of them. Cody Callaway was even better-looking in person. As charming as he looked in the magazine, no picture could do justice to the magnetism that surrounded him, making him appear larger than life.

"I insist that you stay for dinner, Cody," Alfonso had said, and Carina had added her silent pleas.

"Well, if it wouldn't be too much trouble—" he drawled in reply, and Alfonso laughed.

"In this household, there is more than enough for everyone."

He had stayed and Carina had sat across from him at dinner, enthralled with his anecdotes, shy but pleased that he noticed her and teased her from time to time.

Over the years, Cody had added color and excitement to her otherwise boring routine of school and home life. Even after she had finished her schooling and returned to the hacienda permanently, she had looked forward to his visits, eager to listen to his stories and glimpse a freedom she had never experienced.

Looking back she could better understand the crush she had developed—not only on the man, but on all that he represented. Cody was different from anyone else in her life. She found him fascinating.

He had never encouraged her in any way to see him as anything but a family friend. Eventually the infatuation had turned into a comfortable friendship.

She had put her childish dreams away once she

knew what she wanted in her life. She wanted a taste of the freedom that had once fascinated her in Cody. She would always be grateful to Cody for giving her a glimpse of such a life.

However, she couldn't ignore what she had heard tonight, couldn't take the chance that by not getting word to Cody she might be contributing to his death.

She was not sorry that she had attempted to warn him. The only thing Carina regretted was that the warning had come too late to save him.

The first thing Cody saw when he managed to open his eyes were a pair of black eyes watching him worriedly. He blinked and groaned, the pain from the back of his head insistently making itself known.

"Cody? Are you all right?"

He closed his eyes again. That voice. He thought he had dreamed that Carina had come to his room, but she was still here. What the hell was she doing, hovering? Didn't she know he had the daddy of all hangovers? How could he entertain some innocent little—no, wait a minute. He hadn't been drinking. He and Carina had—

Cody opened his eyes again, trying to figure out where he was, where *they* were. He was lying on his back. With a sudden flash of memory he reached beneath him, but he knew before he felt along his waistband that his pistol was gone.

"Where are we?" he muttered in a gravelly voice. Damn, that was an original line if he had ever heard one. The universal question of all time, he supposed, pushing himself up on his elbows, then edging his legs over the side of the bed.

"Don't try to move, Cody. You may have a concussion. You need to lie still.'' Carina placed her hands upon his shoulders.

He ignored her efforts to restrain him, and forced himself to sit up and look around. ''Forget my head. I need to know where we are.''

As far as he could tell, they were in a one-room cabin. The sound of heavy rain falling against tin made him look up at the roof. From the obvious age of the place, they should be thankful the roof didn't leak.

The last thing he remembered was seeing the moon and thinking they were through the worst of it. Then one of the shadows had moved and—

He glanced around at Carina who was watching him with concern. ''Are you all right?'' he asked.

She nodded.

''Can you tell me how we got here?''

''Two men brought us. They tied me up and blindfolded me. I have no idea where we are. We seemed to have traveled for hours.'' She, too, glanced up at the roof. ''I think we were very fortunate to arrive before the rain started. We were in the back of an open pickup.''

Cody eased himself off the bed and gingerly made his way to one of the shuttered windows. ''Something tells me we weren't left alone here. Where are the men who brought us?''

''I haven't seen them. When the rain started, I heard them talking about leaving before they got stranded. I think we must be in an isolated part of the mountains. I peeked out the door earlier, but couldn't see anything at all.''

Cody rubbed the back of his head, feeling the large knot there, and cursed under his breath. He pulled open the shutter over the window and attempted to peer out, but the night and rain blocked his view.

He turned. "So why didn't they kill me? They had every opportunity."

"I don't know. I heard them discussing that they were only to guard against your escaping through the underbrush. I think they were more surprised than we were to see them."

"I wish to hell I knew what's going on...who's behind this."

"Perhaps we should leave here before someone comes back," Carina offered.

He had already thought of that. Had he been alone, Cody would have acted on the idea, but he couldn't go off and leave Carina, and he didn't dare drag her out into the elements without a clue to where they were or how far they were from help.

"Let's wait until morning. Maybe the weather will have cleared some by then." He prowled around the room, noting the antique wood-burning cookstove, which Carina must have stoked. There was a kettle of water steaming on top, while a small fire danced in the fireplace nearby.

He walked over to the sink and grabbed the pump handle there. After a couple of pumps, water came gushing forth. A row of canned goods sat on a shelf above the sink.

"At least we won't starve," he muttered.

"Are you hungry?"

He filled a glass with water and drank before answering. "No, just thirsty." He turned and looked at Carina, who had risen and was standing beside the only bed in the room. "Have you had any sleep?"

She shook her head. "I couldn't. I was afraid you might need something and I wouldn't hear you."

"Then you'd better try to get some rest. We may have a strenuous walk ahead of us when light comes."

She nodded, obviously seeing the sense in his suggestion. He watched as she stretched out on the bed where he had been a few minutes earlier. With a little sigh she closed her eyes, obviously exhausted. He walked over to her and picked up the folded blanket at the foot of the bed. He spread it over her, then turned away.

"Okay, Callaway," he muttered to himself. "You're always so good about getting yourself out of tight places. What do you intend to do now?"

He would be much happier if he had some idea where they were. How long had he been unconscious? He rubbed the back of his head. Whoever had slugged him knew what he was doing. He hadn't broken skin, but had inflicted damage.

Cody paced between the fireplace and the window, watching for any sign of light, artificial or from the sun. Once in a while he would glance at the sleeping girl. Had he been alone he would have handled all this so differently. He wouldn't think twice about getting away from here and finding a place to watch for anyone returning. If the weather let up, he would suggest that they leave the cabin, rather than sitting there waiting for their abductors to return.

The rain continued to beat down on the tin roof, creating a monotonous drumming. Eventually the sky lightened to a heavy gray, but the visibility was scarcely increased through the rain and haze. By midmorning the wind had picked up, causing the small cabin to shudder in the sudden blasts.

Cody went outside at first light and explored the area surrounding the cabin. Bluffs rose directly behind the cabin. He eventually found the trail with the recent tire tracks that marked their entry into the valley-like canyon. There was no sign that anyone else had been here in a long time.

Obviously they couldn't depend on a transit system to get them out of there. The cabin blended so well into the bluffs that it disappeared from view within a few hundred yards. Even the smoke from the chimney was camouflaged by the gray stone behind it.

By the time he returned to the cabin, he was soaked and more than a little disheartened.

Without saying anything to him when he burst inside the cabin and slammed the door, Carina filled a large mug with coffee and silently handed the steaming cup to him.

"Thanks," he said gruffly, reaching for the hot liquid.

"You need to get out of those clothes, Cody," she said softly, handing him a worn but clean towel and the quilt from the bed. She turned away and busied herself at the stove.

He knew she was right, but he didn't like the idea of stripping down. However, his choices were limited. With a muttered curse he sat down and pulled off his boots, then shucked out of his pants and unbuttoned his sodden shirt.

After briskly rubbing the towel over his chilled body he gratefully wrapped the quilt around him, draping one end over his shoulder, and sat down in front of the fireplace.

"Did you get some idea where we were?" she asked, filling a plate with hot food and handing it to him.

"Not a clue," he muttered. He placed the mug on the table and began to eat. When he was finished, he glanced up at her. "Aren't you going to eat?"

"I already have, while you were out." She turned away and walked over to the window. "Do you think we should attempt to find our way out of here?"

"Not in this weather. We're somewhere in the mountains, and they become treacherous after a hard rain. There's too much danger from flash flooding or softened trails that suddenly break away."

She turned back and met his eyes for the first time since she had awakened. "I've made things worse for you, haven't I?"

He glanced up from his contemplation of the fire dancing in the fireplace. "In what way?"

"Those men would not have been able to harm you. You would have heard them coming, as you did me, and been prepared. I've placed you in more danger, rather than helping you."

"You did what you felt you had to do, *chula.* I know you meant well, but a young girl like you shouldn't be exposed to this kind of thing—" he waved his hand to encompass the primitive cabin.

For the first time since they had been together, he saw a glint of amusement in her black eyes. "I don't consider twenty particularly young, Cody. Perhaps where you come—"

"Twenty!" Carefully setting the hot coffee down on the table, Cody came to his feet. "What are you talking about? You can't be twenty."

She raised her right hand and did a quick cross over

her heart with her left one. "I swear I am. How old did you think I was?"

He shrugged and turned away, feeling the heat of embarrassment steal across his face. "I dunno. Fourteen or fifteen, maybe. Just a kid."

She laughed, a light tinkling sound that Cody had always found to be infectious. "I may be young, Cody, but not *that* young!"

He forced himself to look at her again, this time with eyes that assessed what he saw, rather than what he remembered. Suddenly he felt old, much older than the ten years that made up the difference between them. Regardless of her age, Carina appeared to be untouched by life and some of the tough knowledge that can rip away the innocence of a young person.

He winced at the reminder.

"What's wrong?"

"I'm sure that Alfonso has missed you by now."

"Oh! That's probably true. Perhaps he will be looking for me," she started excitedly. Then, as though remembering the rest, she said, "What if he's the one who had you brought here?"

"Actually, that thought has crossed my mind. Is it possible that we're on part of his land?"

"I don't know. I haven't been able to tell much from the doorway and the window. I know that I've never seen this place before."

He rearranged his clothing in front of the fire, pleased at how quickly they were drying. If he did have to greet his captors, he would much prefer wearing more than his skivvies.

To preserve the little modesty he had managed to hang on to, Cody readjusted his quilt and sat back down. Motioning to the other chair he said, "Maybe you'd better sit down and tell me a little more about yourself. I seem to have missed something over the years—such as your growing up."

Carina sat down and folded her hands. "What would you like to know?"

"I thought you were a schoolgirl, obviously. Start there."

She cocked her head to the side, as though thinking. "Well, I did attend a parochial boarding school in Monterrey, until I graduated three years ago. Then, I attended the university in Mexico City for two years. At the moment Alfonso and I are at odds. I've had an offer to attend a university in the states. He wants me to stay here and get married."

"Married!" Cody repeated before he could stop himself. All right, there was no reason for her not to consider the matter at twenty, he supposed. "Is that what you want?"

She shook her head vehemently. "No way. I've been drawn to working with a special-education training, to help children with speech impediments to talk. I'm very interested in this and would like to make working with children a career. But Alfonso is so old-fashioned. He wants me safely married." She made a face. "He's already found me a husband. Hah! Someone that *he* approves of, of course."

"Do you know the man?"

"Yes. He's someone I've known for years, but I have absolutely no desire to marry him! He's too old, for one thing."

Cody decided not to ask her what her idea of too old was, for fear she might think he was ready for retirement, himself. "I see."

"The problem with Alfonso is that he is too protective of me. He always has been. He treats me like a child. He doesn't trust my judgment.''

''I wonder why,'' Cody drawled.

''You see? You do think I should not have tried to warn you.''

''That hardly matters at this point, now, does it? What matters is what Alfonso will do when he finds you. If he *is* behind all of this, he'll see your attempt to warn me as a betrayal. If he isn't behind it, he'll feel that your reputation has been compromised. Either way, your brother is not going to be pleased with either one of us over this little deal.''

''How can you joke when your life could be in danger?''

''I'm not joking, and it's both of our lives, sweetheart. Do you think they're going to allow you to walk away from here, just because you're a woman?''

''I suppose not. Perhaps it's because I thought Alfonso was behind this that I have been feeling safer. He would never do anything to harm me. This I know.''

''I thought I knew your brother pretty well, *chula*, but now I'm not certain of anything. I suppose the best thing that could happen would be if—''

He never got to complete that sentence. The door burst open behind them and three men stepped into the room with guns pointing at them. Cody slowly came to his feet and turned, deliberately placing himself between the gunman and Carina. The quilt settled around his waist and effectively hobbled his movements.

Well, hell. Once more he had been caught without his pants on. This was getting to be a habit he didn't much care for.

The first man inside the door said, ''Get your hands over your head, Callaway, and keep them there.'' The slight movement was all the quilt needed to slither to the floor, leaving him standing there in his briefs.

Three

"So you are the famous Cody Callaway," drawled the man standing before him. The other two closed the door and leaned against the wall, smirking.

"I'm afraid you've got the advantage," Cody replied in a lazy tone. "I don't believe we've ever met."

"Ah, yes. I definitely have the advantage now, don't I?" He nodded toward Carina. "Who is this woman? I wasn't expecting to find you with anyone last night."

Cody shrugged.

"As for my name, I doubt it means anything to you. I am Enrique Rodriguez. Kiki, to my friends."

Cody fought to maintain a passive expression, but he could not control the sinking sensation he felt in his chest. Here was the man he had been searching for, but this was the not the way he wanted to confront him.

"Are you responsible for our being here?" Cody asked.

Kiki nodded, smiling. "This was not the original plan, of course. But my men did very well. They have brought you here so that I may deal with you, myself. I have long wanted to meet one of the sons of Grant Callaway, face-to-face."

"Did you know my father?" Cody asked in an attempt to buy some time for them. He shifted slightly, his body now behind the table. If he could keep Kiki talking long enough to better shield Carina, perhaps she would have a chance to get through the next few minutes.

As soon as he had heard the name of their abductor Cody knew he was a dead man. From everything he had learned about him, Cody knew that resentment had twisted Enrique Rodriguez's mind as well as his entire perspective on life. There would be no reasoning with him.

"Oh, yes. I knew the high-and-mighty Grant Callaway. I went to him with a business proposition years ago. I explained how he owed me and my family. With the money he could have given me, I would have been able to make a success of my business, but he turned me down." Kiki wiped the back of his hand across his mouth. "But he paid for his arrogance," he growled. "I made certain of that. Just as I intend to make every one of you Callaways pay. You're all the scum of the earth."

So his suspicions had been correct. This man was responsible for the death of his parents. He had discovered the truth, but there was no way to let his brothers know...unless he could convince Rodriguez to let Carina go.

Without losing eye contact Cody shrugged his shoulders in a nonchalant manner, and said, "So? There's no reason to involve my girlfriend. She has nothing to do with any of this."

Kiki spit. "She's trash. Otherwise she would have nothing to do with such slime as you."

A slight movement at one of the windows caught Cody's eye. Someone was out there. Was it friend or foe? At this point it didn't matter. He had to try something. He rammed his hip against the table, forcing it onto its side, then grabbed Carina as the table toppled and shoved her behind it. The loud discharge of pistols filled the room, but he didn't allow the distraction to stop him from making a dive for Kiki's knees. The force of his body knocked Rodriguez off balance. The pistol in his hand went flying.

Cody straightened, bringing his right fist up with all his strength, and connected with the man's jaw.

Rodriguez folded like an overextended accordion being released. Dimly Cody had been aware of glass shattering and the door bursting open once more. Now he spun around in time to see the other two men with their hands over their heads.

He smiled at the newcomers, who were holding guns pointed toward the intruders. "Hey, Freddie. Am I ever glad to see you!"

Three more men came inside, one wearing a uniform. "I understand you are having some problems here?"

Cody nodded. "As a matter of fact, I have reason to believe this man—" he nodded to Enrique Rodriguez who lay unconscious on the floor "—is responsible for years of harassment and possible murder with regard to my family. I've been down here gathering evidence on this man and trying to locate him. Obviously he found me first.'' He rubbed his stinging fists, then looked down at his hand, surprised to see that his knuckles were bleeding and beginning to swell.

''Then you wish to press charges against him?''

''You bet. For kidnapping and attempted murder. If Carina hadn't—'' Carina! He spun around and saw her huddled against the table, her head buried, her shoulders shaking.

He strode to the overturned table and knelt down beside her. ''Are you all right?''

She looked up and saw him. With a look of relief, she threw her arms around him. ''Oh, Cody! I thought they had killed you. There was so much noise and shouting. I saw you move toward that man and—'' She shuddered, burying her head into his shoulder.

He awkwardly patted her on the back. ''You're okay, baby. I believe the cavalry got here in time.''

He continued to kneel there beside her, while the authorities took Enrique's men away. In an effort to calm her, Cody lifted Carina in his arms and walked over to the bed. When he attempted to lay her down, she clung to him with a sob. He sank down on the bed and continued to hold her, this time in his lap, while he stroked her hair and murmured soothingly to her.

Looking back on the scene later, Cody could understand Alfonso's first impression when Carina's brother stepped through the cabin door. But his understanding came later, much later.

When he got his first glimpse of Alfonso, he smiled

with relief. "Your timing couldn't have been better, Alfonso," he said.

Alfonso trod silently across the floor, his expression murderous. "Get some clothes on, you son-of-a—" He paused, obviously in an effort to gain some control over himself. "We'll talk about this later."

Only then did Cody remember that he was clad only in his briefs and that Carina was snuggled up to his bare chest as though she had found a permanent home.

"Uh, Alfonso," he began, reaching behind his neck and insistently removing Carina's trembling arms. "I know what this must look like to you, but if you'll just let me explain—"

"I fully intend to hear every one of your explanations, Cody," the man replied in a deadly tone. "But for the moment, I want you to let go of my sister."

Cody spread his arms wide, knowing that this was no time to begin an argument. He had never seen Alfonso in such a rage. "Carina, honey," he murmured. "Let me get some clothes on, okay?"

He knew he had done something else wrong when Alfonso's face darkened even more. Carina lifted her head, her eyes red from weeping, her cheeks moist. "Alfonso?" she whispered, her eyes filled with dread. "Alfonso, please don't hurt him. I couldn't bear it if something happened to Cody."

Cody realized that Carina hadn't seen how Alfonso's men had come to their rescue. She must think that Alfonso had been in charge of their kidnapping, after all.

Wanting to reassure her that her brother had not in

fact plotted to have him killed, Cody began, "Carina, you—"

Alfonso interrupted him. "Shut up, Cody. Just…shut…up." He made a quick motion with his head toward the fireplace where Cody's clothes were spread.

Cody lifted Carina from his lap and put her on the bed, then headed for his clothes. The other men had all left the cabin, so that only the three of them remained.

Cody wasted no time pulling on his clothes, which were thankfully dry by this time. He stamped each foot to make sure his boots were solidly on, then glanced across the cabin. Alfonso was talking to Carina in a voice too low for Cody to hear. No doubt he was reassuring her about his part in the recent events.

"How did you know where to find us?" Cody asked the first question that crossed his mind.

Alfonso reluctantly turned away from Carina and looked at Cody. "As soon as I discovered that Carina wasn't at the hacienda I had men scouring the area, looking for leads. Luckily we made early contact with Roberto Escobedo, whose sister is a friend of Carina's, and he explained his part in helping her to meet you. That's when I doubled my forces in an effort to find you."

"Well, actually, I don't think he understood what—" Cody began, but Alfonso waved him to silence.

"Once we arrived at the cantina, the owner told us about some men who had been looking for you. By that time, some of my other men had located and questioned the two who had transported you in the truck. They very graciously gave us directions to this cabin."

"Then you know that we were forced to come here," Cody pointed out in a carefully reasonable tone.

"Oh, yes. I'm very much aware that Carina had expected to return to the hacienda before anyone had discovered that she was not there."

"She overheard—"

"Come," Alfonso interrupted. "Let's get these fires out and leave this place." He touched Carina's cheek. "I want to get Carina home."

Cody heard the control Alfonso was still using to restrain his temper and decided not to push the matter at the moment. Given time to calm down, Alfonso would no doubt be more receptive to explanations.

Or so Cody hoped.

"Look, Alfonso," Cody said hours later, facing his friend across the massive desk in Alfonso's study. "I know you're upset with me. I know what you must be thinking, but if you would just let me—"

"I am thinking that given my preference I would much prefer to kill you, rather than have to deal with you at all. But since that would not repair the damage done to my sister's innocence or to her reputation, I have reluctantly given up the idea."

"Dammit, Alfonso, there is nothing wrong with Carina's reputation, and as for her innocence…that's what I'm trying to explain—"

"Perhaps in Texas a young woman can be coaxed into meeting a man without her family caring, but not here in Mexico!" Alfonso came to his feet, as though unable to sit still for another moment. "What sickens me is how much trust I placed in you. I befriended you. I did everything in my power to assist you in hunting down this man Rodriguez. And how do you repay this assistance, this trust?'' he asked, slamming his hand flat on the desk. ''By seducing my sister!''

Cody leaped from his chair. ''I did not seduce your sister!'' he shouted, leaning both arms on the desk and glaring at Alfonso. ''How many times do I have to tell you that? She overheard some men plotting to kill me and came to warn me.''

Alfonso made a sound of contempt. ''How ridiculous. How could she hear someone plotting such a thing in my house?''

''I don't know. But she did.''

''If Carina had heard such a thing, she would have come to me immediately with the information.''

''Not if she thought you were behind the plot.''

For the next few moments Cody was afraid Alfonso was going to have a stroke. His color changed with alarming suddenness and he stood there staring at Cody, his mouth moving silently.

Cody started around the desk, but Alfonso backed away, taking in several deep breaths of air. ''Don't you dare try to make me think my sister considers me a killer, because I will never, ever believe such a thing. You are lower than a snake, to suggest the idea in an effort to drive a wedge between us.'' Alfonso strode over to the French doors that opened onto the courtyard of his home. Opening one, he stood with his back to Cody while he stared out at the colorful profusion of the garden.

Cody heard the steady trickle of water from the fountain in the courtyard. He, too, took the moment to get his emotions under control. He wanted to handle this explosive situation with as much detachment as possible.

Without turning around, Alfonso said, "There is no use in your making up lies, Cody. Roberto told me that Carina came to him and begged him to give her a ride to where you were staying. She made it clear to him that she wanted to see you again that night, and that if he didn't take her, she would go alone. She made no mention to him of any plot." Alfonso turned and pinned Cody with a cold stare. "I find it offensive enough that you should betray my family by making an assignation with my sister, but to convince her to come to you late at night—to place her in such unnecessary danger—was reprehensible." Slowly he paced to where Cody stood. "You are not a man. You are worse than a seducer of innocent women. You are a liar and a coward. I hope you rot in hell for what you have done to Carina and to our family."

Cody could not remember a time when he had needed to exert so much self-control over his urge to smash his fist in another man's face. He had never allowed a man to speak to him in such an offensive manner. Never. To have those words come from his friend infuriated him. Alfonso knew better. He knew Cody too well to believe all the things he was calling him. Yet because of his rage over what had happened, he was throwing away their friendship, declaring a state of perpetual enmity between them.

Cody stood there, clenching and unclenching his fists, gnawing on the inside of his cheek, and searched for the wisdom to handle this volatile situation. There was absolutely no doubt left in his mind that Alfonso had meant what he said—he would have preferred killing Cody to speaking to him.

The fact remained that he had chosen not to kill him. Why? Cody knew the answer. Because of Carina.

"What do you want from me, Alfonso?" Cody asked in a level tone.

"What I want and what I insist upon are two different things. If I had my way, I would make certain you never came south of the river again. But I can't. Too many people know."

"Know what?"

"That Carina was with you when you were kidnapped, that the two of you spent the night together in a secluded mountain cabin."

"Alfonso, nothing happened between us. You've got to believe that. *Nothing!* I respect Carina. I respect her very much. I would never, *ever,* take advantage of her."

"Perhaps you did not have the opportunity this time. Of this, I have no way of knowing. Just as I have no way of knowing how often she has slipped away to be with you in the past. This time, through unusual circumstances, the two of you were caught before she could return home."

"Alfonso! Will you listen to me? I am not your sister's seducer. Never, at any time, have I seen her without a family member being present."

Alfonso clasped his hands behind his back and rocked back and forth from his heels to his toes. "Until last night when she suddenly decided to throw away twenty years of training, tradition and maidenly virtue to visit you in your room after midnight. Is that what you wish me to believe?"

Cody sighed, and ran his hand through his hair in frustration. "I told you why she came."

"I know what you told me. Having those men kidnap you no doubt gave you an opportunity to place the blame on Rodriguez. What you want me to believe is that some of the people working for me might be in Rodriguez's pay. What you want me to believe is that my sister, who loves me and who knows that I worship her, thinks I would plot to have one of my friends killed. Do you really think of me as that stupid, to believe such an idiotic story? Please do not insult my intelligence, Callaway. Even my patience has its limits."

Cody threw up his hands. "I give up. Believe what you want to believe. I'm certainly not going to be able to change your mind. I can see that now." He turned and started toward the door that opened into the hallway.

"Where do you think you're going?"

Cody was so angry he wanted to hit something, and knew that he had to get out of there before that "something" became "somebody." The situation was strained enough without his taking a swing at Alfonso. He met Alfonso's gaze with a determined one of his own. *Believe what you like,* he wanted to say. *I no longer care.*

"I'm wasting my time here. I can see that. If I can get a ride to my car, I'm going to check with the authorities to see what they are doing about Enrique Rodriguez. Then I'm going to call my brother and tell him what's happened."

"You are contacting your family?"

Cody heard the sarcasm but couldn't figure out

what had provoked it. "That's right. Do you have a problem with the idea?"

Alfonso smiled, but the smile was far from pleasant. "Not at all. I suggest you invite them to your wedding. We will make the affair as public as possible. There will be no shoddiness regarding this matter to reflect on Carina. There is no reason for her to suffer any more embarrassment than has already taken place."

Cody gave his head a quick shake, thinking his hearing was playing up on him. "What did you say?" he asked, staring at Alfonso in disbelief.

"I believe that you heard me quite well. I have been planning a party for this coming Friday for several weeks now. We will formally announce your engagement at that time. You may invite your family, if you wish. We will discuss the date for the wedding over the weekend."

Cody considered himself a reasonable man. He seldom allowed his emotions to control him, but this was one time that he didn't trust himself to speak right away.

Marriage? Him? Hah! Marriage was the very last thing he intended to experience. Hadn't he made that clear to everyone who knew him?

"Now wait just a damn minute here," he said, moving back toward the center of the room where Alfonso stood, still clasping his hands behind his back. "I'm sorry that Carina got mixed up in all this mess with Rodriguez. I certainly never intended to get innocent people involved. I mean, I have nothing against your sister or anything, Alfonso. She's a real sweet little gal and all that, but I'm not the marrying kind, you see. I like my freedom, and my whole life-style is geared to my being on my own. She'd be miserable married to someone like me and you know it. You can't just go around arranging other people's lives like that. Marriage is a serious business. Nothing to be taken lightly, Alfonso.''

The room filled with silence after Cody stopped speaking. Alfonso continued to watch Cody as if he were some unsavory specimen that he was having trouble identifying. When he finally spoke, he said, ''Carina is the joy of my life. I remember when she was born. Our father died of a heart attack while Mother was carrying Carina. The first time I held her in my arms I promised to protect her, to be the father she would never know. I have done the very best I could to keep that vow.'' He turned away and walked behind the desk once more. He sat down, reached for one of his cigars, rolled it between his fingers, trimmed it, then carefully lit it before inhaling. Cody recognized the insult of Alfonso's not offering him a cigar.

After taking a few puffs, Alfonso looked up at Cody once again. ''There is only one reason my sister would have risked so much for you, Callaway. She must fancy herself in love with you. I don't know how you were able to coax her to your side, but the facts are there and neither of you deny them. The intimacy between you is more than evident—any doubt I might have had was erased when I walked into that cabin and found the two of you together—and you undressed. I would have staked my life on the fact that my sister had never been alone with a man in her entire life.'' He sighed. ''I would have died, obviously. Whatever your magic, you have seduced my sister. The evidence is overwhelmingly against you. If you are any kind of a man at all, you will do what you must to make amends."

"I—" Cody paused, collecting his thoughts. "But, you—" Once again he came to a halt, rubbing his hand over his mouth. "I mean, Carina doesn't really—" Cody stumbled to a complete halt, suddenly aware of the giant hole that had sprung into being before him. Here was the true test of his worth. He knew that he was an honorable man. He knew that he was an honest man. He had always taken his integrity for granted.

Now he was faced with some very disagreeable choices. He did not want to hurt Carina in any way. After all, she had risked her life, as well as her reputation, in an attempt to warn him of danger last night. The fact that he had not needed her protective gesture was moot at this point.

What had happened last night could not be undone. The question was, what did he intend to do about the situation now?

He wished that he could talk to Cole and Cameron. They had always advised him well in the past. He didn't want to make any hasty decisions that would have irrevocable consequences in his life, not to mention in the lives of others.

"Alfonso," Cody began once again, trying to find the words to explain what he felt. "I think we're both too emotional at the moment to be making rational decisions. I think if we give the matter time, give *ourselves* time to cool off and to think with a little more clarity, we can come up with some alternate solutions that would be more beneficial for everyone. Carina mentioned that she hoped to continue her schooling. Perhaps we could wait until after—"

"Absolutely not. Do you think I would allow her to run the risk of being unwed and pregnant—"

"Pregnant! Now wait just a damned minute here, Ramirez. I keep telling you over and over. I have not touched Carina. Not in any way. There is no way she could possibly be pregnant!"

"You forget that I saw the two of you together, with my very own eyes. She was clinging to you, obviously comfortable being around you, while you sat there wearing no clothes. Do not talk to me about how you haven't touched her. I know better."

"Well, she sure as hell isn't going to get pregnant from having my arms around her."

"I never thought she would. But you had several hours of privacy that are unaccounted for. A close intimacy could have evolved by the time I arrived."

Cody felt as if he were caught up in some senseless nightmare where logic and reason were being used against him. He felt like a defendant on the stand who was guilty unless he could prove his innocence.

"Why don't you talk to Carina about this, Alfonso? She'll tell you that nothing happened between us. She'll—"

"She will say whatever you wish her to say, I'm sure of that. She obviously feels obligated to protect you."

"So you think we are both liars, is that it?"

"I think that Carina loves you. Because she loves you, she will do whatever is necessary to protect you. As for you…I believe I've made my opinion of you quite clear."

"You certainly have." Cody couldn't believe what was happening. He struggled to find words to convey his shock. "I'm surprised you would want someone like me to marry your precious sister."

"I want my sister to be happy. She has made her choice. Like it or not, I must accept it."

"Even though you're giving me no choice."

Alfonso removed the cigar from his mouth and curled his lip.

"You made your choice when you spent the night with my sister. Now I expect you to face the consequences. That is, if you're man enough to do so."

Cody had been through a rough twenty-four hours. He had done his best to deal with the startling and tumultuous events with honor. He had done everything he knew how to do to hang on to his control, but his detachment was at an end and his temper flared.

"All right, Alfonso. If you are so damned desperate to get your sister married off, then so be it." He strode to the door, pausing only long enough to look over his shoulder and say, "And yes, you can count on the fact that my family will be here on Friday night to witness the fiasco of your engagement announcement."

Four

As soon as Carina opened her eyes, she remembered that today was a very special day. She lay there for a few moments, luxuriating in the quietness that surrounded her. She knew the silence wouldn't last long. By noon their guests who had a fair distance to travel would be arriving to attend Alfonso's party.

The party had been planned for weeks. She and her mother had insisted that there be a special celebration for Alfonso's fortieth birthday. After much discussion, he had finally agreed, but only if the purpose of the party were kept private between family members.

Carina didn't care, so long as they set this time aside to honor her brother. Thank God Alfonso had known nothing of the plot against Cody. Not that she could get him to discuss the matter with her. In fact, he had refused to discuss the subject the few times she had seen him this week. He would only explain that the men behind the plot were all in jail, where they would no doubt remain. She was sorry that she ever thought Alfonso could have been involved.

He confirmed that Cody would be attending the party tonight, which was wonderful news. She hadn't had an opportunity to speak with Cody since they had been rescued from that cabin in the mountains.

She'd had nightmares the first couple of nights after the incident—dreams of guns going off, people grabbing her—she had been afraid to fall asleep at night. She had wanted to talk about it, first with Alfonso or perhaps Cody, but neither had been available. Gradually the harsh memories subsided and her sleep was made easier because of her busy days.

Everything was ready—all of the extra bedrooms had been cleaned and filled with fresh flowers, awaiting their occupants. Even the buildings surrounding the hacienda had been cleaned. She had noticed yesterday that Alfonso had some of the workers cleaning the small chapel that had been built many years ago. She supposed their visitors would be fascinated with its history and would be going through the various outbuildings, but was surprised that Alfonso had given the matter much thought. When she had peeked inside, she had been surprised to see some of the women polishing and cleaning the altar and mopping the stone floors, while the men scrubbed the stained-glass windows and oiled the wooden pews.

Puzzled by the activity, she wondered if Alfonso intended to hold a special mass in the historic building in honor of his birthday.

Whatever his intentions, she reminded herself, she needed to stop daydreaming. There were still last-minute preparations that needed her attention.

By the time she returned to her room to prepare for the dinner that would accommodate their out-of-town guests, Carina was more than ready for a brief rest. The tension and excitement of the household staff and occupants had continued to build, as more and more friends and relatives gathered at the hacienda. Once she saw that her mother and brother were there to handle greetings and to direct people to their rooms, she slipped away.

Her one disappointment of the day was that Cody had not arrived by the time she returned to her room. She almost asked Alfonso if he had heard from Cody, but at the last minute decided not to mention the Texan to her brother. There was something that Alfonso wasn't telling her where Cody was concerned. Whenever she mentioned Cody's name, Alfonso brushed her remarks aside with impatience and changed the subject. They must have had words, but if so, Alfonso wasn't going to discuss the matter with her.

She could only hope that Cody hadn't changed his mind about attending the party. She had never properly thanked him for being so kind to her during that horrible night.

As soon as she reached her room, Carina slipped out of her clothes and walked into her bathroom. After filling the oversize bathtub with bubbles and scented water, she stepped into its depths and sank down with a sigh, the soothing liquid swirling around her body. She could feel the tension begin to leave the muscles in her neck, shoulders and spine.

She closed her eyes and thought about the dress her brother had surprised her with earlier in the day.

Never had she seen a more beautiful gown. It was

like nothing she had ever had before. This dress was ivory satin decorated with cream-colored lace. The neckline came to the edge of her shoulders, then dipped slightly into a V in front, leaving her neck and upper shoulders bare.

The dress narrowed at the waist, then billowed out into a multitude of tiny satin ruffles edged in lace until it reached the floor. Several petticoats came with it, including one with a hoop in the hem. She would need help getting dressed, her mother had pointed out, and promised to be up later after Carina had had time to rest.

She closed her eyes, resting her head along the rim of the tub. Her thoughts were never far from Cody Callaway. She kept thinking about what he had looked like without his clothes, how he had felt as she had clung to him. She could almost smell the slight scent of his warm body, feel his smooth skin stretched across the muscled plane of his chest. She squirmed with her memories. Of course she was uncomfortable with her thoughts. She had never been in a man's company like that before. She knew it was wicked of her to dwell on the memories, but she was fascinated all the same.

She wondered what it would feel like to be kissed by Cody Callaway. She smiled to herself, allowing her thoughts to drift and whirl around her much like the water that encircled her body.

"Carina? Where are you?"

Carina came awake with a jerk and realized that her bathwater had grown cold. "In here, Mama," she replied, hastily rising and reaching for a towel. Her eye caught the movement of her reflection in the mirror and she paused for a moment, staring at her familiar image. Slowly she wrapped the towel around herself without taking her eyes off the mirror and stepped out of the tub.

Her hair had come loose from the pins she had used to keep the heavy mass piled on her head, so that one long curl fell across her shoulder and curled around her breast.

Oh, if only she were taller! She still looked like a child, standing there wide-eyed. She wanted to be voluptuous and seductive, someone who would catch the sophisticated eye of Cody Callaway and make him aware of her as a woman.

Instead, she looked slender and unsure of herself—much too inexperienced for a man such as Cody.

"You must hurry, Carina, or we will both be late for dinner."

"Yes, Mama," she responded, continuing to dry herself.

When she walked back into the bedroom, she found her underwear and petticoats already spread across the bed. After slipping them on, she raised her arms while her mother dropped the satin dress over her head. Carina slid her hands into the armholes and helped tug the dress in place. By the time her mother fastened the small buttons along her spine and straightened her hem, Carina's eyes had grown wide in wonderment. The creamy ivory was the same shade of color as her own skin. She rubbed her fingertips across the edge of the neckline that rested along her shoulders, feeling as though some fairy godmother had waved her wand and turned her into a princess.

"Ah, Carina," her mother whispered in awe. "Never have I seen you look more beautiful."

She reached for her mother's hand. "How will I

ever be able to thank Alfonso? I can't believe this, can you?''

''Well, we must arrange your hair and get downstairs before he sends someone looking for us,'' her mother said in a practical tone. After Carina sat down in front of her vanity table, her mother pulled Carina's hair high on her head, then allowed it to cascade down her neck and shoulders in a froth of curls.

The dinner bell chimed as they began their descent down the winding stairs. Carina had stuck a gardenia behind her ear while her mother had fastened a double strand of pearls around her neck. She felt as if she were living out a fairy tale—Cinderella had arrived at the ball.

''Ah, Carina,'' Alfonso said, coming to wait for her at the bottom of the stairs. A sheen of moisture in his eyes made them glisten in the light from the massive chandelier overhead. ''You look enchanting, my love. Utterly enchanting.'' He took her hand and raised it to his lips. When he raised his head, he glanced to the side of the hallway and said, ''Don't you agree, Cody?''

Carina hadn't seen Cody standing in the shadowed doorway of Alfonso's study. Now he stepped forward. She tightened her grip on the rail for balance and stared down at him, her heart racing. He was here!

He wore a tuxedo of Spanish design. The red cummerbund accented his trim waistline, the short jacket enhanced the width of his shoulders and the snug trousers molded his muscular legs. She could not read anything from his expression. He stared at her as though he had never seen her before.

Forcing herself to continue down the last few steps,

Carina kept her gaze on him. Why didn't he smile? Why did his mouth appear almost grim?

"Come, Mama," Alfonso said, holding out his arm, "you are just in time for me to escort you to dinner. Our other guests are all assembled." He turned and stared down the hallway. Cody silently held out his arm to Carina.

Tentatively she placed her fingers on his arm, feeling the tensed muscles beneath the finely woven cloth of his jacket.

"Hello, Cody," she said, wishing her voice didn't sound so strained. "I wasn't sure if you would be here tonight."

"Weren't you?" He followed Alfonso down the hallway. Carina slightly lifted the hem of her gown and kept pace with him. She peeked a glance at him, then dropped her eyes. His jaw could be made from a slab of granite, it looked so hard. After that first look at her, he had stared straight ahead.

"I looked for you after we got back from the mountains last week, but Alfonso said you had business to attend to."

"Yes."

"Did it have something to do with that horrible man who had us kidnapped?"

"Partly. I went to Texas to see my brothers, as well."

"Oh."

They arrived in the dining room. Alfonso was already seating his mother at one end of the table. Cody pulled out the first chair at the other end for Carina, next to where Alfonso would be sitting, then sat down beside her.

"Carina, I would like you to meet my brother Cole

and his wife, Allison,'' he nodded to the couple beside him. ''And my brother Cameron and his wife, Janine.'' He nodded to the couple opposite them.

''Oh, Cody! How wonderful. I had no idea your family would be here tonight.'' She smiled at the two couples. ''I am so very pleased to meet you. What a wonderful surprise.''

Both men nodded without speaking or smiling, looking as solemn as Cody. The women smiled. The dark-haired one, Allison, said, ''Your dress is lovely, Carina.'' The red-haired one added, ''I was thinking the same thing. You look radiant.''

Carina could feel her cheeks heating. ''Thank you,'' she murmured, just as Alfonso sank into his chair at the head of the table and signaled for dinner to begin.

''Have you been introduced to the Callaways?'' Alfonso asked Carina.

''Cody just introduced us. Why didn't you tell me they were coming?''

Before Alfonso could answer, Cody said, ''You mean you didn't know?''

''Not who was coming, just that we had two more bedrooms to prepare for overnight guests.'' She smiled at the other couples. ''I can't tell you how happy I am to meet you like this. As busy as you all must be, I'm amazed you found the time to be here.''

''Oh, we wouldn't have missed this party for the world,'' Cole drawled. ''Right, Cameron?'' He lifted his wineglass and made a toasting gesture to his brother.

''Absolutely,'' Cameron replied, lifting his glass in response and taking a swallow.

''Very funny,'' Cody muttered.

By the time dinner was over and the dinner guests began to mingle with the others who had arrived for the dance, Carina felt as though she had been cast in a play without being given a script. There was a definite undercurrent going on during the various courses of dinner. Although the surface conversation between her brother and the Callaway brothers was all very polite, there seemed to be some very pointed remarks that she could not understand in the slightest.

She excused herself as soon as dinner was over, feeling the need to take something for the beginning of a throbbing headache. By the time she made her way back to the massive room, which had been cleared of furniture for the four-piece band and dancing, the place was filled with laughing guests pursuing various pleasures. Several couples were out on the dance floor, others had gathered around a table set up as a bar, still others stood in groups chatting.

Carina paused at the wide archway into the room and looked around, pleased to see that everything seemed to be flowing smoothly. The canapé trays were receiving admiring attention and those working out of the kitchen were efficiently restocking.

"Quite a party."

Carina gave a start, not having seen the tall, solid man come up behind her.

"Oh! Hello. You're Cole, aren't you?"

Cole grinned. "That's right. You've got a good memory."

"Not really. It's just that I've heard so much about you...and Cameron...that it wasn't difficult to figure out which one was which."

"I had no idea Cody was such a chatterbox."

Carina chuckled at his tone of voice. "You must

remember that we have known each other for some time. I've always been interested in his family...and the ranch...and he's been patient enough to answer all my questions, regardless of their impertinence.''

All the while she was talking, Cole seemed to study her, his eyes piercing. His lazy smile belied the serious expression of his gaze.

''Would you care to dance?'' he asked rather abruptly.

Carina glanced toward the crowded dance floor, then smiled. ''I would like that very much.''

Cole led her around the room with an air of command, drawing her out. ''I was surprised to be introduced to so many people who were your sisters and brothers,'' he said, after nodding to one of her brothers and his wife as they passed by. ''For some reason I had the idea that you and Alfonso were the only ones in the family.''

''Oh, no. There are six of us, altogether. Alfonso is the oldest. I am the youngest. I'm the only one left at home, you see.''

''So I gathered. Your other sisters and brothers are married?''

She sighed. ''Yes. Which has been Alfonso's argument whenever I talk about going on with my schooling. He thinks I should be content to marry and care for a family, as Rosie and Conchita have done.''

''You disagree?'' He raised one of his brows.

''Someday I hope to marry, of course. But not now. There is so much more to do in life,'' she said, smiling. ''But now, I'm getting off on one of my tangents, as Alfonso calls them, when we are supposed to be relaxing and enjoying ourselves.''

"How could I not be enjoying myself, dancing with a beautiful woman like you?" Cole responded.

She hated the blush that she knew flooded her face. She knew he was only being polite, but she had never been comfortable with compliments.

"Mind if I cut in, bro?"

Carina could feel her body react to the sound of Cody's voice. Cole glanced down at her, then responded with flattering reluctance. "Well, if you insist, but I figure there are lots of gals around you could enjoy dancing with."

"Then you shouldn't have any trouble finding one," Cody replied. He slipped a very possessive arm around Carina's waist and pulled her to him. Ignoring his brother's amused chuckle, Cody spun her in a series of fast turns that caused her to lose her breath.

When she regained her balance and some air she discovered that he had danced her through the wide French doors out into the courtyard. Although a few couples lingered out there, the light was dim and there was a greater sense of seclusion.

"You and Cole seemed to find a great deal to talk about in there," he said, watching her with a narrow gaze.

"I like your brother. He's friendly and very kind."

"Cole? Hah. He's about as friendly and kind as a barracuda. At least most of the time. I guess he's always been a sucker for a beautiful woman, though."

"Cody?"

"Yes?"

"What's wrong? You've been in a strange mood all evening. Your brother was just being polite. Why does that make you angry?"

"It doesn't. I'm glad you had a chance to visit with

him.'' He slid his hand up her back, then down, as though restless.

''Are you upset with me?'' She gazed into his stormy eyes, wishing he would tell her why he was so disturbed.

''Now why should I be upset with you?'' he drawled.

She was quiet for several moments, thinking. ''I'm not sure. Are you still angry because I came to your room that night last week?''

''I think it's a little late in the day to go over that, wouldn't you say?''

''Then you *are*. I wondered if that's why you left without talking to me again.''

''I wasn't in the mood to talk to anybody when I left here.''

''Aren't you glad that man was arrested?''

''Very.''

''So it worked out all right in the end, don't you think?''

He stared at her for a long moment. ''You think so?''

She looked at him, confused by his manner. ''Don't you?''

He slid his hand up to between her shoulder blades, then made a couple of rapid turns before settling both arms behind her, leaving her little choice other than to rest her hands on his chest.

''Uh, Cody, I don't think Alfonso would like it very much if he saw you holding me in such a manner.''

He muttered something beneath his breath that sounded like ''tough,'' but Carina knew she must have misunderstood him.

With his chin resting lightly on top of her head, he asked, "What has Alfonso told you about tonight, Carina?"

Carina could scarcely think. All she could do at the moment was feel Cody's presence. She hadn't realized how much she had missed the feel of his arms around her until he held her close once again. She could feel the steady pounding of his heart beneath her fingertips, hear his soft breathing, smell the special scent that made up the essence of who he was. How could she possibly concentrate on his question? Something about Alfonso.

She moved her head so that she could see his face. "Tonight? Well, only the closest family knows, but today is Alfonso's birthday, which is why we are celebrating."

"That's all?"

Puzzled at his insistence, she said, "What more could there be?"

He muttered something under his breath that she was almost glad she couldn't decipher. "He told me he would handle it, and like an idiot, I believed him."

"Handle what? Is this about my being with you that night?"

"Yes."

She'd never heard the word more clipped.

"Well, actually, I haven't seen much of Alfonso this week. Every time I attempted to explain why I was there and what I tried to do he waved my explanations aside, as though he knew all about it. I assumed the two of you discussed the matter and he understood what had happened."

The band completed the song they were playing. Instead of going into another one immediately, as they had been doing all evening, there was a drumroll and a harmonious blast of trumpets, causing everyone to take notice.

Cody turned so that they both faced the end of the room, where Alfonso joined the bandleader on the dais. He stepped in front of the microphone.

"I hope everyone is having a good time this evening," Alfonso began with a smile. The room erupted in clapping and cheering. He waited for everyone to become quiet before he continued. "We have a very happy announcement to make this evening, something of a surprise that I hope you all will enjoy. We always feel blessed when our friends and our family come together in celebration. Therefore, we decided to take this opportunity to share another event."

He looked out over the sea of faces, his gaze meeting Carina's. He held out his hand. "Carina, would you please join me?"

She froze, wondering what he was doing. She had assumed that he had decided to tell his guests about his birthday, but there was no reason for her to be there, was there?

The people stepped aside, leaving a wide aisle for her to move through the crowd. She glanced up at Cody, but could read nothing in his expression. With as much grace as possible, she left the courtyard and walked to the end of the room.

Alfonso took her hand, then turned her to face the waiting crowd. "There are times when it is difficult for a brother to admit that his sister has grown-up." Carina nibbled on her bottom lip and attempted to hang on to her smile, reminding herself that no one had actually died of embarrassment. "As many of you know, Carina recently finished her studies at the university in Mexico City."

Oh, my gosh! He had changed his mind! He was going to allow her to go on with her education! And he had chosen to surprise her with the news tonight. She almost grabbed him in an exuberant hug as she heard him say, "Now she is ready to move on to the next stage of her life."

She could feel the bubble of excitement climb within her. She could hardly refrain from laughing out loud. So this was the reason for the very special dress. He was willing to honor her wishes and allow her to make her own choices.

"It is with great pleasure and an enormous amount of pride that I invite you to witness the next part of our festivities, the wedding of my very precious sister, Carina, to Cody Callaway."

The unexpected news stunned the room, but Carina could not fully appreciate their reaction. She had to deal with her own. She stared in horror at the man who still stood beside the fountain in the courtyard watching the scene being played out inside.

Scattered clapping accompanied by the buzz of excited voices filled the air. Carina saw Cole and Cameron move toward Cody as though in protection.

If this was some kind of bizarre joke, there was no one laughing.

Alfonso's voice sounded once more over the microphone, drowning out the noise and her swirling, chaotic thoughts. "May I present the bridegroom, Mr. Cody Callaway?"

Despite everything she could do, Carina's knees buckled. She would have fallen if Alfonso hadn't grabbed her around the waist with one hand while he held out his other hand to the man threading his way through the milling crowd, his brothers no more than a step behind him.

Somehow she managed to focus on Cody's face…on his eyes, which were snapping with fire and suppressed emotion. Nimbly he leaped up on the dais beside her, his arm snaking around her waist, lifting her away from Alfonso as he pulled her tightly against his side.

"Are you all right?" he asked in low tone.

"All right? Of course not. How could I—" she turned and looked at Alfonso "—How could he—"

Meanwhile, the fun-filled crowd applauded Cody's possessiveness and cheered him on.

Still at the microphone, Alfonso said, "Now, then, if you will follow our bride and groom across the way to the family chapel, we will continue with the night's festivities."

The crowd began to move away, leaving Alfonso standing there with Cody and Carina. Cole and Cameron were nearby.

"This wasn't the agreement and you know it," Cody said as the noise abated.

"Care to explain what's going on?" Cole asked from a few feet away.

Alfonso faced Cody, then allowed his gaze to take in the possessive way Cody held Carina to him. "I would say that it is obvious, wouldn't you? We're about to witness a wedding."

"But, Alfonso," Carina began, "this can't be. Why, Cody and I, we aren't—" She looked at Cody's stern countenance and shuddered, "We can't do this. Why are you—"

"Because he has the upper hand and intends to use

it,'' Cody said. He glanced at his brothers. ''I should have figured on something like this happening, but I had hoped he would have second thoughts about the whole situation after having a few days to reconsider.'' He stepped off the dais, then turned and lifted Carina down.

''You knew he planned to do this?'' she asked Cody, shocked.

''Not exactly. I agreed to his announcing our engagement tonight. He's the one who decided to make a circus out of the event.''

''Our engagement! But Cody, how could you agree to such a thing? We are not engaged. We have never discussed it. How can—''

''That's enough!'' Alfonso said. ''Whether you discussed the matter or not, you most certainly should have before you chose to slip out to see him whenever you could. It sickens me to think that my sister would stoop to such behavior.''

''Alfonso! What are you saying? There is nothing between Cody and me. Nothing! How can you do this? I thought you loved me. I thought you were going to allow me to continue with school. Why would you—''

''Come! We're wasting time. Our guests are waiting for us in the chapel.''

''I don't care! You can't just—''

''Carina,'' Cody said quietly, ''I appreciate the fact that you are no more enthused about this little merger than I am, but the fact is that you're wasting your breath. Your brother isn't the least bit interested in hearing the truth. He's found you a wealthy husband and isn't about to let go.'' He glanced over at Cole with a half smile. ''He kinda reminds ya of a terrier who won't let go once he's caught something, doesn't he?''

Cole didn't return the smile. ''Cody, are you going to let this character get away with this? He has no legal right at all. You know that.''

Cody looked at Carina for a long time without saying anything, before he turned back to Cole. ''The way I figure it is, she's a hell of a lot better off with me than with him. At least I'll listen to her, which is more than he seems to be capable of doing.''

''No!'' Carina said. ''I can't let you do this, Cody. This is not at all what you want.''

Cody stared at Alfonso, who met his gaze without flinching. ''Let's just say I like the alternatives even less, all right?'' He glanced at his brothers. ''Well, it looks like I've got me a couple of best men here. Let's get over to that chapel and get this little matter taken care of.''

Without a backward glance, the three men walked off, leaving Carina standing in the empty ballroom with Alfonso. Slowly she turned and faced her brother.

''I have loved you all of my life. You have been the father I never had—you've been my friend, my confidant. But if you make me marry Cody Callaway under these conditions, I will never forgive you, do you understand me?''

''Carina, listen to me—''

''No. You listen to me. You and Cody must have discussed all of this last week, but you did not consider consulting me about my feelings or my desires. You went ahead and planned the whole thing around me.''

''I assumed you would lie to protect him.''

"I don't have to lie. Cody Callaway has never been anything but a complete gentleman with me. For you to use what I did—without Cody's knowledge or permission—against him is reprehensible. If you have any feelings for me at all, Alfonso, you will go over there and explain to those people that there has been a mistake and that there is not going to be a wedding."

She waited, knowing that she was fighting for her very existence. She didn't have to wait long.

"I cannot do that, Carina. Surely you can see that. It is too late."

"It is *not* too late. Only your pride will suffer, Alfonso. But if you force me to go through with it, not only my life but Cody's will be permanently marred."

"Nonsense. You are much too dramatic, little one. It is just because of the surprise that you are so upset. But I felt it would be better so. Now, come. We must not keep them waiting any longer."

Carina felt as though a blast of arctic wind had entered the room, swirling around her until she was numb with shock and despair.

Cody was waiting to marry her in the chapel, but only because her brother had forced him into agreement. How could she face the man she admired, knowing that she was being forced upon him?

Alfonso took her arm and began to lead her out of the room, across the garden area and into the chapel, where Cody waited beside the altar with the priest.

There was no place for her to run, no person who could help her. Once again Carina felt the sense of helplessness that had oftentimes swept over her when she disagreed with Alfonso's choices for her.

She scarcely noticed the candlelight and flowers

that had transformed the chapel into a fairyland. All she could see was Cody, his gaze trained on her face, waiting to see what she would do.

All of her dreams and her fantasies of her future exploded into bleakness as she heard the small organ begin the slow music that would accompany her down the aisle.

This wasn't what she had thought her wedding day would be. How could she have imagined herself marrying a cold-eyed man, without notice, without a trace of courtship, being urged down the aisle by her brother who had betrayed her on the most profound level?

The deep inner trembling that had begun at the first wave of surprise and horror had increased until her entire body shook. Only Alfonso's firm grip on her elbow kept her from falling. With the inexorable movement reminiscent of a nightmare, Carina moved ever closer to the altar and the men waiting there.

She focused her attention on Cody, whose face seemed to have softened in the light from the multitude of candles. His lips turned up at the corners in a slight smile of self-mockery that she found endearing, given the circumstances.

When she reached his side, Cody took her hand and turned toward the gentle man who would perform the rites of matrimony. Cody's hand was warm as it enveloped her icy one. He squeezed her hand slightly, as though for reassurance, and for the first time since Alfonso had made his startling announcement, Carina found herself taking a slow, deep breath of air.

This was Cody. Whatever happened in the future, she knew that she could trust him. At the moment, that trust was the only thing she had to cling to.

She was going to be his wife.

Five

Cody allowed the traditional words of the age-old ceremony to calm and soothe him while he held Carina's hand in his.

He knew that his brothers were just behind him, in the front row reserved for his family. He was thankful for their presence.

Earlier in the week, he had discussed Alfonso's demands with Cole and Cameron, looking for a better solution to the problem. Neither one of them had thought he should allow himself to be pushed into an engagement, even a short one.

Normally he would have agreed with them, but they didn't know Carina. She didn't deserve the embarrassment of being jilted even before the engagement had been announced. He had felt certain that once Alfonso calmed down the three of them would be able to talk about what had happened and—more important—what hadn't happened. He had hoped that Alfonso would then agree to allow the engagement to stand a few weeks before Carina ended the alliance, which would effectively save face for the family.

So he had talked his brothers into being there tonight—for moral support—having no premonition they would witness his marriage to Carina Ramirez.

During their walk to the chapel Cole and Cameron had strongly advised him to stand up to Alfonso, regardless of the repercussions. He listened and he understood their concern, but all the while he remembered the panic on Carina's face when she had realized what Alfonso had done.

He certainly didn't consider himself hero material, but he had known at that moment that he must do something. He couldn't just leave her to face all these people on her own, with a fiancé who refused to become a bridegroom.

He glanced down at the young woman beside him. Her mother and sisters had met her just inside the chapel and placed a thin veil over her head, effectively masking her features and expression when she came toward him down the aisle.

However, nothing could hide from him the pain in her eyes once she reached his side and met his gaze. She did not have to tell him that she had never intended her warning to create this situation. How could she have known that her decision that night would have so many serious and long-lasting repercussions?

Somehow they would work this out. Once married, he would be able to take her away from her brother's influence. He would take her back to the family ranch, then decide what to do. Other people had managed to salvage something from arranged marriages. There was no reason why he and Carina couldn't work out something as well.

When the ceremony concluded, Cody was encouraged to kiss his new bride. He carefully folded the veil up over her head, away from her face. Rich color rushed into her cheeks when he bent toward her, which pleased him. As pale as she had been earlier, Cody had been concerned that she was going to faint on him.

With the slightest hint of a wink and grin, he slipped his arms around her and lowered his mouth to hers. He felt her lips quiver when he first touched her, then all he was aware of was the softness, the yielding, the sweetness that was Carina.

A rush of emotion hit him. Raising his head he looked into her eyes and in a voice meant for her ears alone said, "I will always be here for you, Carina. You can count on me, no matter what happens."

Her eyes anxiously searched his and obviously found what she was seeking because she smiled, the most natural smile she had given him for some time. "Thank you, Cody. I'm glad."

There was no more time for the exchange of confidences. They were swept to the back of the chapel in a swell of organ music and on through the gardens to the ballroom, where they were surrounded by the delighted guests, all wishing them well. Cody kept Carina tucked firmly against his side, aware that the slight trembling he had felt in her earlier had never stopped.

Once again, the small orchestra began to play. This time Carina circled the floor in the arms of her new husband, while the guests watched from the sidelines.

"Are you okay?" he asked after they made the first circuit of the dance floor and she had not spoken.

"I'm not certain," she whispered, her eyes wide. "Is this real?"

He grinned. "As real as it gets, honey."

"I don't think I can take too much more of having people stare at me."

"You don't have to. I'll take care of it."

As soon as the dance was over, Cody made their excuses and whisked her up the stairs amid a great many ribald remarks. He paused only long enough to say a few words to Cole, who nodded and gave him a pat on the shoulder.

Once upstairs, Carina led him down the hallway to her room, then paused in embarrassed confusion. "Where are you going to sleep?"

"If I know Alfonso, and I think I do, I'll bet my clothes have been transferred to your room. Care to place a small wager?"

"But surely he—" She shook her head without saying more and opened her bedroom door. Cody remained in the doorway, leaning against the doorjamb with his arms crossed. Carina hurried into her dressing room. He responded to her muffled sound of dismay with a half smile.

She came out of the dressing room with her hands clasped, a worried expression on her face. Cody straightened and stepped inside the bedroom, hooking his foot on the door and closing it behind him without glancing back.

"Don't look so upset, *chula.* You don't have anything to worry about from me, remember?"

She walked over to where he stood in the center of

the room. "I will never forgive Alfonso for this. Never."

"Well, that gives us something in common right off, doesn't it?" He walked over to the French doors and opened them. Sounds of music and laughter drifted up from the courtyard.

"This is where you were the night you heard those men talking?" He didn't really care, but he thought it might help to get her mind off their present predicament, at least for a few minutes.

She hesitated, then joined him. "Yes."

"Alfonso doesn't believe there were any men. Did he tell you?"

She stared up at him in surprise. "No men? But of course there were. Why else would I have risked going to find you, if there were no men?"

He let his silence answer her.

She continued to look at him, until comprehension slowly engulfed her. "Oh, no! He couldn't have thought that— Why, he couldn't have believed that— Oh, Cody, that's why he did all of this," she said, waving her hand at her dress and at his clothes hanging in her closet.

"You got it."

"But this is terrible! How could he not have believed me when I tried to explain?"

"Because you didn't immediately go to him with your suspicions. Alfonso refuses to believe that you might have thought he could have wished me harm."

She whirled away and paced to the other side of the room. "Yes. It was very stupid of me. But I was so frightened, and I was afraid of making a mistake that might cost you your life." She spun around, her full skirt swirling. "Even so, look what has happened to you! You were forced to marry me because of my foolish behavior.''

''Not forced, exactly. I mean, nobody held a gun to my head. Let's just say I was persuaded, okay?''

''But this isn't what you want!''

''It isn't what you want, either.''

They stared at each other from opposite sides of the large room in a moment of shared revelation, recognizing that they were much like comrades at war with a common enemy.

Eventually Cody held out his hand and said, ''You're going to need help getting out of that dress, I suspect. I have a hunch you probably don't want my assistance. Would you like to call your mother?''

''No!'' Carina glanced around the room helplessly, obviously remembering when she had dressed earlier in the day. ''My mother must have known about this, and yet she didn't say a word. How could she do this to me?''

''You don't know that for sure. I have a hunch Alfonso planned his little surprise very carefully in order to lessen any resistance he might have aroused.''

''But my mother and sisters had my veil—''

''Your mother had just found it when I arrived at the church. Your family—all but Alfonso, of course—think that this is a true love match, that I have been secretly courting you and petitioning Alfonso for his permission for a long time. Your mother told me how delighted she was that you were going to be with me. For some reason, she seemed to believe you would be very happy being married to me.'' His grin was meant to be teasing, but she was too agitated to notice.

Carina reached around to the back of her dress, then made an impatient sound. ''My mother can't understand my desire for more education. So she assumes that marriage would be my only goal.'' She walked over to him and turned around. ''I would much prefer your help than to have to speak to anyone else at the moment.''

He decided not to point out her less than gracious acceptance of his help. Solemnly Cody began to work on the small buttons down her back.

''I thought we might leave here fairly early in the morning and drive to the ranch. It's my home, although I'm seldom there. Now that I have a wife, I need to make some decisions about certain things.''

She glanced over her shoulder. ''What things?''

''Oh, just some work I've been doing. It isn't too conducive to a strong home life. Maybe it's time for me to resign and move back to the ranch on a permanent basis.''

''Is that what you like to do? Ranch?''

The dress began to fall away and she grabbed it to hold the top in place. She hurried into the dressing room.

Cody sat down and pulled off his shoes, which were not as comfortable as the boots he generally wore. He stretched and flexed his toes with a sigh of relief.

''The foreman runs the ranching part of things,'' he replied, raising his voice slightly so that she could hear him. ''I always thought that someday I might start raising horses.'' He ran his hand through his hair. ''Who knows? Maybe now is the time to look into the idea more fully.''

Carina came out of the dressing room tying the

sash of her robe. Without looking at him, she walked over to the vanity and sat down. She removed the flower from her hair along with the various pins, and began to run the brush through its long length.

"Cody?"

"Hmm?"

Still without looking at him, she asked, "You're expected to sleep here with me, aren't you?"

He made no attempt to hide his amusement at her tone from her. *A guy could get a complex, if he didn't watch himself.* "That's the general idea, I think."

"You would be very embarrassed to have to find another place to spend the night, wouldn't you?"

He leaned back in his chair and in the mirror he studied the nervous and fretful young woman who refused to make eye contact with him. "I'm sure I'd survive. Is that what you want me to do?" he asked, curious to know how honest she would be with him.

She placed the brush carefully on the table in front of her before studying her hands and saying, "I don't want to do anything else that will cause you problems."

Cody took his time coming to his feet, and even more time to walk over to where Carina sat. He placed his hands on her shoulders and waited until she looked into the mirror and their gazes met.

"Carina, I know that you don't know much about men, and it's obvious that your mother didn't discuss much with you regarding marriage. So what I need to do is to let you get used to sharing your life with a male. I know that wasn't what you had planned. As far as that goes, this isn't what I had planned either, but we need to start this marriage in the way we mean to go on. Sooner or later we are going to become intimate.''

He could feel her shoulders tense at his words.

Without changing the pitch of his voice, which he had chosen in a deliberate effort to soothe her, he continued. ''However, we don't have to do anything about the matter tonight. We're both tired and more than a little undone by the suddenness of it all. What I suggest is that you go on to bed and try to get some sleep. I bet by morning you'll be feeling better about things, or at least will have gotten used to the situation a little more.''

''But where are you going to sleep?''

''I thought I might take a long, hot shower, then maybe stretch out on the other side of that bed over there. That thing's big enough to sleep a whole bunch of people. I doubt that either one of us would know the other one was there.''

He kept his eyes steady on hers, willing her to understand that he would not under any circumstances take advantage of her.

In a moment he felt her shoulders slump beneath his hands. She looked ready to drop, now that the tension had left her body. He reached down and lifted her into his arms and carried her over to the bed.

The covers had been turned back. He lowered her onto the bed, brushed her slippers off her feet and, with a deft twist of his wrist, unfastened her robe and whisked the soft garment away while he pulled the covers to her chin with his other hand.

''Get some sleep, honey. We'll talk more about this tomorrow.''

He turned away and had taken only a couple of steps when he heard her say, ''Cody?''

He forced himself to turn around once again, making certain that his expression remained impassive. "Yes?"

"Thank you," she whispered.

He gave her a grin and a thumbs-up sign before he walked into the bathroom and closed the door.

He leaned against the door with his eyes closed, feeling the relief of finally being alone for the first time in hours. When he opened them, he dispassionately stared at his image. Now that he didn't have to pretend, he wearily noted that his smile had long since disappeared. *You were pretty convincing, there, old buddy,* he told his image. *Almost had me fooled, and I knew how you were feeling. So the little gal's safe, is she? You're going to treat her like a sister, huh? You're going to pretend that seeing her in that filmy nightgown and robe didn't affect you, that watching her comb out her hair didn't make you want to bury your head in that glossy mass of curls. You're just a regular Sir Galahad, aren't you?*

He reached inside the shower stall and turned on the water, making certain that only cold water came pouring out. He tugged at the tie he had worn, tossing it on the marble counter before he pulled off the jacket in jerky movements. He removed the rest of his clothes, thinking about the woman lying in bed in the next room.

So he actually thought he was going to climb into that bed without blinking an eye, turn over and go to sleep as if his wife weren't lying there an arm's reach away.

His wife. Even the words set off a tingling within his body that he couldn't ignore.

Irritably he stepped under the icy deluge in an attempt to get his mind off his desires and on to what he intended to do about this fiasco of a marriage. The first thing he wanted to do was to get away from Alfonso Ramirez. The man had created enough havoc in his life for one lifetime.

Once he returned to the Circle C, he'd call his boss and discuss the situation with him. Somehow he couldn't see leaving Carina there at the ranch alone with Aunt Letty while he continued his work.

He gradually added warm water to the spray beating down on him, feeling the soothing relief on his battered body. He couldn't find the answers tonight. Perhaps there weren't any answers. Regardless of her age, Carina Ramirez Callaway was still a child in many ways. He had to give her some time and some space without taking advantage of the intimate nature of their relationship.

He had never had a tougher assignment in his life.

Carina lay there listening to the muted sound of the water and tried not to imagine what Cody must look like standing beneath the spray. She felt as if her body were on fire and she shifted restlessly on the bed, wondering what she could do to force her mind into a peaceful blankness.

He had looked so handsome, so austere, as he stood beside her in the chapel, repeating the vows in a firm voice. Nothing seemed to bother him, whether it was an attempt on his life or the sudden acquisition of a wife.

She envied him his ability to deal with life head-on without wavering. She turned her head slightly, looking at the French doors standing open across the room. She could hear the muffled sounds of conversation and laughter. Obviously everyone had enjoyed Alfonso's party and the impromptu wedding ceremony.

Carina wondered if she would wake up in the morning and discover that all of the events of this evening had been part of a dream. She might open her eyes and discover that the party was scheduled for that night. Could her subconscious possibly have dreamed that she would marry anyone, especially Cody Callaway?

Not even her subconscious could be so creative.

The bathroom door opened and Carina realized that the sound of running water had ceased several minutes before. Without moving her head she peeked over the covers and briefly saw Cody's silhouette in the doorway as he turned off the light, leaving the room in darkness except for the moonlight around the balcony.

Cody moved silently toward the French doors. Carina could feel her heart pounding as she watched him. In the brief glimpse she had been given of him, she knew that he wore only a small towel around his hips. He paused at the open doors for a few moments, watching the activities below, before he gave a barely audible sigh and quietly closed them.

Concentrating on keeping her breathing as even as possible, Carina watched as Cody moved to the other side of the bed. Her eyes reflexively closed in shock when she saw him nonchalantly drop the towel beside the bed and slide under the covers.

The bed was large enough that he was still a considerable distance from her, but all Carina could think about was the fact that Cody had come to her bed wearing nothing.

She fought to swallow without a sound, holding herself as still as possible. He had promised not to touch her, hadn't he? He had never gone back on his word, not since she had first met him.

The mattress beneath her quivered, signaling Cody's movement. She waited, not exactly certain of what she expected him to do. After a moment, the bed settled down and she risked the slight movement of her head to look in his direction. The light from the glass doors gave enough illumination for her to see him quite clearly.

He lay on his stomach with his head beneath the pillow. She could see the broad expanse of his shoulders and the way his back tapered down to where the sheet covered his narrow waist. The white sheet made a sharp contrast to his darkly tanned skin.

Carina found herself studying him with fascination. This man she had known for years, and yet did not know at all, was her husband. He had the right to lie there beside her. She now carried his name, just as she wore the ring that he had slipped on her finger during the ceremony in the chapel.

Remembering the ring, she lifted her left hand and studied the unusual piece of jewelry carefully. Although wide, it had a delicate look because of the filigree design. She had never seen anything so beautiful, nor so unusual. When had Cody gotten it? Had he known that he was to marry her tonight? Somehow she didn't think so, although he had hidden his reaction well.

With a soft sigh, she closed her eyes and allowed her body to relax. She could hear the sound of Cody's soft, even breathing and was surprised to find it reassuring as she drifted off to sleep.

The next time she opened her eyes they widened in surprise. Dawn light filtered into the room. Cody was watching her as he lay beside her, propped on his elbow, his head resting in his hand. She gazed up into those blue eyes of his, which had haunted her dreams the night before, and saw an expression there that she'd never seen before.

"Good morning," he murmured, slowly lifting his hand and with his finger nudging a wisp of hair away from her cheek. "Did you sleep well?"

She blinked. She had never heard that particular tone in his voice, either—it was warm and sensuous and caused her body to quiver.

Carina nodded, unable to speak.

He began to run his fingers through her hair as she began to relax.

"I'm afraid I can't say the same," he replied in a low voice, filled with self-mockery. "I kept waking up to find myself in bed with this beautiful woman. Despite all the rumors to the contrary, that just isn't my life-style. I found it downright disturbing." He grinned at her and she saw the teasing twinkle in his eyes.

"I found it a little strange, myself," she admitted.

He moved his hand to the side of her face and trailed his fingers along the curve of her cheek, traced the line of her jaw and down the length of her throat, eventually pausing at the demure neckline of her cotton nightgown. Mesmerized, Carina neither stiffened nor attempted to pull away. As though encouraged by her lack of objection, he slowly leaned down and pressed his mouth gently against hers.

Carina could feel something inside of her letting go, as though a part of her were melting. Quivery sensations rippled through her body in gentle waves causing her to shiver. Cody shifted slightly and slid both of his arms around her.

Carina felt engulfed in a swirling sea of feelings, all of them new, different and exciting. She shyly placed her arms around Cody's shoulders, and slid her fingers into the silkiness of his hair.

He made a deep sound of pleasure, delighting and encouraging her, so that she allowed her hands to explore him more fully, from the broad expanse of his back to the hair-roughened texture of his chest. When her fingers accidentally brushed against his nipple he shuddered.

Cody untied the ribbon at the neckline of her gown, loosening the garment so that it slid off her shoulder, exposing her breasts.

Carina knew she was blushing. How could she not? No one had ever looked at her so intimately before.

Cody lowered his mouth to her throat, leaving a trail of kisses to her breasts.

She forgot to breathe when he first touched his tongue to the tip of her breast. She had never known how sensitive that part of her body was until now. Exhaling on a shaky breath, she ran her fingertips across his chest with a sense of wonder.

"Ah, Carina," he whispered, inching her nightgown down, until she was fully exposed to his gaze. "You are so lovely. How could I have ever thought of you as a child? You are a woman—a perfectly formed...enticing...heart-stopping...woman." He interspersed his words with soft kisses on her breasts, her stomach, her belly button, her abdomen....

She stiffened at this newest intimacy, but he murmured soothing sounds while his fingers continued to work their magic over her body. She sighed and shifted restlessly, allowing her knee to fall to the side.

Cody leaned over her, finding her mouth again, no longer hiding his passion. She returned his kiss with innocent abandon.

His hands, never still, began to massage and circle at the top of her thighs where the melting sensations seemed to grow stronger. She wanted something more, something only he could give her, but she didn't know what that could be.

She whimpered and, as though he understood, Cody slipped his finger into the waiting softness. She gave a little jolt of delight and surprise at his audacious move. She lifted her hips to him in an unconscious rhythm, wanting to continue feeling the indescribable sensations he aroused inside her. His movements quickened, his tongue repeating the steady rhythm he had begun lower. She shifted, wanting to be closer to him. He increased the pace of movement until she felt a searing shock sweep through her, causing her body to stiffen like the bow of a hunter. She let out a soft, keening cry of surprise and release.

Carina couldn't believe what had happened just now. Cody held her tightly, stroking her hair, murmuring something beneath his breath. She listened, trying to hear his words, until finally she understood that he was apologizing to her.

She pulled away and looked into his eyes. "Why are you sorry?" she asked, when she could find her voice.

"For taking advantage of you. I didn't mean to let this go so far. It's just that—" his eyes burned, still hot with passion "—I've never been in such a situation before. I thought I had more control, but I—"

"Are you saying that what we did just now was wrong?"

"Well, no. Not wrong. Just, uh, inappropriate under the circumstances."

"We are married, Cody. You have done nothing that a husband would not do with his wife, have you?"

"Of course not. I mean, well, look, Carina. I'm older, more experienced, and I should know better. I don't want to take advantage of this situation. Neither one of us wanted to get married, but the fact is, we are."

She studied him for a long time in silence. "You don't want me," she finally said in a low voice, as though thinking out loud.

His laugh was not one of amusement. "Honey, if I didn't want you so damn bad, I wouldn't be hurtin' right now. But that's not the point. We barely know each other. You know nothing about the world. I know too much. You're an innocent, and I don't want to destroy that innocence." He rolled away from her and sat up, reaching for his jeans. "But I came damn close and I'm not very proud of myself."

"What are we supposed to do?" she asked to his back, as he stood without turning around.

"I wish to hell I knew," he finally muttered, stalking into the bathroom and slamming the door.

Six

"Carina," Cody drawled, dropping his arm companionably around her shoulders, "I'd like you to meet Letitia Callaway, better known in the clan as Aunt Letty."

They stood in the middle of a glass-enclosed room with a view of a patio that eerily resembled the one at Alfonso's hacienda. Carina smiled at the older woman who had been watering plants when they walked into the room. The woman registered surprise when she first saw them standing there. The surprise rapidly became shock, when Cody continued.

"Letty, my love, this is Carina Ramirez Callaway...my wife."

"Your—! Cody! What are you talking about?" Letty strode toward them, frowning.

Cody grinned his familiar lighthearted smile. A quick glance told Carina that the smile never reached his eyes. "I know, Letty, I know. You would have been there, if you'd known it was going to be a wedding. Well, I have to tell you...it took us all by surprise, didn't it, *chula?*" He gave Carina's shoulders a slight squeeze.

"I am very pleased to meet you, Miss Callaway," Carina said politely. "Cody has told me so much about you."

"Hah! I just bet he has," Letty replied with a snort. "And none of it any good, I'm sure." She looked at Cody for a long moment, then shook her head. "Married! Of all things! You were the very last person I would have guessed would be gettin' married any time soon."

Cody laughed. He sounded a little more relaxed now, which eased Carina's tension a little.

"This is a beautiful room, Miss Callaway. I—"

"My name's Letty...you might as well get used to saying it." She studied Carina for a long moment. "Carina, is it?" Shaking her head with resignation at Cody, she said, "She's just a child."

"She's older than she looks, Aunt Letty," he replied. "I thought she was about sixteen or so, myself, but she's twenty."

"I'm not talking age and you know it." Letty took Carina's hand. "I bet you're still attending classes, aren't you? In some private girls' school?"

"Not exactly, although I went to a private high school. I've recently finished my second year at the university in Mexico City."

Letty eyed her doubtfully. "Your family let you live there alone?"

Carina could feel herself flushing. "Well, not exactly. Alfonso rented an apartment for my mother and me. One of his men stayed there with us and drove me to and from school."

Letty glanced back at Cody. "About as close to convent-bred as you can find in this day and age. You ought to be ashamed of yourself."

"Dammit, Letty, I haven't done anything wrong. I tried to explain to Alfonso but he—" He stopped, running his hand through his hair. "Ah, hell. Why do I even bother trying to explain? It's too late, anyway."

"I would like to remind you, you uncouth renegade, that your language is not acceptable in the presence of ladies." With that Letty tugged on Carina's hand and said, "Come, my dear, let me show you around the Big House. I'm certain you would like to see your new home." Letty turned her back on Cody and drew Carina with her.

Cody stood there watching the two women leave the room. How in the hell did that woman manage to reduce him to a stammering schoolboy with visions of his mouth being washed out with soap? He could stand up to a kidnapper with a gun, he could face the dangers of working among drug smugglers, but Letty could ruffle his composure every time.

No matter. He was home now, with all that word signified. Letty was a part and parcel of the surroundings. Carina would have to get used to her, so she might as well start now. In the meantime, he would go get their bags.

They had stayed at Alfonso's hacienda that morning long enough for Carina to point out what she wanted packed and shipped to her in Texas. Since neither one of them wanted to see Alfonso, they had stayed upstairs to oversee some of the packing before venturing into the other part of the hacienda.

When they finally came down with their luggage Alfonso was nowhere around, which suited Cody just fine! To think that he had always considered Alfonso his friend. Some friend, betraying his own sister like that—forcing her to marry....

Cody paused, the trunk of his small car halfway raised, suddenly struck by something. He was angry at Alfonso, not because Alfonso had forced *him* to marry as much as because Alfonso had forced Carina. He lifted the bags from the car and closed the trunk, his mind caught up in his own reactions. Absently picking up the bags, he nudged the front door open and walked inside, heading for the wide stairway to the second floor.

Carina was the one who had been treated unfairly...like a child, without regard for her thoughts or feelings. None of the women he knew, from his aunt to his sisters-in-law, would tolerate such treatment. Of course, she had been upset. Who wouldn't have been?

As if that weren't enough, she had assured him that she wanted his life to continue as it had before, even though her dreams of an education and career had been dashed.

He was halfway down the hallway when he heard Letty's voice and was reminded of the suite of rooms in his wing of the sprawling house. Oh, no! He had meant to explain— He needed to—

The word he muttered beneath his breath was short, profane, and worthy of a vigorous mouthwashing.

He paused in the doorway of his room and leaned against the doorjamb, listening as Letty explained.

"Now this is the master suite in Cody's wing of the house. The dressing area is in here..." Cody watched the women disappear into another room, but he could still hear the tour guide's strident tones. "The bathroom is really quite something. Cole had all the plumbing updated and the fixtures remodeled a few years ago. If you ask me it was a big waste of money, gettin' all these fancy things, but then, again, I have to admit I've enjoyed my tub that swirls hot water around so briskly. After I've spent a few hours in the garden, that Jacuzzi-thing feels pretty good."

Cody shook his head, grinning. Letty had never admitted to anyone else, as far as he knew, that she approved of anything about the remodeling. What an old fraud she was!

When the women walked back into the room, Carina was the first to spot him. She stopped, looking at him uncertainly.

"Oh!" Letty exclaimed. "There you are. It took you long enough. Carina tells me most of her things are being shipped, which makes some sense, I'd say. I told her Rosie could help her unpack, but she insists she can do it."

She glanced at the two of them, who were continuing to stare at each other in silence.

"Well. I'm certain you two could eat something. I've never heard Cody turn down food. I'll just go down and tell Angie you're here."

Without taking his eyes off Carina, Cody murmured, "You do that, Aunt Letty. We'll be down in a few minutes."

He straightened to let her pass him, then hooked his heel around the door, letting it close behind him.

Carina started toward him. "I, uh, didn't know

what to say to your aunt when she showed me this room. I mean, it's obvious it's yours and I don't want to take your room away. After all—"

"Carina?"

"Yes?"

"Stop worrying about things, all right?" He slipped his hand to the nape of her neck, feeling the weight of her long, silky hair against the back of his hand. Slowly, but steadily he pulled her toward him until he had both arms around her. He brushed his lips against hers once…twice…and then settled them more firmly, as he tasted and teased her delectable mouth.

She had tensed beneath his hand when he first touched her, but had not resisted when he pulled her closer. With his kiss, she seemed to relax and melt against him, as though she trusted him.

Trusted him! Cody jerked away from her as though he had been burned. With his hands on her upper arms he watched as her thick black lashes slowly left their resting place on her flushed cheeks and fluttered open, revealing those damnably compelling black eyes. His gaze wandered down to her mouth, still moist from their kiss.

Cody groaned.

"What's wrong?" she asked.

He just shook his head.

"I know I'm not experienced, but if you would show me how you want me to kiss you, I could—"

"Honey, you don't need any lessons, believe me. You do quite well on your own. Either that, or you're a hell of a fast learner."

He turned away, his shoulders stiff, and walked over to the window.

"Are we going to share this room?" she asked, after several minutes of silence.

"Not if I can help it," he muttered under his breath.

"Did you say something?" she asked.

He turned back to her, hoping he had himself under better control. "We'll work out something, *chula.* I don't know what we're going to do just yet." Afraid to touch her for fear he couldn't control his reactions, he said, "Let's get something to eat. I never can think on an empty stomach." He waved his hand to indicate she should precede him, so that he had the excruciating pleasure of walking behind her down the hallway and stairs, the view of her delectable derriere, swaying in front of him, a constant reminder of what he wanted but knew better than to pursue.

Good old Alfonso—his buddy, his pal—had a lot to pay for.

Letty joined them for lunch, which eased the tension for Cody. As usual, Letty had jumped in with both feet to help them manage their lives.

"I hope this means you intend to hang around the ranch more, Cody. Now that you've got a wife, you can't continue to gallivant around the countryside all the time, whoopin' it up with all your wild friends."

"What a lovely picture you paint of me, Aunt Letty. I'm touched."

"Surely you don't intend to drag Carina along with you. She would be—"

"No, Letty. I don't. I'm still thinking about what we can do now that we're married. You have to admit the circumstances are unusual. I mean, most people who get married have had time to adjust to the idea, make plans...that sort of thing. This whole business was kind of sprung on us."

Letty turned to Carina. "What were you planning to do before all of this happened?"

"I really didn't have any plans. When Alfonso refused to allow me to continue my education I stayed at home, helping around there."

"Why in tarnation wouldn't he let you finish your schooling?"

"He said I didn't need any more education. That I would marry and have a family and be busy with them."

"That's the biggest bunch of hogwash I've ever heard. Why, an education is just as important—maybe even more important—if you're going to be training young minds, than if you were out working somewhere."

Cody added, "What Carina wants to do is work in the field of speech therapy."

"Oh?"

"She was telling me that she had hoped to convince Alfonso to send her to school in the Chicago area."

Letty turned from gazing at Carina sympathetically and narrowed her eyes toward Cody. "So why don't *you* send her?"

"What?" He replaced his coffee cup in his saucer before he spilled its contents.

"You heard me. From what you were telling us, this gal risked her neck...and lost her reputation...trying to save your ornery hide. And what does she get for it? Stuck here with a footloose husband and a bossy old woman."

"I wouldn't consider you exactly old, Letty," Cody drawled, grinning.

"Don't get smart-mouth with me, now. Do you intend to settle down and stay here at the ranch full-time?" She leaned on the table and faced Cody without blinking.

"I don't know if I can, Letty. You see, I—"

"Oh, I see a lot of things, young man. Mostly I see that you don't have the sense God gave a goose. Carina is without a doubt the best thing that could have happened to you, and you don't even know it. She went from one domineering, opinionated man to another."

"Hey, wait a minute. I'm nothing like Alfonso. I'm not telling her what to do. I married her, damn it, I didn't purchase her. She's got a mind and a will of her own. She can do anything she pleases. You make it sound like I intend to chain her up in my room or something."

Letty's harshly lined face seemed to crinkle, then crack. Cody stared at her in shock as the lines rearranged themselves into a big grin, as she said, "Prove it!"

In all the years he had known Letty, Cody couldn't remember seeing her smile so broadly before. Oh, there had been a few times when the corners of her mouth might quirk up for a split second, but Cole had once suggested it was no more than a gas pain. Cody stared at his aunt as if she had just turned from a frog into a prince...or in this particular case, a princess.

"Prove it?" he echoed, thoroughly confounded.

"That's right. Let's see you put your money where your mouth is."

"Meaning?"

"If you're so all-fired liberated that you won't stop your wife from doing what she truly wants to do, then why don't *you* send her up to Chicago to school?"

Cody stared at his aunt, convinced she had finally cracked after all these years. Her eyes sparkled and she sat there, still smiling at him, as if the joke were on him, if he could just see it.

Letty had always liked to get the best of him. He took pride in the fact that she rarely managed to do so, and he wasn't about to admit that she might have gotten the upper hand this time.

"Actually, I've been thinking along those very same lines, myself." He lied, with commendable self-possession given the existing circumstances. "However, I haven't had an opportunity to discuss the matter with Carina." He glanced at his watch. "We've barely been married twenty-four hours. I assumed we would take a few days to, uh, to—"

"Honeymoon?" Letty asked.

"Well, no. Not exactly. I mean, there's no reason to rush into a— Dammit, Letty. It's none of your business, and I don't even know why I'm discussing it with you. Whatever we decide will be between us, do you understand? I—"

"Cody?"

Carina's soft voice punctured his ire, releasing the build up of steam into a sizzling hiss that escaped from his lips. He turned to his wife. "Yes?"

"Were you really thinking about sending me to school?"

Her eyes sparkled with hope and with excitement. He looked into their depths and was lost. His gaze flickered to her lips and down the graceful line of her neck. He swallowed. "Sure...if that's what you want."

"Oh, Cody! I can't believe it. Last night I thought my dreams were over, that I would never be happy—"

There was no doubting her sincerity. It played hell with his ego. He had been escaping the clutches of possessive women his whole life. He had lost count of the number of women who had done everything in their power to get him to make a permanent commitment to them. Each time he had run, feeling nothing but relief that he had managed to escape. Now his wife could hardly wait to get away from him.

He didn't like the feeling that gave him. It left a bad taste in his mouth. He took a bite of Angie's cherry pie and *slowly* chewed, in an effort to buy himself some time.

Of course Letty had to jump back in. The two women were already considering phoning the university, to see if she could still register for the spring semester. They talked about getting records transferred, about appropriate clothes for that far north, about a place to live.

"Cody, why don't you two buy a place up there? There's no reason to rent, when you could own a place."

"While you're arranging my life so swiftly, Letty, you might want to take into consideration that I would have nothing to do in Chicago."

Letty waved her hand in dismissal. "Of course, you wouldn't. I wouldn't expect you to stay up there. Just help Carina get situated. She's going to be too busy to look after you, anyway. This way she can concentrate on her studies and you can practice curtailing some of your more outrageous activities—if you have a mind to, that is.''

''Well, thank you for the invitation to plan a little of my own life.''

''Oh, quit puffing up like some ol' horny toad, Cody. You're not the sulkin' kind. Besides, this is all your idea, anyway. Didn't you just say so?''

''Buying a place in Chicago didn't suddenly pop into my mind, no.''

''Well, of course, that's up to you. But it's just such a waste to pay rent, when you can own a place. Then Carina could fix it up any way she pleased and not have to worry about some fussy landlord.''

He looked from Letty to Carina. ''Would I at least get to have visiting privileges?''

Carina stared at him uncertainly, then smiled. ''You're teasing me, aren't you?''

Slowly he grinned at her. ''Yeah, I think I am.''

''You don't mind if I go to Chicago?''

He sighed, confused by all the conflicting emotions that had been running through him during this conversation. Less than twenty-four hours ago he had been incensed that a bride was being thrust upon him. Now he was feeling abandoned because she was blithely planning to stay out of his life.

Wasn't this what he wanted?

He could continue his work unhindered. He could attend Enrique Rodriguez's trial, keeping Carina's involvement to a minimum because of the distance. He could, in effect, retain his bachelor status, at least for another year or two.

''No, *chula,*'' he said after a long silence. ''I don't mind if you go to Chicago. I think it's a great plan.

I want you to be happy. I want you to be a person in your own right, not just my wife."

Carina came around the table and hugged him, her eyes moist with happy tears. "Oh, thank you, Cody. I am so happy...thanks to you."

He hugged her back, his eye caught by the pleased look on Letty's face. When she saw him watching her, she winked and gave him a thumbs-up signal.

Her approval made him feel a little better.

But not much.

Seven

"Oh, Cody, look at the view! I had no idea Lake Michigan was so large. It could be the Gulf of Mexico."

Cody sauntered over to stand beside Carina and look out the plate-glass window of the condominium. "You'd notice a difference if you were in it. This is freshwater...the Gulf is saltwater."

"Oh, this is so beautiful. What do you think, Cody?"

He hadn't taken his gaze off his wife. "About what?"

"Do you like the apartment?"

He glanced around. "It's all right, I guess. A little small."

"Small! Cody, it has over two thousand square feet. That's huge."

"I suppose. Guess I'm used to the Big House."

She walked across the massive living room and disappeared through the kitchen doorway. "This kitchen is wonderful," she announced. "I can't believe it. A place to myself. I can spend all the time I want in here."

He followed her to the doorway and looked inside, watching as she opened cabinet doors, the refrigerator and oven doors, and checked the microwave and dishwasher. When she caught him staring at her she laughed. "I feel like I'm in a fairy tale."

"Oh, yeah? Which one, *Beauty and the Beast*?"

She shook her head, her eyes dancing. "Of course not. *Cinderella*!"

He blinked. "Are you saying you see me as some kind of prince?"

She danced over to him and hugged him. "Oh, yes. You make a wonderful prince, Cody. Tall and very handsome and—".

His mouth covered hers, effectively muffling her next words. Once again she melted against him, a habit that increasingly frustrated him. Damn! He wanted this woman like none he had ever known. In just a few weeks, she had insinuated herself into his life so completely that he couldn't remember what he had done without her.

He was aware of every breath she took, every movement she made. He listened for her delighted laugh, finding ways to provoke it. He found excuses to touch her—brushing a wisp of hair away from her face, running his hand over her shoulder, hugging her—and as often as possible, kissing her.

He felt like an addict, craving a fix.

Meanwhile, she treated him like an indulgent uncle.

She pulled away from him with another hug, and said, "Are we going to buy this one?"

They had looked at dozens of places and time was running out. After a flurry of paperwork and phone calls, Carina was enrolled in school. Finding a place for her to stay was a must.

"Do you think you could be happy here?"

"Oh, yes!"

"I'll admit I like the security in this building. Would you be afraid to stay here alone?"

She shook her head. "But I won't be alone all the time, will I?" She looked wistful.

"Of course not. It's just that I can't walk away from what I'm doing right at this time. I've already extended my leave twice. As soon as I get you settled, I've got to head back to Texas."

She spun away from him and headed down the hallway toward the bedrooms. He had already looked at them. There was a large master bedroom with private bath, another bedroom that would serve as a guest room, also with private bath, and the third could easily become a study.

He followed her into the master bedroom. She stood in the middle of the room turning in a small circle. "Oh, Cody, we need furniture, and dishes, and linens and— I can't believe how much."

"Don't worry about it. We'll go tell the realtor we've decided on this one. It shouldn't take long to sign the papers. We'll spend the next couple of days shopping. I thought women enjoyed that."

"But we're spending so much money," she pointed out.

"*Chula,* I've got three trust funds that I've never touched. I've never had to. In addition, I get a third of everything generated by Callaway Enterprises. Don't worry about breaking me. It won't happen."

She came to him and took his hand. "But it's all your money. I've contributed nothing."

"Alfonso sent the papers to transfer the money he had been investing that your father left for you. You're not exactly a pauper, darlin'."

"Could I have control of it?"

"Certainly."

Her eyes widened. "Aren't you going to tell me how I don't know anything about managing money?"

He grinned. "Don't worry. You'll learn—one way or the other."

"Oh, Cody, I am so happy and it's because of you. Then I feel so guilty. I've been given so much, while you've gotten nothing."

He picked up her left hand and kissed the wedding band she wore. "What do you mean, I've gotten nothing? I have a wife. That's good enough for me."

She stared at him doubtfully. "Are you sure?"

Once again, he pulled her into his arms. "Don't ever doubt it, darlin'. I wouldn't have it any other way."

Their hotel suite had two bedrooms and Cody had not allowed himself to think about entering her bedroom there. He had promised her time...and space...and he was determined to give it to her, even if it killed him. He had never heard of anyone dying from too many cold showers, but there was always a first time.

Now they would have a place of their own. He liked the feeling that gave him. Oh, he loved the ranch. He had a special feeling for the land, a feeling that neither Cole nor Cameron seemed to share. They were content to establish homes elsewhere and occasionally visit the Circle C.

He had always known he would spend his life living on the ranch, but he was just now realizing that he liked owning a place that was just his and Carina's. Since she planned to continue her courses through the summer, she would get her degree in eighteen months.

Although he would need to continue what he was doing on the border until the present operation was concluded, he would still be able to fly to Chicago to see her on a regular basis. Thank God for the company jet; he wouldn't have to plan his visits around an airline schedule.

Letty had been right to insist that Carina be given a chance to make her own decisions. Cody was enthralled with Carina's blossoming personality. Free of restrictions for the first time in her life, she seemed to float—her obvious joy encompassing everything and everyone around her.

Cody could get lost in the moment, if he were to allow himself. He could forget about all the promises he had made to her and to himself. He could become a permanent part of her life.

Did he dare?

A week later Cody let himself into their new apartment. He had been out at Midway Airport talking to the pilot and arranging his flight back to Texas. Now he had the unpleasant duty of telling Carina that he was leaving tonight, although he knew she had been expecting him to leave any day.

Last night had been their first night in their new

home. When it was time for bed, Cody had taken the coward's way out and slept in the guest bedroom.

What the hell was wrong with him, anyway? He was acting like some adolescent kid with his first crush, stammering and stuttering, feeling awkward and ridiculous.

Carina hadn't said anything about the sleeping arrangements to make him think she wanted him to stay with her. Somehow he had gotten himself all tied up in the situation, needlessly complicating what was really a simple relationship.

They were adults, weren't they? Surely they could sit down and sanely discuss the matter. Of course they could…soon. In the meantime, he would continue his role of casual companion, at least for this last night they would have together for awhile.

Cody paused in the doorway, his gaze drawn to the dining alcove. His heart sank at the sight that greeted him. The small round table had been draped with a lace cloth, silver candlesticks held flame red candles already lit, their bright color matching the red roses he had given Carina two days ago—on her first day of classes. Now they were arranged in a low bowl between the candles, seductively scenting the air.

Their new china, crystal and silverware sparkled in the candlelight, and red linen napkins were intricately folded on the plates.

A tantalizing scent of savory ingredients drifted from the kitchen.

Cody groaned. How was he going to be able to maintain a semblance of casual companionship in an atmosphere like this?

"Cody? Is that you?"

"It had better be," he replied, pocketing his key and moving toward the kitchen.

Carina came out of the kitchen and met him. She wore a filmy, full-skirted dress with long, flowing sleeves and a high, ruffled neckline.

"You look sensational."

Her face lit up. She glanced down at the pink dress. "Oh, do you like it? I wanted something special, but I'm not used to buying clothes on my own." She touched the sleeve. "I was hoping it was all right."

He took her hand, brought it to his mouth, and placed a kiss across the knuckles. "It is more than just all right. You have exquisite taste. If you don't believe me, just look around you. You have an innate sense of style."

Draping her arm over his shoulder, he pulled her closer, eager to kiss her. A loud buzzing sound erupted in the kitchen.

"Oh! The roast is ready. Are you hungry?" she asked, stepping away from him. In a whirl of flowing material she fled to the kitchen.

"Oh, yeah. I'm very hungry," he offered, more to himself than to her. He felt as if he were starving for another taste, another touch. He would be leaving her in a few hours, with no idea of when he would return. How could he possibly walk away without—

Carina came out of the kitchen carrying a laden tray. Cody reached her in two long strides, taking the heavy weight and carrying it to the table, where she placed the separate serving dishes in their designated areas.

She took the tray from him and headed for the kitchen. "I bought some wine today," she said over her shoulder. "Would you like to open it?"

He followed her into the kitchen. "My, you *are* being daring. Wine, yet!"

He listened for her chuckle, and smiled to himself when he heard it. "If you must know, I explained what we were having for dinner and the nice man suggested some wines. He let me sample them, so I would know the one I liked best."

"What nice man?" he asked suspiciously.

She handed him the wine. "The one at the liquor store."

"Humph." For a moment he had envisioned his naive little wife blithely accosting some stranger on the street. He should have known better.

Cody discovered that he actually had an appetite for food as soon as he began to eat her meal. "I had no idea you could cook," he said, pausing to sip the wine. He had to admit that she had made an excellent choice.

"Are you being insulting?" she asked, raising her brows.

"Not intentionally. Why?"

"I thought every young girl was taught how to cook. How else can she supervise what goes on in her kitchen?"

"Most of the women I know admit they get lost in a kitchen."

"Really?" Never had her smile appeared sweeter. "But then, it wasn't their cooking skills that attracted you to them, was it?"

He almost choked on his wine. He felt just like he suddenly had been clawed by a baby kitten he had been stroking gently. "I was paying you a compliment," he pointed out with dignity.

"By comparing me to your other women? Not likely."

"Hey, what are we talking about here? I don't have any other women."

She eyed him for a moment over her wineglass. When she finally put the glass down, she asked, "You don't?"

He kept his gaze steady. "No. You are my wife. There is no one else in my life."

"But I'm not your *real* wife. I mean, it isn't as though you chose me or wanted to marry me, or—" Her voice trailed off.

Cody pushed his chair back with careful movements and stood. Then he walked behind her chair and slid it away from the table. When she looked up at him he grinned, saying, "And if you're going to add that I don't want you, then you're wrong, *chula*. Very, very wrong." He picked her up—his arms around her waist and beneath her knees—and started down the hallway toward the bedrooms.

"Cody? What do you think— We're in the middle of dinner, Cody. Why—"

His mouth effectively silenced her. He could taste the wine on her lips, smell the scent of her new perfume, feel her tremble, hear the catch in her breath, and when he lifted his head, he could see the smile of encouragement on her face.

Knowing that she wanted him pushed him over the edge.

Even in his urgency, he carefully removed her dress and matching slip, her hose and shoes, until only her bra and panties remained. He undressed, breaking all of his previous records for speed, then knelt beside her.

"You are so beautiful," he whispered, spreading her hair over the pillow...trailing his fingers along the edge of her bra...sliding his hand behind her to unfasten that particular garment.

"I feel beautiful when you look at me that way," she admitted. She sounded a little breathless. And shy.

She shivered when he lifted the bra away. With his finger he lightly touched the pink crest now revealed, watching it draw into a tight nub. Cody leaned over and flicked his tongue across the rosy peak. She shifted restlessly.

He reached beneath her and pulled the bed cover and sheet down, then over her. "Are you cold?" he whispered. She shook her head, but her skin continued to ripple with goose pimples. "Let me warm you," he murmured.

He fought the clawing need deep in his belly, determined not to rush her, not to take advantage of her as he had on their wedding night.

He ran his hand across her body and down her side—soothing and yet arousing, reassuring and encouraging her to respond to him.

She was so sweet. He could no longer resist kissing her. This time he placed his kisses all over her body as he explored her, memorized her, possessed her with his lips.

"Oh, Cody, oh, please...I want you to— Oh, yes, please..."

When he moved over her and allowed her to feel how strongly she affected him, she lifted her hips in silent supplication. How could he resist such honesty when he wanted her equally as much?

He bent her legs and knelt between them, then

slowly leaned forward until he was stretched out over her, resting his weight on his forearms. She pulled him down so that she could kiss him, her mouth searching, her tongue imitating the motions he had taught her.

She was small...small and so tight he was afraid for her, but she wouldn't let him draw away. Instead, she locked her heels together around his thighs, forcing him to complete what he had started.

He felt her flinch when he broke through the thin barrier and he hated himself for hurting her, but, oh! she felt good. He felt her warmth surround and enfold him. Never before had Cody experienced anything like this.

There was no more time to savor the spiraling sensations. He had waited too long, spent too many restless nights, endured too many cold showers to deny himself for another moment.

Each movement made him groan with pleasure and when she seemed to go up in flames all around him he lost the small amount of control he had maintained. He joined her in the conflagration.

Not wanting to crush her, he rolled until she lay on top of him, still joined. He pressed her against him, enjoying the slight weight of her, as she cuddled so intimately against him.

He couldn't seem to keep his hands still. As though they had a mind of their own they continued to stroke, to fondle, to caress, until he could feel himself growing hard inside her once again.

She lifted her head and stared at him, her eyes wide in astonishment. He grinned and slowly lifted his hips, causing her to gasp. She was still sprawled across him. Lazily, he positioned her knees on either side of his hips, then eased her away from him until he could find her breast with his mouth.

She tightened her knees, hugging him with her thighs, and he began to move in a smooth, rhythmic motion. His hands rested on her hips, guiding and mutely instructing her.

He wasn't at all certain that he ever would get enough of her, not if he tried for the next hundred years.

She was so perfect, this small, innocent person. His wife.

Carina took over the rhythm, increasing her movements until he was wild, straining, fighting for and yet not ready to accept the culminating release that was rapidly overtaking them.

When the release struck, Cody felt as if he were drained from his toes upward, leaving nothing but a shell. He couldn't believe what had just happened. He had never been able to reach two such dizzying climaxes in such a short time. What had this woman-child done to him?

He lay there, gasping for air, wondering if his legs would ever be strong enough to carry him out of there.

"Carina?" He managed to get out after two tries.

"Mmm?"

"*Chula,* there's something I meant to tell you," he paused between every two words in an effort to find air enough to talk.

She raised her head and looked at him. "We're not married?"

Her question caught him off guard and he choked, laughing. When he was finally able to speak again, he said, "As far as I know we're definitely, legally married."

"That's nice," she murmured, allowing her head to rest on his chest once more. "I'm very, very glad."

He could feel the slight movement of her hand caressing him, and his heart seemed to swell in his chest with new and overwhelming emotion.

"I don't want to leave you," he admitted.

"Then stay," she replied softly, not looking at him.

"I can't. I meant to tell you earlier, but seeing you and—and well, everything, made me forget. I'm leaving tonight. I should have been at the airport an hour ago."

She jerked her head up and stared at him. "Tonight?"

"Yeah. Now, as a matter of fact."

She glanced down at the two of them so closely entwined, and grinned. "Like this?"

He shook his head, a feeling of despair slipping over him. Never had he felt so pulled in opposite directions. He had given his word that he would return tonight. He needed to be in Mexico no later than tomorrow night. He had spent years infiltrating this particular group and there was no one to take his place. He had to be there.

But not now! he wanted to cry out. Not when he had moved his wife fifteen hundred miles from where he would be. He reminded himself that she would be much safer up here. He also reminded himself that she needed this time on her own, needed to know that he would not be oppressive and dictatorial as her brother had been.

"You never finished your dinner," she finally said.

''I know. You were just too distracting,'' he admitted ruefully.

She sighed and shifted, allowing him to sit up. ''When will you be back?''

He headed toward the shower, not trusting himself to look at her and still have the strength to leave. ''As soon as I can possibly get away. You can count on that.''

Eight

Cody stared out the window of the plane at the clouds drifting past the wing tip, feeling as though he had spent most of the past eighteen months in the air between Texas and Chicago. He had thrown himself into his work in an almost desperate effort to bring about a successful conclusion to the sting operation the DEA had set up with his help.

He ran his hand over his face. The past two weeks had been hell. He couldn't remember the last time he had been in a bed for a full night's rest. He had gotten into the habit of napping wherever he could, in whatever was available at the time—a chair, a couch, a bench. When he finally got a couple of days' break, he had grabbed it, taking time for only a quick shower and some clean clothes.

He closed his eyes, his thoughts on Carina. He hadn't seen her in almost six months, the longest they had been separated since the wedding. Six long, grueling months.

Even their telephone conversations had proven to be frustrating. One of her first questions when he called would be, When was he coming to see her? Invariably his answer would be painful for him. He didn't know. After that, she would have little more to say, merely answering his questions in monosyllabic words.

She didn't understand what he was doing and why it was so important. He couldn't tell her the whole truth. In the past few months Alfonso had become a part of the scene, which had devastated him. Alfonso, part of the drug cartel? How could Cody tell his wife that he was diligently working to put her brother behind bars?

Never had Cody so misjudged a man as he had Alfonso.

Alfonso had sent several messages to Carina through Cody, but she never made any comment when he passed them on to her. Cody had kept his distance from Alfonso, using his supposed attitude regarding the forced marriage as an excuse for his continued aloofness. What a hell of a situation to be caught up in! Worrying about Alfonso, and Carina's reactions, had been the cause of a great deal of his sleeplessness these past several months.

He felt so isolated. Somewhere in the time since he and Carina had married, Cody had discovered that he no longer wanted his self-imposed isolation. How ironic that he now had no choice.

He closed his eyes, entertaining himself with memories of their times together during her first year in

Chicago. He smiled to himself, allowing his mind to drift and to dream....

If he were to single out the most anticipated moment of each visit, it would be that instant when she first saw him. He couldn't begin to describe the rapidly changing expressions that raced across her face, but joy seemed paramount.

Another welcomed event was waking up with her in his arms each morning. He never grew tired of that aspect of their relationship. On the contrary, he could hardly wait until the time they would be together every day and every night for the rest of their lives.

Each trip he had made north had brought them a little closer. Resisting his need to keep her in bed with him for his entire stay, Cody virtuously had planned outings for them. Sometimes he would take her shopping, delighting in buying her things she would not buy for herself. They attended movies, plays, museums, and explored the many aspects of the city.

However, he much preferred the times when they were alone.

He found her shyness endearing. As responsive as she was during their lovemaking, she never initiated anything, always waiting for him to show her what he wanted from her. He smiled at some of those more intimate memories and stirred restlessly in his seat. Although she appeared prim and dressed very properly—even at home—she came alive in his arms.

He was looking forward to their time together these next few days. He felt as if he were escaping from the reality of his life and indulging in a fantasy where there was no evil to combat and conquer.

Carina had done well in school. She would be graduating in a few weeks, thank God, and would be returning to Texas. Unfortunately, everything on the border was heating up. The timing for her return was all wrong. One of his reasons for breaking away now was to talk to her about her plans.

His boss knew he would be finished with this type of work once this sting operation was concluded. Cody hoped that he would never have to tell Carina what he had been doing in Mexico nor the part he had played in Alfonso's arrest.

He had decided not to tell her he was coming on this trip since he had canceled two of his previously planned visits. She probably wouldn't have believed him, anyway.

He had decided to go directly to the campus and wait for her to finish with her classes. They would go home together and make up for the months they had been apart.

He could almost feel the silkiness of her long hair as he ran his fingers through its thick length. He fell asleep with a smile on his lips.

Carina stopped to speak to her instructor before leaving the classroom. There were only three more weeks before finals. She was excited and filled with anxiety at the same time. For several minutes, the instructor discussed with her some of the points she had raised, then Carina left the room and started down the hallway.

She would never regret having moved to Chicago and continuing her education. Her internship at a local speech clinic had already convinced her she had chosen the right field, but at what price?

The move might have cost her her marriage. What

marriage? she reminded herself. For the first year she had been here she had kept herself so busy she didn't have time to miss Cody when he wasn't there. Back then, he had flown up to see her every few weeks, seemingly as eager to be with her as she had been to have him there.

They never talked about their feelings for each other. She was too shy to tell him how much she had grown to love him, especially when he showed no indication of wanting to hear such a declaration. He was so self-assured, so self-sufficient. She knew that Cody Callaway needed no one, not even a wife.

He showed her a great deal of attention whenever he visited. She blushed at some of her memories. She had discovered some things about men as her circle of friends increased. She better understood their needs and drives, and knew that Cody could want her without necessarily loving her.

Most of the time she could accept the truth of their situation. Other times, she felt lonely and bereft.

She had been so upset the last time he had canceled his proposed trip to see her that she could scarcely talk. As soon as she had hung up from that conversation, she had burst into tears and cried for hours.

Why did life have to be so complicated? Surely to be in love with your husband wasn't such an unusual circumstance. She shook her head in an effort to break her chain of thought.

''Carina? Hey, Carina, wait up.''

She glanced over her shoulder and saw Chad, one of her classmates who worked with her at the clinic.

''Hi, Chad. What's up?''

''I'm walking these days. My car finally gave up the ghost last week and went to that old parking lot in the sky.'' He piously held his hands beneath his chin in a prayer-like position and looked heavenward. ''My buddies and I had a ceremony for the old geezer. That car was older than I was, you know. It was more like a friend. We'd been through a lot together. To commemorate the loss, Charlie made a wreath of empty oil cans and Dave said an eulogy at the junkyard.''

Carina laughed as Chad held the door open for her. She ducked under his arm and stepped outside. The brisk breeze, so familiar to the area, whipped her ankle-length skirt around her legs.

She fought with her skirt and the loose hair blowing around her face at the same time.

''Need some help?'' he asked, laughing at her efforts.

She looked up at him and saw the teasing glint in his eye. ''I can just imagine what sort of help you would give me!''

He obligingly wiggled his brows in a mock-villain way and growled, ''You are safe in my presence, me beauty, never doubt that.'' Chad dropped his arm around her shoulder, effectively holding her hair in place. ''Where you headed?'' he asked, matching his steps with hers.

''Home. I don't have to go to the clinic until Monday. How about you?''

''I'm supposed to be at the clinic within the next half hour. I was hoping you were going that way so I wouldn't have to take the bus, but—''

''No problem, Chad. The clinic isn't that far out of the way. So what did you think about the prognosis on the Moreno child?''

They talked about their assigned cases as they

wended their way across campus, comfortable with their casual companionship.

Cody watched them coming toward him. They were so absorbed in their conversation they were oblivious to their surroundings.

He hadn't recognized her at first, because he hadn't expected to see her with anyone—especially not a man. An icy dread seemed to fill his chest. The cozy way she was tucked under the guy's shoulder irritated him, but he wasn't going to jump to any hasty conclusions.

Once she saw him, he would know.

So he waited beside her car and watched the couple approach him.

Carina raised her head after finding her keys in her purse and saw Cody casually leaning against her little sports car, his legs negligently crossed at the ankles, his arms folded across his chest.

"Cody?"

Her face registered shock. Nothing more.

"Cody! What are you doing here? Why didn't you call and let me know you were coming?"

Cody watched her shrug the man's arm from her shoulder and hurry toward him. He was glad he wore his sunglasses; they masked the pain he knew must show on his face. Slowly, he straightened to his full height.

"Hello, Carina."

She stopped a few inches away, not touching him. "How did you get here?" she asked in a breathless voice.

"Took a cab. Thought I'd surprise you." He glanced past her. "Guess I did, huh?"

She spun around. "Oh! Cody, this is Chad Evans,

a classmate of mine. We work together at the clinic. Remember I told you I've been putting in twenty hours a week there this semester?"

"I remember." He held out his hand. "Cody Callaway."

Chad took his hand and grinned. "Oh, I knew who you were. I've heard about you from Carina."

"Oh?" He glanced down at her. She watched him without expression. There was no sign of welcome in her face, no indication that she was glad to see him. The icy dread in his chest grew larger. "I'm afraid you have the advantage, then. Carina's never mentioned you."

Carina spoke up. "I've offered Chad a ride to the clinic. He's temporarily without transportation."

"Hey, no problem," Chad said, backing up a couple of steps. "You didn't know your husband was here. I understand how it is. You've both got a lot of catching up to do. Look. I'll take a bus and—"

"Don't be silly," she said. "If you don't mind the tiny back seat, you won't have to wait for a bus in this blustery weather." She looked at Cody with a level gaze as if she were expecting him to make a comment. Instead, he stepped back and waited for her to unlock her car.

Carina and Chad kept up a spirited dialogue on the way to the clinic, making Cody feel old and totally out of touch. The two students obviously shared friends and associations that meant nothing to him. He rubbed his raspy jaw, wishing he had shaved.

Why hadn't he gone directly to the apartment and gotten some sleep, rather than rushing to the campus like some lovesick swain wanting a glimpse of his own true love after months of being away from her? He felt a little foolish given the circumstances.

He had wanted her to experience freedom. He had wanted her to feel as though she had had a choice. Had she already made her choice? Did it include him?

They pulled up in front of a small whitewashed building. Cody crawled out of the car so that Chad could get out of the small back seat. Once he stood on the curb, Chad held out his hand. "I enjoyed meeting you, Cody. I don't have to tell you what a special person Carina is. You're very fortunate."

"I think so," Cody replied quietly. He waited for Chad to turn away before he got back into the car. "I think this car shrinks every time it goes through the car wash," he grumbled, fastening the seat belt and straightening his legs.

She smiled. "It's a fun car for me, though. It's just my size. I've enjoyed having it, even if I did try to talk you out of buying it for me. You were right."

"I'm glad you're enjoying it."

"Where would you like to go?"

He sighed. "I haven't given the matter any thought. All I could think about was getting here."

"You look tired," she said, studying him.

"Yeah."

"Then we'll go home and I'll make you a good dinner. Can you stay long?"

This was worse than anything he had imagined. He had braced himself for her irritation, ire, anger. Instead, she was treating him like an acquaintance, with aloof politeness.

"A couple of days," he mumbled. He leaned his head back against the headrest and watched as she efficiently guided the car into the flow of traffic and headed downtown.

He loved watching her hands. They were so small, so graceful. He loved to feel the silkiness of them, the—

"Carina?"

She gave him a quick glance, as though she heard a new note in his voice. "Yes?"

He stared at her hands and realized that he didn't want to know. But he had to ask. "Why aren't you wearing your wedding ring?"

"Oh, I was in a hurry this morning. I took it off to put some cream on my hands and forgot to put it back on."

"Does that happen very often?" He kept his tone as casual as he could.

"Does *what* happen often?"

"Forgetting to wear your ring."

"I haven't really thought about it."

She didn't say anything more for several blocks, and Cody decided to leave the subject alone. He was too tense and tired for a rational discussion and she was in a mood he had never seen before.

They parked in the underground parking lot beneath the building and rode the elevator to their floor in silence. He pulled out his key and opened the door. Once inside, Carina headed toward the kitchen. "I'll start dinner," she said over her shoulder.

"Carina?"

She stopped. With seeming reluctance she turned back to face him, but said nothing.

"What's wrong?"

She raised her brows. "I don't know what you mean."

"You're different."

"From what?"

"From the way you usually are when I come see you."

She crossed her arms. "Perhaps I am. Nobody stays the same, Cody. We change. We grow. We become different people. You, of all people, should know that."

"What's that supposed to mean?"

"A wife was a novelty to you, at first. Playing at marriage was a game, setting up house together, hurried visits back and forth. And then you stopped coming." She turned and went into the kitchen.

He followed her to the door and leaned against the doorjamb, his hands in his pockets. "I'm here now."

She began pulling items from the shelves, the refrigerator, the cabinet. "I know," she murmured, pulling out a knife and beginning to chop the vegetables in front of her.

"You don't seem to care."

She jerked her head up and looked at him. "Oh, I care, Cody. That has been the problem for me. I care. I miss you. I want to see you. You promise to come, then beg off. I feel as though I'm hanging in limbo, not knowing what to do, how to plan. Yes, I have my freedom, but only to a degree. I am part of a marriage that isn't a marriage. I have a husband whom I rarely see. What do you expect from me?"

He shrugged. "I suppose I wanted you to be happy I managed to get here."

Slowly, she put the knife down and came toward him. Sliding her arms around his neck she went up on tiptoe and whispered, "I am very happy you are here, Cody," just before her lips pressed against his.

Cody grabbed her and held her tightly against him, desperate for her. He teased her mouth open and plunged his tongue inside, showing her how much he had missed her, how much he wanted her, how empty he had felt.

The kiss went on and on, until Cody thought he was going to explode. He lifted her in his arms and carried her to the bedroom, peeling their clothes away, feverishly touching and tasting, exploring and caressing, his breath harsh, his longing almost devouring him.

She responded almost as feverishly. Cody lost all coherent thought, lost in the passionate present, surrounding himself with this woman who had become more important to him than life itself.

Their passionate coming together rapidly escalated, crescendoing into cries of release, and they clung weakly to each other as if they were survivors of a tempestuous storm that had almost destroyed them.

For long minutes they lay there. Cody felt drugged, unable to think beyond the moment. Eventually their surroundings impinged on his consciousness, and Cody realized he hadn't bothered to pull back the covers. They lay across the spread with total disregard for the delicate fabric.

He nuzzled her ear. "I've missed you, *chula*."

"I've missed you, too."

"I'm sorry everything's so mixed-up right now."

She pulled away so she could see his face. "Mixed-up?"

"With my job and everything. My project should have been completed months ago, but it keeps dragging on and on."

"This job is very important to you, isn't it?"

"The commitment I made to stick with it is, yeah."

She sighed, then rolled away from him.

"Where are you going?" he asked, leaning on one of his elbows.

She pushed her hair behind her shoulders and walked away from the bed. "To get a shower and finish the meal I started."

Cody watched her bare backside until she closed the door to the bathroom. What was going on? She had been with him every step of the way in their lovemaking. How could she walk away with such seeming indifference now?

For the first time in his life he felt used, then discarded. He hated the feeling...and he hated the dread that had taken up permanent residence in his chest.

He went into the other bathroom and showered. When he returned to their bedroom, he found an old pair of his jeans and a shirt he'd left from one of his previous visits.

He found Carina in the kitchen. She was wearing a satin lounging robe of sapphire blue. Her hair was haphazardly piled on top of her head, with curling wisps falling around her ears and the nape of her neck. She looked adorable to him. She also looked aloof.

By unspoken agreement they kept their conversation casual, mostly limited to putting dinner together, his flight, her classes. Neither seemed to want to discuss anything personal.

Dinner, as usual, was a delight. Cody savored every bite, feeling the strain and weariness slip away from him while they ate. Carina made coffee and they sat in front of the fireplace while they enjoyed their after-dinner drink.

Once again Carina's attitude and actions denoted a shift in their relationship. In the past they had sat on the couch together, where she generally ended up in his lap.

Tonight she sat in one of the matching wing chairs.

He lounged on the couch and watched her gaze into the small fire he had started earlier. Her profile fascinated him. He wished he were an artist and could capture the purity of her face—the way her nose tilted upward so slightly at the end, the clean line of her jaw and patrician neck. The soft glow of the firelight brushed her cheeks. Her mouth... He almost groaned at the wave of feeling that washed over him when—

"Cody?" she asked in a husky voice, still gazing at the fire.

"Mmm?"

"Did Aunt Letty ever get in touch with you?"

"About what?"

"My message."

"No. I haven't talked with her in a while. What was the message?"

Her smile was sad. She still didn't look at him. "It is no longer important."

"Tell me, anyway."

When she turned her head, he caught his breath in shock. The pain reflected in her eyes caught him totally unprepared.

"A few months ago I tried every way I knew how to contact you without alarming your family. I needed you so much, but I couldn't—" Her voice broke and she looked away for a few moments before continuing, "I couldn't find you anywhere."

Cody sat up, leaning forward, his elbows resting on

his knees. ''What happened, *chula?* Why were you looking for me?''

She bit her bottom lip, in an obvious effort to gain control. After swallowing a couple of times and taking a few deep breaths, she said, ''I had a miscarriage four months ago.''

Cody shot off the couch and was leaning over her before he was conscious of moving. ''Oh, Carina, no! I didn't know. How—?'' He reached for her and saw her stiffen. Stricken by her instinctive reaction, he carefully moved away from her and sat down on the couch once again. ''Will you tell me what happened?''

She looked down at her hands folded in her lap. ''I didn't even know what was wrong at the time. I'd been spending long hours at the library doing research work. I hadn't been feeling well for several weeks, but I thought I had the flu. I missed you so much and you had already called once to say you weren't going to be able to come to Chicago, after all.''

She paused, but for the life of him Cody couldn't think of a single word to say. She had been alone and had needed him, and he hadn't been there for her.

''What happened?'' he asked gruffly.

Her eyes were steady when she said, ''I was at the library and started having terrible abdominal pains...like cramps, only so much worse. The librarian called an ambulance and I was rushed to the hospital, but there was nothing anyone could do. They kept me in the hospital for two days. That's when I tried to reach you. I didn't want to alarm Aunt Letty, so I just asked her to have you call me if she heard from you. I gave her the number, but didn't tell her it was a hospital. I never heard from you.''

Once again she looked down at her hands. "When I got home I was so upset. I felt guilty because I hadn't known I was pregnant. I blamed myself for not questioning the symptoms sooner, even though the doctor said there was nothing I could have done to prevent what had happened."

"Oh, God, Carina. I'm so sorry." He wanted so much to take her in his arms, to hold her. He hated to think of what she must have gone through all alone. The pain must have been devastating. The shock of the news was slowly giving way to his own sense of loss for a child he had never known existed.

"I thought we were being so careful," he murmured, almost to himself. "I thought—" He stopped, shaking his head.

"I've done a great deal of thinking about our situation since then," Carina continued, her voice firmer. "For the first time I realized what it meant to be independent and on my own, truly on my own." She gave him a small smile that almost broke his heart. "It has taken me a long time to grow up...much longer than most women my age."

When she looked at him again, he could see the inner strength that she had drawn from these past few months. "I've been blaming Alfonso for my situation, but I can no longer do that. Alfonso was acting from the highest motives. He was protecting me from my own foolishness in thinking you needed to be rescued. You and I have both paid the price for my poor judgment, and for that I'm sorry." She looked back at the fire. "I'm sorry for many things, but not for the opportunity to get to know you better, to be your wife, to grow up."

Cody wanted to interrupt, to explain to her that—

What could he explain? That she had been brave to act in the way she had? That she had touched him in a way that no other human being had managed to do?

"I've been offered a job here in Chicago, Cody," she continued, "with the clinic where I've been working this spring. At first, I told them no, but they insisted I consider their offer for a few days. So I have been. And what I realized is that I don't want to go back to Texas and live at the ranch if you're not going to be there. I am willing to commit to this marriage, but only if you are."

"Otherwise?"

"I will stay in Chicago and allow you to continue the life you so obviously want."

"Does this mean you want a divorce?" Cody was surprised to hear his voice sound so calm, when his heart was pounding so hard in his chest he felt his breath was being shaken out of him.

"That would be up to you."

"I don't want a divorce," he stated harshly.

"What do you want?" she asked softly, her gaze on him.

Cody came to his feet, unable to sit still. He began to pace. "I want us to be together. I want us to have a home…and a family." He pivoted on his heel and stared at her across the room. "I love you, Carina. I love you with all my heart."

She stared at him, obviously shocked, and he realized this was the first time he had ever said the words out loud…to anyone.

Slowly she came out of her chair and walked over to where he stood by the large plate-glass window. When she reached him, she took his hand and raised it, pressing her lips to his palm. "I love you, too,

Cody. It seems as though I've loved you for most of my life.'' She stared at his anguished expression. ''But it doesn't really change things, does it? Not for you, anyway. Your work comes first.''

''I was doing this work before I ever met you. I've told you that. All of this happened with you at a time when I was least prepared to have a relationship with anyone. I can't just walk away from my job...not at this point in my investigations.''

She closed her eyes for a moment.

''Do what you must, Cody. I won't try to stop you, because I know it would do no good.''

''What about you, *chula?* Will you come back to Texas?''

She had never released his hand. Now she placed another tender kiss in his palm, carefully folded his fingers over the kiss, and let go of his hand.

''No, Cody. I cannot sit and wait for your occasional visits, with nothing to occupy my time when you are not there. I'll stay in Chicago. Perhaps some day we will be able to arrange our lives to better suit our desires. In the meantime, I have an opportunity to do the work I have trained for.''

''It won't be for much longer,'' he said eagerly, then dropped his head back and stared at the ceiling with a groan. ''How often have I said that since we've known each other?'' he muttered in frustration. Looking at her once again, he said, ''We can work this out, *chula.* I know we can. We love each other.''

She turned and looked out at the night. ''Sometimes I wonder if love is enough.''

Nine

One Year Later

Carina rushed through the side door of the clinic, already late for her next appointment. No doubt the waiting room was full. She had spent too much time at the hospital this morning, but she had needed that time to reassure the parents of six-year-old Jamie that he could be taught to speak again.

She pulled off her coat and started down the hallway.

"Carina! Thank God you're here."

She paused by the receptionist's desk. "I know. I'm going to be backed up for the rest of the day."

"It's not that. Your brother-in-law has called twice. He wants you to call him right away. He said he tried the hospital but you had already left, so he called back here."

Carina felt as though a giant hand had grabbed her, squeezing all the air from her lungs. She forced herself to battle the shock that had swept over her with Helen's words. "My brother-in-law?" she repeated in a careful tone.

Helen handed her a slip of paper. "Here's the number where you can reach him."

Numbly Carina took the pink slip and stared at it. Helen's excellent penmanship carefully spelled out the name Cole Callaway, the date and time of each one of his calls, and a number.

"Thanks," she mumbled, turning away.

"I hope nothing's wrong," Helen responded.

"So do I," Carina replied.

Her heart thudded in her chest, hammering at her ribs. Why would Cole be calling her?

She had not seen or spoken to Cody's family, with the exception of Aunt Letty, since her wedding. She had no idea what they thought of her continued stay in Chicago. She and Cody had never discussed their reactions.

Nevertheless, she knew she felt defensive. How could anyone understand that she and Cody had chosen to live apart, to live separate lives with minimal contact between them?

There were times late at night when she lay awake staring at the ceiling, wondering where he was, what he was doing and with whom. Carina had doubted the wisdom of her choice to remain in Chicago, but had to continue to remind herself that she would have been just as alone at the ranch with nothing to occupy her time.

She glanced at the slip of paper in her hand. She wasn't at all certain that she was ready to hear whatever Cole wanted to say to her. Since he had never made an effort to contact her before now, the matter must be urgent—to have prompted him to call the hospital and her office looking for her.

Had something happened to Cody? They had only spoken by phone a few times during the past few months.

Perhaps Cole was just relaying a message—a message that Cody had chosen not to give her directly.

She sat down at her desk and picked up the phone, her hand shaking. She had to start over twice before she got the right sequence of numbers. The phone rang once before it was answered. The deep voice sounded enough like Cody to increase her heartbeat even more.

"This is Carina Callaway," she managed to say, relieved to hear that her voice sounded a great deal more calm than she felt.

"Carina! Thank you for returning my call so promptly. I wasn't sure—" He paused, as though unwilling to finish that statement. His next words paralyzed her.

"I wanted to let you know that Cody's been hurt. I'm afraid I don't know much about the details. He was flown from McAllen late last night to a San Antonio hospital. He's in surgery now. I came to Cam's office to try to notify you. The rest of the family is at the hospital."

She kept trying to swallow the lump in her throat. "How bad is he?" she forced out.

His silence was worse than anything he could have said. Finally, in a voice rough with emotion, he replied, "Not too good. A bullet caught him in the chest, another in his hip. They weren't certain of his other injuries."

"You mean he's been shot?" Her voice rose and she immediately fought for control. "I thought he was in an automobile accident. What happened? Where was he? Who—"

"I'm afraid I don't know any more of the details…just that it happened in Mexico and that someone down there had enough authority to get him across the border so that he could be taken to a hospital here in Texas." He paused, and she realized that he was fighting for control, as well. "They, uh—" there was a long pause before Cole continued "—they almost lost him on the flight up here."

Carina jammed her fist against her mouth to stifle the cry that came to her lips. When she could trust herself to speak, she replied, "I'll be there as soon as I can get a flight."

"The jet's on its way to Midway Airport. It should be landing there within the hour."

"Thank you, Cole. Thank you for calling."

There was a moment of silence before he said, gruffly, "I thought you would want to know."

She squeezed her eyes in an effort to hold back the tears that threatened to fall. "Yes," she managed to say before they hung up. Carina couldn't let go of the phone, but continued to sit there hanging on to the only link, however tenuous, she had with Cody.

Forcing back the tears, she stood and carefully picked up her purse—as though she could hold the shock of Cole's news at bay by concentrating on practical details.

She paused at Helen's desk. Taking a deep breath, she forced herself to speak calmly. "Helen, I'm afraid

I've got to leave.'' She forced herself to take another couple of breaths before she continued. ''My husband—'' her voice squeaked and she stopped, gnawing on her bottom lip ''—has been hurt. I must go to him,'' she managed to get out.

''Oh, Carina, I'm so sorry! I'd hoped it wasn't bad news. Is there anything I can do?''

Carina closed her eyes, trying to think. After a moment, she said, ''You'll have to rearrange the appointments, see if there's anyone available to cover mine. I don't know when I'll be back.''

''Let us know how he's doing, all right? And don't worry about anything here.''

''Thanks, Helen.''

Numbly Carina went through the motions as she drove herself home. She thought about all the shopping she had done these past few weeks, all the plans she had made in her determination to reestablish her marriage.

Why had she taken so long to make up her mind that Cody was more important to her than anything else in her life? Why hadn't she made more of an effort to find him and tell him that she was coming back to Texas, had already given her notice of resignation at work...that she loved him and wanted to be with him, regardless of his other commitments?

She pulled into the underground parking lot at the apartment, got out and hurried to the elevator. Once she reached the apartment she paused, forcing herself to think about what she would take.

Carina pulled some clothes out of the closet and tossed them onto the bed, opened drawers and emptied them, searched for shoes and other accessories.

Then she went into the bathroom and gathered her personal items and threw them into a cosmetic bag.

She retrieved her luggage from the hallway closet and began to pack, all the while praying, "Hang on, Cody. Please hang on. I'll be there as soon as I can. Oh, darling, don't leave me now that I've finally realized how much I need you."

Less than an hour after she had talked with Cole, Carina was on her way to Midway Airport. The sleek jet was being refueled when she arrived. She was used to bringing Cody to the airport to catch the plane. This would be her first time to fly alone. She grabbed her suitcase and hurried across the Tarmac.

The pilot met her at the top of the steps. "Here, Missus Callaway. Let me have your bag."

"Thanks, Sam." The muscles in her arm leaped and jerked after having the weight removed from that arm. She went over to one of the seats and thankfully sank into it, strapping herself in.

"Do you need anything before we take off? It'll be about another fifteen minutes or so."

She shook her head, closed her eyes and rested her head on the headrest.

Her mind kept racing around, filled with questions that couldn't be answered. What could have happened that would have caused Cody to be shot? He would never tell her exactly what he did, just referred to investigative work. Why hadn't it ever occurred to her that he might be involved in something dangerous, especially after the night she had heard those men plotting to kill him? He had later explained that the man who had kidnapped them had a vendetta going against the Callaways and now that he was behind bars with a long-term sentence, there was nothing more to fear.

She had believed him.

"Oh, Cody, please be all right."

She couldn't imagine what the world would be like without Cody somewhere in it. She loved him so much...loved him as a woman now, and not as the child she had once been.

She looked down at the gold wedding band that gleamed on her left hand. She touched it lightly with her other hand. She remembered how upset he had been to discover her not wearing it. She had been childish to take off the ring the day after her miscarriage, out of spite, anger and pain.

His strong reaction had made her ashamed of herself. Since that day she had never taken it off again. During the ensuing months of loneliness, of waiting for his phone calls, of wondering how much truth there had been in his declaration of love that last weekend they had spent together, the ring had represented hope to her. He had given it to her, insisted she wear it despite their continued separation, as though the symbol of their marriage had some magical quality for him. Sometime during the passing months she had begun to feel the same way.

She heard a noise and opened her eyes. The pilot stepped inside the plane and closed the hatch, then disappeared into the cockpit. Soon she felt the vibration and heard the sound of the plane as they prepared for takeoff. She waited, eventually feeling the thrust of the small plane's power engines as it rapidly built up speed, then lifted away from the ground, quickly gaining altitude.

This was the hardest part, when there was nothing

to do but to sit and wait…and remember. She closed her eyes again and remembered the way Cody looked the first time she saw him, all golden and glowing with vitality and life.

"Please take care of him, God," she whispered. She touched the ring as a talisman and waited to reach her destination.

Cameron and Janine met her at the airport in San Antonio.

"How is he?" were her first words when she stepped off the plane.

"He's hanging in there," Cameron responded. "The surgery went well, according to the doctor, but there was considerable damage. If your brother hadn't acted so quickly, Cody would never have gotten out of there alive."

They were walking toward Cameron's car. Carina stopped walking and stared at him. "Alfonso? Are you saying that Alfonso was there when Cody was shot?"

With a slight tug, Cameron urged her forward. "That's right. He's at the hospital now."

Carina couldn't take all of this in. She had neither seen nor spoken to Alfonso since the night she and Cody married. She had resisted every overture he had attempted. She had kept in touch with her mother through letters, but had made no attempt to see her because of Alfonso.

And now he was at the hospital!

Once in the car, Janine said, "I almost didn't recognize you when you stepped off the plane. You made a lovely bride, but wow! Look at you now."

Carina smiled, knowing that Janine was trying to

distract her. "It's probably just the hair. Once I started to work full-time I decided to find a simpler hairstyle." She ran her fingers through her hair that fell in soft curls around her face, ears and neck.

"That's part of it, I suppose. But you look so—oh, I don't know what it is...sophisticated, maybe, uh—"

"Sexy?" Cameron suggested with a sly grin at his wife.

Janine laughed. "That, too. Has Cody seen your new hairdo?"

"No."

Cameron and Janine exchanged glances but said no more.

At the time she had her hair cut off, she had wanted a completely different look. Obviously she had achieved her goal. Her clothes were considerably different, as well. She felt as though she had finally moved into the twentieth century, wearing bright colors and current fashions.

She knew that part of the change was to give herself more self-confidence. She liked her new look. In her present concern for Cody, she had forgotten that he had not seen her new appearance. From Cameron and Janine's reaction, perhaps she should have warned him.

It was too late now, but it probably wouldn't matter. No doubt they had exaggerated their reaction in an effort to get her mind off Cody.

"Have you seen Cody since he was brought in?" she asked, leaning toward the two people in the front seat.

They pulled into the hospital parking lot and parked. Cameron replied, "No. He was still in recovery when we left to go to the airport." He opened her door and helped her out of the car. She walked between Cameron and Janine, comforted by their presence, needing others who loved Cody around her. They rode together in silence up to the proper floor and when they stepped off the elevator she saw Cole and Alfonso standing at the end of the hall, talking. Both men turned and watched her as she approached.

Alfonso had aged considerably during the past couple of years. His hair was almost completely silver now, and there were deep furrows across his forehead and down his cheeks. When he saw Carina his face brightened with surprised recognition and love that had her choking with sudden emotion.

This was her brother...the man who had raised her, nurtured her, protected her. He was here now, at a time when she desperately needed emotional support.

With a small cry she ran into his open arms. He held her tightly, his face buried in her hair, and they clung to each other for timeless moments before Carina lifted her head and looked up at him. Tears streamed down his face and she stared at him with wonder. She had never before seen Alfonso cry.

"Cody?" was the only word she could force past the lump in her throat.

"They have him in intensive care, still heavily sedated," Cole said from somewhere behind her. "They're allowing one person at a time with him for a few minutes once an hour. I was in a few minutes ago."

"How was he?"

Cole shook his head. "I can't tell. They have him hooked up to all kinds of machines. His chest and thigh are heavily bandaged, one side of his face is swollen and discolored. He looks like he's been through a rough time."

Carina looked at her brother. "Cameron said you were the one who brought Cody here?"

Alfonso nodded. "Yes. I was just explaining what happened to Cole."

Cole said, "Look, why don't the two of you stay here and catch up on everything while we go get something to eat. We won't be gone long."

Alfonso answered. "All right."

"Can we bring you something?"

"Nothing, thanks."

Carina watched the Callaways walk away, then felt a slight tug on her arm. She glanced around.

"There's a small waiting room over there that's empty," Alfonso said and led her into the well furnished room.

"Can you tell me what happened?" she asked, sinking into one of the chairs.

Alfonso sat down beside her and took her hand. "Yes. It is time that you should know."

She watched him as he rubbed his hand over his face.

"For years," he began, "Cody and I have been working at cross purposes." He paused for a moment. "It's been a case of the left hand not knowing what the right hand was doing."

"I don't understand."

"Are you aware of what Cody was doing in Mexico?"

"Investigative work, he said."

"Do you know who he was working for?"

"No."

"The United States Drug Enforcement Administration."

She stared at Alfonso in bewilderment. "Cody is an agent?"

"Yes...working undercover."

"Oh!"

"What you need to understand is that I've been doing the same kind of work for my own government, deeply undercover."

Carina stared at him as if she had never seen him before. How could she have been so unaware of yet another similarity between her husband and her brother?

"So we began to watch each other, suspect each other, until we finally learned the truth."

"When did you learn the truth?"

"A few weeks ago."

"You thought he was a drug dealer?"

"Of course not. I thought he was Cody Callaway of the Texas Callaways who enjoyed flirting with danger. Only as all our plans began to fall into place and come to a head did our bosses see fit to inform us that as brothers-in-law we were also working for a common purpose."

She glanced down at her hands. "Cody never told me."

"He couldn't."

She looked up at him. "But you can?"

"Now I can, because it is over. We successfully completed what we set out to do. After considerable time, difficulty and tremendous effort, we were able to gather several members of the cartel together where they could be arrested."

"Is that when Cody was shot?"

Alfonso sighed. "Unfortunately, yes."

How could he have been doing something so dangerous for so many years without her knowledge? During the years Cody had come to visit with Alfonso, he had joked and teased with her, as though he never took anything seriously.

"Those men I overheard?" she finally responded.

"Ah, yes. We were able to trace them eventually. They had been hired by Enrique Rodriguez to follow Cody and report his whereabouts. My men knew them and thought I had hired them, but I knew nothing about their being on the premises until several weeks later."

"Were they involved in the drug war?"

"Not really. They were hired guns willing to do most anything for a few extra dollars."

"Does Cody know they were identified?"

"Oh, yes. He never lets anything rest until it's resolved. He came to me with the information when he had proof. That was one of the many times I tried to contact you in hopes of getting you to accept my apology for what I had done to both of you."

"Cody accepted your apology?"

"He didn't seem to care. He was more interested in the fact that we had located and captured the men." He looked away from her for a long moment before returning his gaze to her. "I need to tell you that Cody was shot because of me."

"You had him—"

"No, no. Please don't misunderstand. I was the one who told the cartel members they were under arrest. Agents from both countries immediately stormed the room, but one of the drug men pulled his gun. Cody leaped between us, knocking me to the floor and catching the bullets meant for me."

Carina stared at him, tears running unheeded down her face.

"I immediately yelled for help and worked to stop the bleeding. We had helicopters standing by to transport prisoners out of there. We managed to have Cody airlifted out of there as well and flown across the border, then transported here."

"Why? Why would he have done such a thing?" she asked, almost to herself.

Alfonso sighed. "I asked him the same thing, before he lost consciousness."

"Did he answer you?"

"Yes. He looked at me and said, 'Because Carina loves you.'"

Ten

"Mrs. Callaway?"

Most of the family was there in the waiting room when the nurse appeared in the doorway, but everyone knew which Mrs. Callaway was being addressed. Carina came to her feet, her eyes on the woman's face. "Yes?"

"You may see your husband now."

Carina was trembling so hard she could scarcely stand. "Thank you." She glanced around the room at Cole and Allison, Cameron and Janine, Aunt Letty and Alfonso. Each of them gave her a soft word or nod of encouragement, giving her strength to follow the nurse out of the room.

They walked down one of the hallways and through a pair of swinging doors marked *ICU No Admittance*, then into one of the rooms. Carina moved slowly over to the bed and looked down at Cody. She fought for control. This was even worse than she had imagined. No one could have prepared her for the shock of seeing him lying there, his skin gray. If the various machines surrounding him had not been making their steady beeping sounds, she would have thought he was dead. Only his hair gave off a certain brightness against the starkness of the pillowcase.

He was attached to a series of wires and tubes. She was almost afraid to touch him for fear of dislodging something. Gingerly she picked up his hand and lifted it to her lips.

"I love you, Cody," she whispered.

He didn't stir, but then she hadn't expected a response. She had just needed to say the words to him.

He had saved her brother's life. Despite everything that had happened, he had known how much she loved Alfonso. How could he have sacrificed his own safety to save her brother? Didn't he know how much she loved him, too?

"I sincerely hope this means that your work in Mexico is finished," she whispered. "I'm going to be very selfish, my darling, and insist that you spend more time with me. I need you so much."

The nurse came back in a few minutes and Carina left. But only because she had to. She had every intention of returning as often as possible.

She loved this man, and she would do whatever necessary to preserve their relationship.

Cody felt as though he had been trampled by a herd of elephants. Angry elephants, at that. One of them seemed to be resting its foot on his chest, pinning him to the ground. He moaned and attempted to change positions, causing pain to shoot through his hip and down his leg.

In the midst of his agony, someone took his hand and brushed it against something soft and warm. He fought to open his eyes, then blinked in an effort to clear them.

Where was he, anyway?

Carina's beautifully shaped black eyes stared back at him. He smiled, or at least he made the attempt. His face felt stiff and swollen. He watched her place a kiss on his knuckles and realized he was now witnessing what he had felt a few moments ago.

Carina. She was so often in his thoughts that he found nothing unusual about seeing her beside him now. He had been dreaming about her only a few moments ago.

"Hi," he tried to say, but his throat was too dry. He licked his lips and tried again. "Where are we?"

"A hospital in San Antonio."

He frowned at that news. San Antonio? What was he doing there? The last thing he remembered was—what? where? He closed his eyes in an effort to concentrate.

"The doctor said you're doing amazingly well. He's quite pleased with your progress."

Good for the doctor. What sort of progress had he been making? "What are you doing here?" he finally asked, opening his eyes once more.

"Being with you."

"Aren't you supposed to be working?"

"I took some time off."

"Oh."

He allowed his gaze to wander around the room, which was large and rather luxurious. He couldn't remember ever having been in a hospital before as a patient. Lying flat on his back was a new perspective. He wasn't at all impressed.

He closed his eyes, wishing the pain would go away. There was something important he needed to do…or say….

"Carina?"

"Yes, darling?"

He must have said her name out loud. He smiled to himself and returned to that place where there was no pain….

The next time he opened his eyes the room was dark except for a night-light. Carina was still there, watching him, a slight smile on her face. She looked…he searched for a word, wondering why his brain felt so sluggish. She looked…happy…yeah, that was it. Happy and content, as though her fondest wish had been granted.

"So what am I doing here?" he finally asked.

"How much do you remember?"

He thought about that for a while. "Not much. Was I in a wreck?"

"Not exactly."

"Then what?"

"I believe the official phrase is that you were injured in the line of duty."

"Line of duty—" He paused, thinking, and images began to appear. After several minutes of silence he sighed, "Oh, yeah. Line of duty." He looked around the room again, avoiding her eyes. "Was anyone else hurt?"

"No."

He closed his eyes. ''That's good,'' he murmured, drifting away once more....

Light filled the room when he woke up again. Carina sat in the chair beside his bed. ''Don't you ever go home?'' he asked gruffly.

She had been reading a magazine until he spoke. At his words she looked up and smiled. ''Once in a while, why?''

''I just wondered.''

He shifted, trying to find a more comfortable position. ''How long are they going to keep me in here?''

''Until you're well enough to go home.''

''When will that be?''

''They haven't said.'' Carina picked up a glass of water. She held the bent straw to his lips. He managed to sip, enjoying the cool, refreshing feeling of the liquid as it eased his thirst.

He allowed his eyes to drift closed, when something different finally registered on his consciousness. He blinked his eyes open once more. ''Your hair! What did you do to your hair?''

She tilted her head slightly before saying, ''I had it cut off.''

''I see that, dammit! Why?''

She eyed him, her expression sober. ''Don't you like it?''

''Carina, I've always loved your long hair. I could never leave it alone. I can't believe you cut it off without even mentioning anything to me.''

He sounded like a sulking child and he knew it. Damn, he felt so helpless. He hated lying there in bed, every movement taking an enormous amount of his limited energy.

"It will grow back, you know," she said after a moment.

He shut his eyes. "It doesn't matter. You've got your own life to live. I don't have any right to comment." That was what he thought. It wasn't how he felt.

After several minutes of silence, he searched for a new topic. "How's work?"

"Always there," she replied.

"Isn't that the truth? No matter how much you do, there's always something more that needs to be done."

"Is that what's kept you in the business?"

He raised one of his brows. "What business?"

"The undercover business."

"How did you know about that?"

"Alfonso told me."

He looked at her, trying to figure out her mood from her expression, but she was giving nothing away. "You spoke to Alfonso?"

"That's right."

"When?"

"After he brought you here. He stayed until you were out of intensive care, then he returned home."

"Did you ever forgive him for forcing you to marry me?"

"Yes."

He found himself smiling. "I'm sure he was relieved."

"I got the impression that you forgave him a long time ago."

He started to shrug, but the slight movement made

him wince. He touched his bandaged chest and made a face. "I just didn't like the way he went about things, that's all."

"Why didn't you tell me the two of you were working together?"

"Because I couldn't. Besides, for the longest time I didn't know he was on our side. I thought he was one of them. I had to deal with the probability of arresting my own brother-in-law. My boss didn't have to be quite *that* secretive!"

"Speaking of your boss, I spoke to him when he came to check on you. He told me that you had put in your resignation effective as soon as you made these arrests."

"So?"

"So, it looks like you're now unemployed."

He thought about that for a moment, then smiled. The idea sounded good to him. Very good. "Looks that way, doesn't it? Guess I'll be able to spend some time with you now." He eyed her a little uncertainly. "That is, if you're willing to have me come." He glanced down at her hand and was surprised at the relief he felt when he saw her ring glinting on her hand.

He closed his eyes, not wanting to react to her, not wanting to feel what he always felt in her presence…a longing so intense that he ached with it for hours.

"You won't have far to travel."

His eyes opened. "What do you mean?"

"I've resigned my position. I talked with the office a couple of days ago. They've already found a replacement who can start right away. Looks like I'm unemployed, too."

Damn. He wished his chest would stop hurting. He

struggled to push up on his elbows but couldn't handle the strain on his chest muscles. "Hey, there was no reason to quit your job because of what happened to me. I don't need you to—"

"I didn't quit my job because of what happened to you. I tendered my resignation at least four weeks ago. I had decided to surprise you with the news on our anniversary."

"Anniversary?"

She grinned. "Um-hm. We have an anniversary coming up in a few weeks. By the time you've done your physical therapy on your hip and allowed your chest to heal, I'm hoping you'll be well enough to leave the hospital and help me celebrate."

He could feel an easing of an age-old pain in his chest. This one had not been caused by a bullet wound. No, he had carried this one ever since the day he had seen her coming across the campus with a guy named Chad.

"Is that what you want?" he asked gruffly.

"More than anything I can think of," she replied, smiling, while tears trickled down her cheeks.

Several weeks later, Cody stood at the entrance of the hospital. He had finally been given a clean bill of health. His chest gave him a twinge or two now and then, and he still walked with a slight limp, but the doctor assured him that if he took it easy he would have no problems with the chest wound. The limp would disappear with continued exercise.

He had been in daily phone contact with Carina for the past two weeks. She had returned to Chicago to pack and have their belongings shipped to the ranch. She placed their condo on the market and tied up all the loose ends before making her move south permanent. Then she drove back, arriving home yesterday so that she could pick him up this morning when he was released.

He paused for a moment, filling his lungs with air, glad to be out of the hospital environment. He could have left before now, but his boss and doctors had insisted he rest and regain his strength. He knew he had been pushing himself for a long time now. He had been exhausted and run-down before all of this came to a conclusion.

He hated to admit that the doctors had been right. He hadn't felt this good in a long time, a very long time. Part of his mood was because he was going to see Carina. He hated going a day without seeing her. Two weeks had seemed like an eternity. Never again would he allow himself to go through the hell of not being with her for a year!

A car pulled up and he recognized it as Carina's car. He grinned and started down the steps, watching as the car door opened and Carina stepped out. Cody caught his breath and stared.

She wore a flaming red dress that lovingly displayed her trim figure and a pair of heels so high that she swayed when she walked. Three men across the street stopped to stare at her and one motorist came to a screeching halt before he hit the car in front of him, whose driver was straining to get another glimpse of her retreating form.

This was not the same woman who had been practically living at the hospital while he was there, wearing jeans and no makeup. Now she wore dark shades that covered the upper part of her face, somehow calling attention to her delectable mouth. Her lips looked soft and very kissable.

Slowly he made his way toward her, wondering if she was aware of the danger she presented to traffic in the area. From her expression, she appeared to be unaware of anyone but him.

She lowered her glasses and peered over their dark rims. Her large black eyes gazed up at him before she went up on her toes and kissed him oh-so-gently on the lips. She smiled at him and said, "If you would like, I can drive."

The men across the street shot him varying looks of admiration, irritation and envy. He could certainly understand their reaction. "That's quite a dress you're wearing, honey. It could set off a riot with very little provocation."

She laughed. "I bought it especially for today, sort of as a celebration. Do you really like it?"

"If we weren't in public, I'd show you exactly how much I like it," he replied in a husky voice. He rested his hand in the small of her back while they walked to the car.

After she helped him into the passenger seat, she walked around to the driver's side. Just as Carina opened her door, Cody heard a wolf whistle from some punk on a motorcycle. Then he became aware of Carina sitting down beside him in her short, snug skirt.

"It's a damn good thing I've got a strong heart, darlin'. Otherwise, I'd be going into cardiac arrest," he drawled, looking at the expanse of leg showing.

"Are you talking about my dress?" she asked, starting the car.

"Yeah, partly. There isn't much to it, is there? I mean…isn't it a little short?"

"C'mon, Cody. This is the style."

"Hmm. I wonder what your mother would think."

She adjusted her glasses without offering an opinion, then pulled out of the parking space. He kept watching her legs while she shifted gears, then his gaze wandered up to her face. "Thanks for arranging to get me out of there. Another day and I would have been clawing the walls."

"I told the doctor you would have round-the-clock supervision and attention, if he'd let me bring you home."

He grinned. "And what did he say?"

She glanced at him out of the corner of her eye. "You really want to know?"

Faint color filled her cheeks, which he found rather intriguing. "Yeah."

"Lucky fellow," she said, attempting nonchalance.

He threw back his head and laughed, then held his chest.

"Are you in pain?"

"Well, there's pain and then there's *pain.* Are we going to the ranch?"

"Uh, well, no. Cole suggested we go down to South Padre Island to the family condo for a few days. Since that's almost three hundred miles from here, I thought we would have a leisurely dinner, stay at one of the hotels tonight, then travel tomorrow. We don't have to be anywhere at any particular time, which is nice."

"Sounds like a good plan."

She gave him a quick smile, almost a nervous smile, he decided. He wondered what she was up to.

* * *

Hours later they sat sipping their coffee in the dimly lit restaurant. Once again Cody decided that Carina appeared to be a little nervous. Was it because they would be going back to the hotel soon?

If he didn't know better, he could almost imagine that his sweet little wife had intentions regarding him...seduction intentions. If so, he was going to sit back and enjoy watching her technique.

They finished their coffee while Cody admired the way the candlelight caressed the contours of her face. She picked up her purse and played with the catch for a moment. Finally she looked at him from beneath a thick fringe of dark lashes. "Are you ready to go?"

"Anytime you are," he replied, flashing her a smile that seemed to fluster her.

Cody placed money on the tray next to the bill and stood. He helped her out of her chair and motioned for her to walk in front of him. Once outside the restaurant he opened the passenger door and waited patiently while she got in, then quietly closed the door. When he crawled in beside her from the other side he said, "That is one eye-catching outfit you're wearing, *chula.* The only problem I have with it is the number of eyes it catches. Some of those men back there almost fell off their chairs when you walked by. I mean, I like short skirts, and I like snug-fittin' short skirts, but I'm not at all sure I like other men watching *my wife* in a short, snug-fittin' skirt."

"Are you saying that you don't want me to wear this dress?" The expression in her eyes gave him pause. He thought for a minute.

"No, ma'am, I'm not. What I *am* doin' is statin' my preference about some things. What you choose to do about what you wear is strictly your business."

Neither one of them said anything more. When they reached the hotel, he handed the car keys over to the parking attendant and escorted Carina inside. He was enjoying the exercise he had gotten today, but recognized that he didn't have his full strength back, which was frustrating. He was tired and didn't like it. Not at all, given the circumstances. He was with his wife and he had definite ideas on how he wanted to spend the evening, every one of them calling for energy and stamina. He absently rubbed his chest and sighed.

As soon as they reached their suite, Carina excused herself and went into the bathroom. Cody wandered over to the window and looked down at the river that wound its way through the downtown area of San Antonio.

After a few minutes he went into the bedroom. He heard water running and decided she must be taking a bath, which could take a while. He sat down on the side of the bed and took off his boots. Then he stripped off the rest of his clothes and stretched out, pulling the covers to his waist. After all his complaining at the hospital, he had to admit that there were times when a bed was downright useful. This was definitely one of those times.

After flipping on the television with the remote control he clicked through various channels. He didn't really care about watching television, but he knew he was a far cry from being ready to sleep. He didn't see that he was left with very many options from which to choose at the moment.

Although the water had shut off in the bathroom, he could hear soft, swishing movements and pictured Carina in the large tub, relaxing. He was tempted to offer to join her. After all, it wouldn't be the first time they had bathed together. Then he remembered his recent wounds and decided to wait a few more weeks to indulge in that particular exercise.

While he stared at the television screen he remembered the times they had spent together, which didn't help his state of mind nor other parts of his anatomy in the slightest.

He heard the bathroom door open some time later, but didn't immediately look around. Chastising himself for being a coward, he glanced away from the television only to discover she had not come out of the bathroom.

A wisp of scent teased him, and he recognized the cologne he had bought her on one of his trips to Chicago. He remembered the day they had chosen the seductive scent, as well as the evening when he had given her a physical demonstration of the various points on the body where cologne could be applied with tantalizing results.

He almost groaned out loud.

He clicked past three more stations and had paused to watch a commercial when she finally walked out.

Cody gave her a casual glance to let her know that— Every thought in his head flew out the window.

"Oh my God," he murmured, not certain if he intended that as a prayer for help or praise for the sight before him. Cody had grown used to Carina's white cotton nightgowns. He had found them endearing as well as innocently provocative.

The gown she now wore was anything but innocent. Made of material so sheer he could scarcely see it, the color was the same deep black as her eyes. Her coral-tipped nipples shone through the black lace at the top. The slightly darker circle of her navel was not concealed, nor was the thickly curled triangle at the top of her thighs. The gown opened on both sides from hem to waist, exposing the length of her leg and hip.

"Is that what you've been sleepin' in these days?" he asked, sounding hoarse. "It's a wonder you haven't died of pneumonia."

She came toward him, seemingly untroubled by his comments. She slipped under the covers and stretched out beside him. With a hint of a smile and a twinkle in her eyes, she said, "No one will ever see me in this but you, Cody."

He had to swallow before he managed to say, "I sure as hell hope not. I'd hate to have to kill a man at this stage in my life."

She turned so that she faced him, propping herself on one elbow. "I wanted you to find me sexy."

"If I found you any more sexy I'd explode," which was exactly what he thought he was going to do. He wasn't certain he could handle this kind of stimulation, not after the past year of celibacy. Reminding himself that he had just gotten out of the hospital, he carefully pulled her closer to his side and nuzzled her under her chin.

"Are we going to watch television?" she asked, in a voice filled with amusement.

He hit the off button of the remote without looking while placing kisses along the side of her neck. He heard her sigh and felt her touch him at the same time. Her touch sent him up in flames.

He placed his trembling hand on her thigh and felt the shimmering material that was the only thing between them. Sliding his hand along her leg he could feel the tiny ripples of sensation on her skin as the combination of smooth, silky material and roughened palm aroused her.

Once again, she ran her fingertips up and over his heated flesh.

"Where did you learn to do that?" he asked, remembering how shy she had been.

She gazed at him out of heavy-lidded eyes. "I read in a book that you're supposed to do what gives you pleasure and that sometimes the other person will gain pleasure from it as well."

"You enjoy touching me?"

He saw color flood her cheeks once more, and he grinned. Despite their time apart, she hadn't changed all that much.

She nodded her head, watching him with wide eyes. He studied her for a long moment, then said, "Okay. Then be my guest." With that he stretched out beside her and tugged her closer.

She looked at him, startled.

"Show me what else the book taught you," he coaxed, knowing his grin was more than a little wicked.

The smile quickly left him when she proceeded to follow his instructions with infinite attention to detail. "Oh—uh—Carina, honey. I can't handle that right now. It's been so—o-o-o-h—long and I don't want to—uh-uh-uh—o-o-h..."

Later he didn't remember when she carefully had straddled him without putting pressure on either wound. She seemed to hover above him, light as a butterfly, while he filled his hands and his mouth with her. He forgot about everything but the two of them together again. There were no more thoughts, only feelings...and what he felt encompassed a multitude of pleasurable sensations too numerous to count.

When he could no longer contain himself he stiffened and cried out, aware of her pulsing movement gripping him, draining him completely.

"What is it?" she panted, concern filling her eyes. "Are you hurt? Did we do something—"

He scarcely had the breath to laugh. "Yeah. I'd say we did something, all right." He waited for more air before he added, "My gently reared darling has turned into a tiger in bed."

She edged away from him, stretching out along his unwounded side. "Is that good?"

"Oh, *chula*...honey, it sure ain't bad!"

Cody woke up the next morning with a stripe of sunshine on his face. With a silent groan he stumbled out of bed and jerked the draperies closed, then felt his way back to bed.

Dimly he was aware that he hadn't obtained much sleep the night before. Technically speaking, he hadn't obtained *any* sleep the night before, because the sky had already lightened before he had fallen into an exhausted rest, his arms securely around Carina.

She hadn't stirred just now when he got up. Nor did she stir when he returned to bed and slipped beneath the covers. He leaned on his elbow and gazed down at her.

They were back together again and this time he was determined to keep them together. She had given up her job, a job he knew was important to her. They needed to discuss the future.

While he had been convalescing, he had asked Cole and Cameron what they thought about establishing a speech-therapy clinic in San Antonio. Both of them had been enthusiastic about the idea. So perhaps he had an anniversary present of his own.

When she opened her eyes and saw him watching her, she smiled. He had never seen anyone more beautiful.

"How are you feeling?" she asked.

"Content. At peace with my world. How are you feeling?"

"Very much the same. I was talking about your injuries."

"Considering all our activity last night, I feel surprisingly well rested." He yawned and leaned back on his pillows. Playing with one of her wispy curls that he found very endearing, he said, "I was watching you sleep and thinking about how much I love you and how scared I've been this past year that I was going to lose you. Thank God you chose to honor your marriage vows, even if they were made under protest."

"Cody! That isn't true. I was angry at Alfonso for forcing you to marry me. I had hoped that someday you would perhaps want to marry me, but I wanted it to be your decision." She shook her head. "I know you felt trapped, that you had never thought of me in that way. You were very honorable, marrying me under those circumstances."

He reached for her and pulled her in his arms. When she was arranged to his satisfaction, he said, "I want to tell you a story." He lifted her hand and placed a kiss on her ring finger.

"When my folks were killed, my whole world fell apart. I was angry with everybody and at everything. My life had changed in a way that I hated but could do nothing about. I remember one night, in particular. My Aunt Letty came into my room late, hours after everyone else had gone to bed. I don't know how she knew I was still awake. At the time I think I was convinced she had X-ray vision eyes that could see through walls and across the miles. That lady never missed much.'' He placed a light kiss on Carina's nose. ''Looking back, I realize that she probably checked on me every night without my knowing it.

''I was sitting on the window seat in my room staring out at the stars, wondering if maybe two of those stars might be my mom and dad. I didn't have a very clear idea of exactly where heaven was and how a person got there.

''I expected her to tell me to get to bed, that I had school the next day. Instead, she pulled up a chair and sat down beside me. She began to talk.

''Even now, I'm surprised at what she told me, because—as you well know—Letitia Callaway is one of the most unsentimental people you would ever hope to know. She started telling me about how my mom and dad met. She told their story as a sister watching her brother fall head-over-heels in love, courting a beautiful young girl. She told me about the time when her brother came home excited that his love had agreed to marry him.

''Then she reached into her pocket and pulled out an object. It was too dark for me to see what it was, but she held it on her palm and said, 'Your dad bought your mom the most gorgeous ring, ornately decorated with stones, and she told him that although she found the ring quite beautiful, she wouldn't be comfortable wearing it. Her hands were small and slim. So then he went out and bought her this,' my aunt told me and held out her hand.

"I felt something drop into my palm and I looked at it. It was a small gold filigree ring. I remember staring at it and hurting inside, real bad. The last time I had seen that ring my mama had been wearing it. She never took it off. Aunt Letty told me that she wanted me to have that ring to remind me of the wonderful love my parents had for each other and for the three of us boys. I remember her saying, 'Cole and Cameron were given a few more years to build memories of their parents than you had, Cody. You need something more tangible as a reminder. So keep this ring, knowing who it represents and what it represents.'"

Cody smoothed his palm across Carina's cheek. "Even at ten, I knew the tremendous gift my aunt had given me that night. She had given me back my belief in life and in the future. She had given me love in its most tangible form. I carried that ring with me until the day I placed it on your hand."

He took his thumb and gently wiped away one of the tears from her cheek, but more replaced it.

"Even when I didn't fully understand my feelings, I knew that somehow it was right for you to wear this ring." He lifted her hand and placed another kiss across her fingers. "This ring has always symbolized eternal love to me, and you were the embodiment of that love. I was too much of a coward to admit it for a long time."

"You are anything but a coward, Cody."

He shook his head. "Aunt Letty knew the minute she met you how I really felt about you. She knew because she saw that ring on your finger. She also knew that I had to give you your freedom or neither one of us would ever have a chance to be happy together.''

Carina smiled. ''She's quite a woman, isn't she?''

''The last of a dying breed. Tougher than a boot but she would do anything in the world for you. To her, family is *everything.*''

''Family's important to me, too, Cody.''

''I know, honey. That's why I'm so glad you've worked out your differences with Alfonso.''

''What I mean is, a family of my own is important to me. That's why I was so devastated when I lost the baby.''

In a quiet voice, Cody said, ''I'm not saying that I wasn't upset about the miscarriage, because I was... sorry because of the baby and sorry that you had to go through all of that alone. I intend to spend the rest of my life making up for those lonely years we weren't together.''

''Be careful what you promise, now. I might keep you so busy training horses and children that you'll dream of the days when you were a loner.''

He pressed his lips against hers, paused and whispered, ''Don't count on it,'' before his mouth found hers once more.

Epilogue

Cody sat with his feet propped up on the porch railing, his chair resting on the back two legs, and gazed out at the rolling hills around Cole's Austin home. Cole and Cameron were in similar positions on either side of him. Each of them was contemplating the fact that they had eaten entirely too much food off the recent Thanksgiving table and were now paying for it.

"The Cowboys played a hell of a game," Cameron said into the quiet surrounding them.

"Sure did," Cole agreed. "They'll make it to the Super Bowl this year for sure."

"You say that every year," Cody reminded his brother.

"So? They've got a strong team this year, better than I've seen in a long time."

Knowing what he was provoking, he said, "Well,

if you ever get tired of backing the Cowboys, you might switch to the Oilers. They've been doing great this year.''

''Wash your mouth out, boy,'' Cole growled, causing Cameron and Cody to laugh.

''You know,'' Cody said after another lengthy silence, ''I think I actually miss not having Aunt Letty here, even though I'm sure she's enjoying her cruise. It just isn't the same, not having her point out all our shortcomings. Can't you just hear her, if she could see us now?'' He pitched his voice into a falsetto. '''That's no way to sit in a chair. I didn't raise you to act like a bunch of heathens. You know how to behave.'''

''You sound just like her,'' Cameron said with a grin.

From behind them a soft, young voice said, ''Daddy?'' Three chairs hit the porch at the same time, three pairs of boots scraped the floor and three sets of eyes turned to see who wanted them.

Sherry Lynn Callaway came toddling toward them, her mother hovering just behind her. Cody swooped down and picked up his thirteen-month-old daughter. ''Hello, precious,'' he cooed. ''Did you have a good nap?'' He glanced around and saw that his wife and both brothers were grinning at him like a bunch of fools.

''What's wrong with y'all?''

Cole cleared his throat, Cameron shuffled his feet and Carina patted his cheek. ''Not a thing, Cody. Not a thing. Would you like to entertain your daughter? We've got a hot game of Spades going on inside.''

''Sure,'' he said, settling back into his chair, this

time with all four legs on the ground. He placed Sherry on his knee.

"They're really adorable at that age," Cole admitted, and nobody within hearing argued with him.

"I've been meaning to tell you," Cameron began slowly, "Janine and I are adopting a little boy."

"That's great, Cam," Cody said, rubbing his daughter's back.

"He's almost two. We told them that age didn't matter. I figure the only way I'm going to be able to keep up with you two is to get 'em on the hoof, so to speak."

"Hey," Cody replied, "Don't look at me. We were married almost four years before we started our family."

Cole gave Cody a lopsided grin. "Hell, son, it just took you that long to figure out what you were supposed to be doing."

"You feel safe with me sitting here with my hands full."

Cameron chimed in. "You have to admit that once you got the hang of things you haven't wasted much time. Clay's barely three, Sherry just turned one and Carina is pregnant again."

Cody grinned. "Can't argue with the facts, can I?"

"Trisha is excited at the idea of having a baby brother," Cam went on. "She wants several more. I'm sure so that she can boss them around."

Cole looked out over the hills. "The folks would be proud to see the families we're raising. I just wish they could have seen us the way we were today all gathered around the table."

"I don't know about you, but I hear myself talking to one of the kids and I sound just like Dad used to,"

Cody said. "I guess that's part of being family, repeating the same stories, passing on the sayings."

"They taught us about love," Cam said thoughtfully. "It was a lesson worth learning."

Cody glanced over his shoulder and saw that Carina had come to the door again, no doubt to check on her daughter. With his heart in his eyes he answered his brother without taking his eyes off his wife.

"And worth waiting for," he added softly.

* * * * *

TEMPTATION TEXAS STYLE!

One

He should be used to pain by now. Tony shifted gears and grimaced. After all, he'd been part of the rodeo scene since he was fifteen years old...fifteen years ago.

He was a fool for continuing to enter the bullriding events at his age. He was getting too old to punish himself like that, as his body at the moment kept telling him.

He'd left Fort Worth four hours ago. Another hour should see him pulling in at the gate to his place, thank God. He was more than ready to stop the punishment he'd been putting himself through trying to drive. His pickup had a stick shift. Every time he'd had to use the clutch, his left ankle had let him know that he'd done a number on it.

The damn thing was either sprained or broken.

He'd probably have to have Clem cut off his boot once he got home.

Rodeoing played hell with his wardrobe as well as his body. Despite all the drawbacks, though, he still loved the excitement, the competition, and the recognition that came with the three belt buckles he'd won that proclaimed him World Champion Bullrider for three years running...which was why he kept putting himself through this punishment.

He lowered the sun visor, adjusted his aviator shades and checked the rearview mirrors to make certain the horse trailer he was pulling was okay. Thank God Clem was at the ranch looking after things. Tony would ask him to unload the cutting horse he'd used for the calf-roping events and put him away while he got his blasted boot off and soaked himself in the tub.

Clem had hired on with him three years ago, the same year Tony had bought his spread with his prize money from following the rodeo circuit. So far they'd managed to get along on the ranch without much outside help. Of course, if Tony's plans to expand his stock worked out, he'd be looking for more help. However, that was somewhere in the future.

For now, Betsy Krueger came out from town once a week to give the house a cleaning, and cooked enough food to freeze so he'd have something to warm up and eat during the week. The rest of the time he rattled around the house by himself.

Tony preferred it that way. He liked living alone, answering to no one. Clem had a room in the barn where he slept, sharing his meals with Tony when he wasn't off to town during the evenings.

Tony liked his life. There were no entanglements, no distractions. If he got lonesome and wanted company, he had a raft of relatives scattered across the state.

He came up over a rise in the road and began to slow down. At the bottom of this long and winding drop was the gate to his place, the T Bar C Ranch.

That gate had never looked so good to him. He wanted to throw himself on a flat surface and not move for a week. Not that he could do that. He had a meeting in town on Monday to discuss his plans for the ranch. He couldn't afford to postpone it. However, he could spend tomorrow—Sunday—lying around with his foot propped up. By the following day he should be feeling all right.

He guided the truck-and-trailer rig into the private lane with his usual skill and followed the road among brush, granite outcrops and occasional cacti to where the ranch house, barn, feed shed and storage garage formed a horseshoe around a circular driveway.

He was already swinging the rig in an arc in front of the barn so that he could park the trailer next to the building when he saw a vehicle he didn't recognize sitting in front of the house.

What the hell? He wasn't expecting anybody. At the moment, company was the last thing he needed or wanted.

He stopped the truck and sat for a moment, staring at the faded red van with the Georgia license plates. He tried to remember if he knew anybody from that part of the country. At the moment, no one came to mind.

"You goin' to sit there all night?" Clem asked, sauntering up to the cab of the truck and peering in at him.

Clem Wilson was tall and as skinny as a rail, his skin weathered from years of working outdoors. Tony had no idea how old Clem was, and he didn't care. He just knew there was very little that Clem didn't know about running a ranch. That was good enough for Tony.

He grabbed his Stetson from beside him, opened the door and gingerly lowered himself to the ground.

"Whadya break this time?" the older man drawled without inflection.

"Nothing! I don't think," Tony replied, wincing when he attempted to put some weight on his left foot.

"Bull step on ya?"

Tony bristled. "Of course not. I just came off a little sloppy and landed wrong."

"Before or after the buzzer?"

Tony grinned. "After, of course."

Clem nudged the brim of his hat with his thumb, turned his head and spit, then rearranged the chewing tobacco in his cheek with his tongue. "It's a wonder ya have any brains left, you've scrambled 'em so many times taking them falls."

Tony nodded toward the house. "Who's at the house?"

Clem shrugged. "Some long-lost relative of your mother's. At least that's what she said."

Tony frowned. "A relative of Mom's? Then what's she doing here?"

"She said the housekeeper at the Austin house told her your mom and dad weren't home and gave her directions to your place."

Tony rubbed his forehead. His headache had grown steadily worse in the hours since he'd finished his bullriding stint. He'd hit the ground pretty hard, and it had jarred him. He was tempted to agree with Clem. His brains must be scrambled by now. What he didn't need at the moment was to have to entertain some visiting biddy, and listen to long, rambling stories of the days when she was just a girl.

"Who is this woman—did she say?"

"Christina O'Reilly."

"Never heard of her."

"She said her great-great-grandmother and your mother's great-grandmother were cousins."

"So? That doesn't make her a real relative of ours, for God's sake."

"Never said it did. She's the one claiming to be your relative."

Dammit! This was the last thing he needed. What rotten timing. She would have to show up the week his folks took the younger kids to Disney World in Florida.

"You want me to put the horse up?"

Damn. He'd been standing here stewing over his unwanted company instead of taking care of chores. "Yeah. I'd appreciate it."

"You'd better get off that ankle. You goin' to need some help getting that boot off?"

"I'm not going to bother saving it. I'll just get a knife and—"

"Let me do it. There's no sense in you—"

"You'll be busy out here. I can do it."

"Don't be so bullheaded, hotshot! Git on inside and prop that leg up. Give me fifteen minutes and I'll be in there to help." Clem spun on his heel and strode to the back of the trailer, muttering to himself. Tony was fairly certain he was meant to overhear a few of the more choice adjectives he used—"stubborn," "arrogant," "simple-minded," and a couple that were bordering on obscene. Nope, not a complimentary comment in the lot.

He hadn't expected to hear one.

He would never have to worry about letting his rodeo fame and accomplishments go to his head, not as long as Clem was around to point out his shortcomings.

Tony started walking toward the house, stifling a groan with every step he took. Damn, but that ankle hurt! Add to that the fact that his entire body was one great big ache, already stiffening up on him. Never had the distance between the barn and the house seemed so long. He'd just—

"Oh, my! You're hurt! Were you in an accident?"

He'd been looking down when he heard the voice coming from the front porch. He glanced up and came to an abrupt halt. What the hell was going on here?

The woman standing by one of the square pillars that supported the porch roof couldn't be over twenty-five years old. Her hair was a riot of corkscrew curls and fiery color, springing around her head and spilling over her bare shoulders.

She wore a skimpy tank top—bright yellow—and

a pair of jeans that clung to her slim hips and long legs. Thong sandals were on her feet. Each of her toenails was painted a different color—red, orange, yellow, green and blue.

His gaze returned to her face. Wide-spaced green eyes with a thick fringe of dark lashes stared at him in obvious concern. A sprinkling of freckles decorated her nose.

"*You're* Christina O'Reilly?"

"How did you...? Oh! Mr. Wilson must have told you my name." She danced down the stairs to where he stood staring at her with disbelief and dismay.

"You must be Tony Callaway, Allison's son."

"You know my mother?" His mom had never told him about anyone remotely resembling this person.

Christina gave a quick shake of her head, causing her curls to dance as though they were on springs. "Not yet, but I know a lot about her."

He stiffened. Tony was very protective of his mother and her reputation. If this woman was implying—

"Her mother was Kathleen Brannigan. Kathleen's mother was Moira O'Hara, and Moira's mother was—"

"All right. I don't need a genealogy lesson at the moment, or a recital of my family tree."

The look Christina gave him was tinged with disappointment. "Oh. Genealogy happens to be a hobby of mine. I've been doing it for years. When I decided to visit Texas, I made a list of the names that I had traced to this part of the country. It's fascinating to trace a line, then search to find where that person lives. I've been to Ireland twice and met several people who are distant kin. It's kinda fun since—''

My God, did the woman never shut up? He hobbled past her and grabbed the stair railing, relieved to take some of his weight off his ankle.

''Ohh, you're really hurting, aren't you? What happened?''

He eased up the steps, one at a time. ''I landed wrong,'' he muttered between clenched teeth.

''Landed wrong?'' She repeated his words as though they made no sense to her. ''You mean you jumped out of something?''

''*Off* of something.''

She was moving slowly alongside him as though to encourage him in his efforts. ''What did you jump off of?''

He closed his eyes for a moment, wishing he could let out a bellow of pain. When he opened them he saw a pair of worried green eyes watching him.

''A bull,'' he muttered, making it to the top step and carefully crossing the porch.

''You jumped off a bull?'' She sounded incredulous. ''How on earth did you happen to be on a bull?''

He opened the screen door and waited impatiently for her to enter. ''That's what I do.''

She hurried through the door. ''You're joking!'' She whirled around to face him. ''Nobody spends their time jumping off bulls.''

''I *ride* them. I'm a bullrider. It's a skill, an art, a...'' A slight movement caught his eye and he looked past her shoulder. ''What in the hell is that?'' He pointed across the living room to the animal stretched out on the braided rug in front of the fireplace.

"It's a dog, of course. I know I should have asked if I could bring him—"

"A dog! Now who's joking? That thing is the size of a horse!"

The object of their discussion raised his massive head and looked at them as though aware he was the topic of discussion. Slowly, he unwound his incredibly long legs and stood on snowshoe-size feet before ambling toward them, his long tail knocking over everything he passed as it waved to and fro in a friendly gesture. His head came to Tony's chest.

"Oh, Hercules! Look what you've done," Christina said with patient exasperation. She rushed over to the table next to the leather couch and scooped up the papers and magazines the dog had knocked to the floor. "He's a Great Dane," she explained, "and he's really very gentle. He wouldn't hurt a soul."

"Unless he sat on them," Tony muttered.

Hercules ducked his head and rubbed his chin against Tony's hand.

"See? He's trying to make friends with you."

"Am I supposed to be flattered?"

Christina straightened and gave him a sparkling smile filled with mischief. The smile caught him unprepared because it totally changed her looks. "I'd like to say yes, but the truth is that Hercules tries to make friends with everybody. That's what's wrong with him."

Tony rubbed the massive head. The tail increased its furious movement. "Wrong?"

She nodded, her smile gone. "His original owners bought him to be trained as a guard dog, but it didn't work out. He was too friendly. Hercules loves everybody. Don't you, precious?" she crooned to the monster.

"So how did you end up with him?"

"They were going to have him put to sleep!" she said indignantly. "I was at the vet's the day his owners brought him in. As soon as I heard what they intended to do, I told them I'd take him myself before I'd let them kill him."

"I see."

The screen door squeaked open and Clem said, "I thought I told you to prop that leg up. Don'cha have a lick o' sense?"

"Here, let me help," Christina said, dashing to his side and wrapping her arm around his waist.

Her unexpected offer startled Tony. "Wha-what do you think you're doing?" he demanded, staring at the woman who was now pressed snugly against his side. He pushed her away. "I don't need any help, for God's sake."

He wouldn't have needed any help, that is, if Hercules hadn't decided to pursue his newest friendship opportunity by crowding against Tony, causing him to lose his balance. He began to topple, favoring his injured ankle, until Christina grabbed him around the waist again and guided him the few steps to the couch.

Still off-balance, they both fell, luckily landing on the couch with Tony on his back and Christina sprawled across him.

She didn't weigh much. That was his first thought as he measured her length against his. Her small breasts were pressed against his chest, and from this angle he could see down the front of her tank top, confirming what he'd already noticed the moment he saw her—she wasn't wearing a bra.

One of his thighs was between her legs, and as she squirmed against him, he was acutely aware of other intimate parts of her anatomy.

"Oh! I'm so sorry," she said, wriggling away from him. "Hercules! Leave his hat alone. That's no way to make friends with people."

By the time she'd managed to push away from him and get up, Tony felt that a permanent impression of her body had been stamped upon his.

"You okay, Boss?" Clem asked from somewhere behind the couch. Tony could almost hear the snicker in his voice.

He considered himself a mature male with a fair degree of patience, but he wasn't a saint, dammit, which was what any person would have to be to tolerate Ms. Christina O'Reilly and her horse named Hercules.

"Of course I'm not okay," he bellowed, stretched out flat on his back and feeling like a complete fool. He struggled to push himself up onto his elbows.

He glared at Christina, then turned to annihilate Clem with another glare just as a blur of yellow fur flew past his face and landed on his chest.

"Wha' the—?"

"Oh, Prometheus, not now! I don't think Mr. Callaway is ready to meet you just yet."

A pair of slanted topaz eyes stared unblinkingly at Tony a few inches from his nose. Ears lay flat against a broad, round head. The cat was a solid weight on his chest.

"Prometheus?" he repeated incredulously.

"Well, he wasn't exactly chained to a rock, but he was caught in a horrible trap. He almost died! The vet couldn't save his foot, but he's gotten along just fine without it." Christina leaned over Tony, either unaware or unconcerned that he was given another view of her chest clear to her belly button, and scooped up the short-haired, tiger-striped cat.

Only then did Tony see that the animal was missing a front paw.

"Don't tell me, let me guess. They were going to have him put to sleep and you—"

"Oh, no! I was the one who found him. It was when I was practicing for a marathon. I'd found a route I liked in the country and was following a series of farm roads. I heard him late one afternoon as I was making one of my laps. It was awful. I didn't know how to help him and he was in so much pain. I ran to the closest farmhouse. The farmer helped me by finding a grain sack and putting the cat and the trap inside. He swore that it wasn't his trap. Anyway, I drove Prometheus to the vet's office. The man had to put him to sleep before he could get the trap off his leg. He did everything he could, but there was no way he could save the paw."

"You and the vet must be buddies by now," he said sarcastically, but she took his comment at face value. "Yes, we are. I once thought I wanted to be a veterinarian but discovered I couldn't handle seeing the animals in pain. I couldn't even work in the office, although I've filled in on a few emergencies when his regular help was unable to come in. Filling in like that proved to me I'd made the right decision. I just couldn't be that detached when I knew what they were going through."

"Uh, Boss?"

"Yes, Clem?" Tony answered wearily, this time managing to sit up.

"About your ankle...?"

"Yeah, I know. Get a knife from the kitchen."

"A knife!" Christina echoed, horrified. "You can't mean to—" She glanced down at the cat in her arms and hugged him to her before she stared at Tony's booted foot.

"Oh, for crying out loud," he muttered, looking over his shoulder to make certain Clem was headed toward the kitchen. That's when he saw Hercules pawing at his black Stetson, which he'd placed on the nearby table.

"Hey! Get away from there!"

His sudden bellow startled the dog, the cat and the woman. The dog backed up, bumping into the floor lamp and causing it to swing alarmingly; the cat leaped to the back of an armchair nearby and hissed, the fur on his perpendicular tail standing on end; the woman gave a startled yelp.

"'Deliver me, O Lord, from the evil man and preserve me from the violent man,'" a hoarse, sepulchral voice intoned.

Clem came striding into the room, waving a lethal-looking butcher knife. "What in blue thunder was that?"

Christina clasped her hands and held them rigidly at her waist. "I can explain. I'm really sorry. She's usually very quiet. I mean, most of the time I forget she's around."

"Who are you talking about?" Tony demanded, looking around the room for some demented female.

"Minerva."

"Who in blazes is Minerva?" he shouted.

"'Keep me, O Lord, from the hands of the wicked.'"

"I think your shouting upsets her," Christina said quietly.

Tony counted very slowly to ten and decided to keep going. By the time he reached twenty-five, he believed he could trust himself to speak once more. "Who..." There. He sounded calm "...is Minerva?"

"Clara Bledsoe's mynah bird."

He nodded as though her answer made perfect sense to him. "I see. And who is Clara Bledsoe?"

"My next-door neighbor. Or at least she was. She's the sweetest thing. Eighty-two years young and a joy to know. Full of sprightly fun and energy. Truly a delightful person." She paused for breath, brushing a cluster of corkscrew curls behind her ear. "She broke her hip a few weeks ago and had to move into a nursing home. It was so sad. She had to sell or give away most everything she had accumulated over the years. She has no family. She said I was just like a daughter to her."

This woman was out of her cotton-pickin' mind. Why hadn't he understood that immediately? Shouldn't the multicolored toenails have told him something?

He was determined to humor her in hopes of getting her out of here as soon as possible. "So...because she thought of you as a daughter," he continued her story helpfully, "she gave you her bird?"

"I guess. I mean, they wouldn't let her have Minerva in the nursing home and there was really no one else, you see."

"Oh, absolutely." He shifted on the couch and motioned for Clem to come over. "So, tell me, Ms. O'Reilly. What other surprises do you have for us this evening? A blind Bengal tiger lurking in the van? A deaf rhinoceros, perhaps? I'd rather have some kind of warning, if you don't mind." He was being as pleasant as he knew how to be, given his circumstances.

"There aren't any more," she said quickly. "Honestly. Usually none of them are any trouble at all. The thing is, Mrs. Bledsoe taught Minerva several Bible verses and sometimes when she's disturbed, she starts quoting them."

"What, exactly—besides loud voices, of course—seems to upset Minerva?" Tony asked, looking around the room in an effort to spot the Bible-spouting bird. Once alerted to the presence of another visitor, he had no problem locating her. The cage was sitting in one of the corners by a window, and it held a black bird crouched on a perch, balefully eyeing him.

"That's all, really. Sometimes, when she's in a particularly philosophical mood, she'll offer food for thought, but on the whole, she doesn't say much."

"Thank the Lord," he muttered.

"Amen," Minerva added with solemn dignity.

"C'mon, Clem. Get this boot off."

Clem knelt beside the couch and looked at the expensive boot leather. "Are you sure you don't want to try to pull it off?"

"It won't come off. Not now. Just do it."

Christina hurried around the couch and leaned over the back to watch as Clem carefully worked the sharp point of the knife into the leather. The movement caused stabbing pains all around the ankle. Tony caught his breath and clenched his jaw.

"Am I hurtin' ya?" Clem asked.

"Just get it off, will you?"

"Here," Christina said, holding out her hand to him. "Squeeze my hand when the pain gets too intense."

He stared at her slim hand as though it were a poisonous snake. If Clem dared to laugh, so help him, he'd deck him.

"Thank you," he replied, "but if it gets too bad, I have some bullets in my pocket I can chew on."

He ignored Clem's throat clearing.

She looked stunned, as well she should. "Really? You mean people really do bite bullets?"

"Only in Texas. You ever been here before?" he

asked, trying to ignore the excruciating pain as Clem continued to work on the boot.

"No. This is my first visit."

"We're a different breed of people down here, you know," he confided. "Like no place you've ever been."

She eyed him uncertainly. "In what way?"

"Well, we're not really civilized. Of course, we know how to pretend around other folks when we have to, but most of the time we just enjoy our primitive pleasures."

"There!" Clem said with satisfaction. "Lordy, boy, but you did it up good this time."

Tony looked down and watched as his discolored foot, now free of both boot and sock, swelled before their eyes. No longer restrained by the boot, the blood rushed into the injured area with an insistent throb that made his head swim.

"Shouldn't you get some ice on that?" Christina asked.

Her voice was fading in and out as the room began to spin.

"Good idee," Clem replied, standing. "I'll make him up an ice pack and see if we can get that swelling under control."

The room darkened and shimmered around him. The last thing Tony heard before he passed out was Minerva's eerie voice hoarsely offering her philosophical comment on the moment, "'I will not leave you comfortless.'"

Two

"Mother," Tony said into the phone early the next morning while he was still in bed. "I know you've been promising Katie and the boys this trip for the past two years, but you've got to come home!"

Allison Callaway sounded much too young to have a thirty-year-old son. She also looked too young. People who met her for the first time had trouble believing that she was the mother of a fourteen-year-old daughter and eleven-year-old twin sons.

Young or not, she definitely sounded like a worried parent. "Oh, no, Tony! What happened? How bad is it? Are you in the hospital? Where—?"

"Whoa, whoa, Mom, calm down. I'm not hurt. Well, I sprained my ankle, but that's nothing," he said, dismissing his wimpish fainting spell of the evening before. He'd forgotten to eat lunch yesterday, that's all. His blood sugar had dropped too low and fainting had been the perfectly natural result.

"Then what is it?"

"You've got a visitor."

"Tony Callaway, what are you talking about? You aren't making any sense whatsoever."

Patiently, he attempted to explain. "There's a woman here who came to Texas to meet family members she's found on her genealogy chart. She says that one of her long-gone ancestors was a cousin of one of your long-gone ancestors, and she seems to think you'd be delighted to make her acquaintance."

"Well, maybe I would. What's her name?"

"Christina O'Reilly. She says she's been living in Atlanta for the past five years."

"I don't know of any relations in Atlanta."

"Well, if you have any, she'll know everything about them, believe me."

"Who are her parents?"

"Hell, I don't remember all the names. She rattled off so many last night my head was swimming." Which was the God's truth.

"Tony, watch your language."

"Yes'm. Anyway, she said her folks were killed when she was four and that she was raised in an orphanage. Maybe that's why she's so interested in her bloodlines. Who knows? The thing is, Mom, she's weird."

"What do you mean, weird?"

"Strange...loony...bonkers. She's traveling with a dog the size of a horse that she calls Hercules, a three-legged cat she named Prometheus—don't ask me to try to explain that one. I was never interested in Greek mythology—and a Bible-verse-spouting mynah bird named Minerva.''

Tony stared stonily out the window and waited while his mother laughed her fool head off. When she began to run down, he said, ''I'm real pleased to know you find all of this so blasted amusing. Why don't you do me this big favor...come on home so *you* can entertain Christina and her zoo and get 'em out of my hair.''

''She's there with you now?''

''Oh yeah. She went to your place first and Carlita gave her directions here.''

''Good for Carlita. I'm looking forward to meeting this Christina. She sounds like a wonderful person to me.''

''Glad *you* think so,'' he muttered. ''Then you'll come home right away?''

''Next weekend,'' she corrected gently. ''We should land in Austin around noon next Sunday.''

''But that's a whole week!''

''So?''

''So what am I supposed to do with this woman for a week?''

''Entertain her?'' she suggested helpfully.

''How do you propose I do that? I'm laid up with this ankle. Clem's having to take care of the stock for me until I can get a boot back on.''

''Have you talked to the bank about your loan?''

''I have an appointment in the morning.''

''You know that your dad and I would be—''

''Mom, we've already discussed it. The answer's

no. I'm doing this on my own or not at all... remember?''

''Oh, you're so stubborn! There are times I get terribly frustrated trying to deal with you.''

''I come by it honestly, and you know it.''

''Not true. At least I'm open to discussion and can be reasonable.''

''I was referring to Dad.''

She laughed. ''Point taken. As for Christina, I don't see why you can't have a little compassion for her. After all, you grew up without a father. It seems to me you might be able to understand how she felt growing up without either parent.''

Good ol' Mom. She zeroed straight in to the guilt button. He didn't know how she managed to nail it every time with unerring precision.

''Next Sunday, you said?'' he asked wearily, conceding defeat.

''Yes.''

He gave a big sigh. ''All right, but remember, you owe me big time for this one. I don't know exactly what it'll be, but I'll think of something.''

''Really, Tony, how hard can entertaining be? She's probably a warm and tenderhearted person. How old is she?''

''I didn't ask. I guess somewhere in her twenties.''

''Good-looking?''

''I don't know.''

''Take your blinders off, Son. There's a whole wide world out there besides ranches and rodeos.''

''Don't start. If you're implying that I should become interested in this retro hippy, you're—''

"Do you have any idea how stuffy you sound? Sometimes it's hard for me to believe that you're actually my flesh and blood."

He grinned, thinking about his mother's artistic temperament, her use of bright colors and some of her more outlandish choices of clothing. "Maybe I took after Dad more than I realized. Come to think about it, you and Christina *do* seem to have a lot in common."

"Is she a sculptor, too?"

"I haven't asked. But if she's going to be here an entire week, I'll probably know everything there is to know about her by the time you arrive," he said, rubbing the bridge of his nose wearily.

"You'll do just fine, I'm sure," she said reassuringly. "Do you want to say hello to your dad?"

"Not now. I've got to get going. Tell him hi, give the kids a hug for me. I'll see y'all Sunday."

He hung up before Allison could ignore his response and hand the phone to Cole. He knew that sooner or later he and his dad were going to have to talk, but Tony wasn't ready. In the meantime, he avoided one-on-one conversations with him as much as possible, shielding himself with the noise and boisterous confusion that occurred whenever the rest of the family was around as well.

He glanced at his watch. He should have been up an hour ago. Whatever it was Clem had given him last evening had done the trick. He'd slept through the night without stirring, which was probably why he felt much better this morning. The ankle twinged a little when he flexed it, but with the swelling down, the pain had subsided.

He tossed the covers back and got out of bed, intending to shower and dress. With his first step, however, his foot hit an obstruction lying by the bed. With a yelp of surprise and helpless indignation, Tony landed with a resounding thud on the thick carpet.

Hercules let out his own yelp of surprise and lumbered to his feet, towering over Tony, who rolled to his back and lay reciting the dog's lineage at some length.

Hercules gave him an enthusiastic swipe with his ten-foot tongue to show his appreciation of the attention.

The bedroom door flew open.

"What happened? Are you all right?" Christina rushed in and stared, horrified, at the two of them.

Tony was not dressed for company. He was bare except for a pair of black bikini briefs. He glared at the woman, whose eyes had grown to an enormous size since the last time he'd seen her. He pulled himself off the floor by grabbing one of the bedposts and asked, "What in the hell is that dog doing in my room?"

She wrung her hands. "He wanted to stay close to you. He was worried about you."

"He told you that?"

"He didn't have to. His actions were quite plain."

In a lower voice, he asked, "How did he get in here without my knowing it?"

She offered him a tentative smile. "You must have fallen asleep within minutes after Clem helped you to bed last night. He'd just left when I heard Hercules scratching at your door. I opened it to see if you'd mind if he came in. You were sound asleep. Hercules took advantage of the open door and immediately rushed in. After sniffing your hand and nosing your cheek, he collapsed beside the bed, put his head on his paws and closed his eyes.'' She gave a little shrug. ''He's impossible to move if he doesn't want to go, so I ended up leaving him in here. I'm truly sorry if he disturbed you.''

This morning she was wearing a dress...of sorts. At least there was a skirt. It was a rainbow of swirling colors that hung to her ankles. However, it was so thin that he could see through it. She was wearing some kind of leggings underneath. The top was of the same material but doubled or something, because he couldn't see through it. Thin shoulder straps held the top up. He had a hunch she'd dispensed with a bra today as well.

He wondered if she even owned one.

With as much dignity as possible given the present circumstances, Tony sat down on the side of the bed and jerked the covers over his lap. ''I talked to my mother this morning,'' he said politely, ''and told her you were here. She's delighted you've come to visit.''

Christina's face lit up. ''Oh, I'm so glad. I'm looking forward to meeting her. Did she say when she'd be home?''

''Sunday.''

Her face fell. ''Next Sunday?'' she repeated, sounding dismayed. ''But that's a week away.''

''I know.''

She looked around the room with a sense of uncertainty and concern. "But I can't stay here for a week."

"Why not?"

"Because I don't want to take advantage of your hospitality that way."

He rubbed the back of his neck for a moment before asking, "Can you cook?"

Her brows drew together. Puzzled, she replied, "Certainly."

"Then you won't need to worry that you might be taking advantage. You can cook for us."

"Us?"

"Me and Clem."

She thought about his offer. After a lengthy silence, she slowly said, "I suppose I could."

"Then it's settled." Tony shifted slightly and concentrated on meticulously rearranging the covers across his lap.

"I thought you were upset with my animals," she said after another long silence. She watched him carefully, her hands hidden in the folds of her filmy skirt.

Couldn't put anything past this woman, he thought dryly.

"I'm sure I'll adjust all right once I get used to them," he said, mentally reviewing what he was going to extract from his mother in payment for a week of being a zookeeper.

Christina suddenly broke into one of her brilliant smiles, which seemed to catch him off guard every time he saw one. He thought about what his mother had asked. *All right,* he admitted to himself, *I guess she's good-looking, in a bohemian kind of way.*

Straightening to her full height and facing him unflinchingly, she said, "I took it upon myself to make you breakfast. I hope you don't mind."

Now here was some good news. He'd always relied on his own cooking for breakfast and he wasn't the most inspired chef around. He smiled at her, determined to show her he could be friendly. "That sounds great. I'm starved." He waited for her to leave.

Instead, she asked, "Would you like me to bring it to you?"

What was the matter with her? Did she think he was some kind of invalid? "No!" She flinched and he tried to modify his response by lowering his voice a little. "But, uh, thanks for offering. I'll come get it as soon as I'm *dressed.*" He stressed the last word and had the pleasure of seeing her cheeks turn red.

Had it just now occurred to her that she was in his bedroom and that he was practically nude?

She spun away. Without looking at him she said, "The biscuits should be ready in about five minutes." She stepped back into the hall and jerked the door closed behind her.

He looked at Hercules, who'd been sitting on his haunches observing the conversation like a spectator at a tennis match. Now that they were alone, the dog rose in a welter of legs and ambled over to the bed. He rested his chin on Tony's knee with a sigh, rolling his eyes.

"Biscuits?" Tony repeated to himself thoughtfully,

absently stroking the dog's head. "She can make biscuits? This may not be such a bad trade-off after all."

He gently pushed the dog aside and stood, this time making it to the bathroom without mishap.

Although the day hadn't started well for Tony's sense of order and comforting routine, he had to admit that maybe things weren't going to be as bad as he'd thought.

Christina hurried down the hall, appalled by her behavior and embarrassed that she'd made such a complete fool of herself. How could she have barged into the man's room without so much as a knock?

The shock of finding him on the floor had been almost as great as seeing him undressed.

She hadn't needed a reminder of how strongly she was drawn to Tony Callaway.

From the time she saw him yesterday, Christina had known that Tony was different from any man she'd ever known. She'd been fascinated by his tall, lean body with its wide, muscled shoulders, slim hips and long muscular legs. He'd moved with athletic grace across the ranch yard despite the hesitation before he placed his weight on his injured ankle.

He had a hard look about him, as though he didn't find much in life to laugh about, and a fierce toughness that had been apparent in his attitude toward his injury.

His black Stetson had shielded his face from her view until he'd gotten close to the house. He'd looked up when she'd spoken and her breath had caught.

He had a face that could have been used as a model

for Michael, the militant archangel. It had a purity of sculpted lines and planes—a wide forehead, deep-set black eyes, high cheekbones, a strong jawline and a mouth that tempted her with its sensuous curve.

The shock of seeing such male beauty had shaken her, and in her nervousness she'd rattled on like a complete idiot, making an awful hash of their meeting.

She checked the biscuits and quickly placed them on top of the stove, then went back to mixing eggs for the omelets she was preparing. A stack of finely chopped vegetables, ham and cheese waited to be included in the dish.

It would be a long time before she forgot her reaction when she'd returned to the living room with Clem last night and discovered Tony had fainted.

Hercules had been by his side, nudging him, a soft whimpering sound coming from the dog's throat.

"Blast him anyway," Clem muttered, wrapping the bag of ice around Tony's ankle. "He's gotta be so all-fired macho about his injuries. I knew that pain was gettin' to him, but no, he ain't goin' to admit it to nobody."

She knelt beside Tony, fighting the desire to brush his hair off his forehead. Without the scowl, he looked even more like her image of a sword-wielding angel, his brow gleaming with a faint sheen of moisture, his features at peace.

"Is he going to be all right?" she whispered.

"Not from any smart thinkin' on his part. I can't remember the number of bones he's broke riding in those rodeo competitions. Ribs, arms and legs...once he punctured a lung. To him a sprain ain't nothing.'' He shook his head in disgust.

''Should we try to bring him to?''

''No way. He needs the rest! 'Sides, he's gettin' some relief from the pain. He drove all the way from Fort Worth with this thing hurtin'. Most people would have had the smarts to get a room for a day or two and rest, maybe get the thing x-rayed and wrapped. But this guy don't have a lick o' sense.''

''You admire him a lot, don't you?'' she asked softly.

Clem's eyes cut toward her and he gave her a ferocious frown. ''Admire him? When he don't take care of hisself? Huh! But I knowed him since he was in diapers. Watched him growing up without a daddy. His mama did a fine job of raising the boy. Sure can't blame her for his stubbornness.''

''But I thought Cole Callaway was his father,'' she said, puzzled. According to her research, Cole and Allison had four children—Tony, Katie, Clint and Cade.

''He is. There's no doubt in anybody's mind that Tony's a Callaway...looks like 'em, acts like 'em.'' He shook his head ruefully.

''I don't understand. Where was his dad when Tony was growing up?''

''Playing Mr. Big Shot Callaway of the Texas Callaways, busy running the family's businesses. The family must own a hunk o' Texas. Can't pick up a paper or watch TV that they aren't in the news doing somethin' or another.''

''He ignored his wife and son?''

Clem seemed to realize that he was gossiping about his employer and that Tony would have his neck if he found out. He glanced uneasily at the man who still lay relaxed in front of them and cleared his throat.

"To give the fella his due, he didn't find out that Tony even existed until the boy was almost fifteen. He was practically growed up by then. Ol' Cole did what he could, I'll give 'im that. He married Allison, moved her and Tony to Austin, put Tony through college, but Tony had already developed his independent ways. He still goes his own way pretty much, regardless of what the family might want for him."

"What do they want him to do?"

Clem shrugged. "Dunno. Maybe spend more time with 'em, maybe get involved in the family businesses. Tony's uncle, Cameron, works closely with Cole. Tony is more like his maverick uncle, Cody, who's busy raising horses on the family ranch south of San Antonio. Don't want no truck with the business world. Tony's the same way."

Unable to resist the temptation any longer, Christina lightly brushed Tony's hair back from his forehead. His eyelids quivered and he groaned.

"I think he's coming to," she whispered.

Clem nodded. "Good thing, I guess. He'll still be in a heap o' pain, but I think he's got some pain pills left over from the last time he got banged around. I'll get some and see if we can get a couple down him while he's too groggy to protest."

Christina had been alone with Tony—if she ignored the presence of a curious dog, a haughty cat and a sleeping bird—when he opened his eyes. He blinked at her as though he didn't believe what he was seeing.

"Hi," she said softly. "Remember me?"

He closed his eyes for a moment before opening them again. He looked at the room in confusion. "What happened? Did I fall asleep?"

She nibbled on her bottom lip to keep from smiling. "You're probably tired after your long trip today," she replied.

Before Tony could respond, Clem strode back into the room carrying a glass of water and a capsule. "Here. Take this," he said, thrusting them both at Tony.

Tony pushed himself into a sitting position, wincing when he moved his foot. "What is it?"

"Don't matter. Take it." He continued to hold out the items.

Tony reached for them slowly.

"When's the last time you ate?" Clem asked.

"Breakfast, I think."

"Well, hell, man. How do you expect to keep going without fuel? I'll heat ya up some of that stew." He turned and left the room.

Christina watched Tony look blankly at the capsule he was holding. She held her breath, waiting to see what he would do, then released it when he rolled his shoulders in a shrug and swallowed the medication.

"Guess I was tireder than I thought," he muttered, not meeting her eyes.

Only then did she realize that she was still kneeling beside him as he sat on the couch. She quickly stood and turned away.

Minerva caught her eye. Thankful for something to do, she went over and placed the colorful cloth cover Mrs. Bledsoe had made around the birdcage. When she turned back, Tony was watching her.

"The guest bedroom's at the end of the hall," he said, nodding in that direction. "I'll have Clem carry your bags in."

"I didn't intend to stay this long," she explained a little nervously. "I thought you could tell me when your mother would be home and I'd be on my way."

"It's too late for you to go anywhere tonight. We can talk more tomorrow." He pushed himself off the couch just as Clem brought in a tray with a bowl of savory stew. "I'll eat that in my room," he told him. "Why don't you help Christina with her things and see that she has something to eat, okay? I think I'm going to turn in. It's been a long day."

Christina had found the bowl half-empty when she'd followed Hercules into his room later.

She heard Tony's bedroom door open and hurriedly slid his omelet onto a warm plate, setting it on the table. She was pouring coffee when he appeared in the doorway.

He'd showered and shaved and looked incredibly appealing to her in a blue chambray shirt that stretched snugly across his wide chest, and a pair of jeans that were faded almost white from repeated washings. He'd put on a pair of moccasins that no doubt provided him with a little more comfort than his boots.

"Smells great," he said, flashing a quick grin at

her. "You're definitely worth keeping around for a while."

She knew he was teasing her, knew he was trying to reassure her, but her silly heart raced at his words, anyway.

Of course he didn't mean it. Now that he was feeling a little better, he was putting himself out to be more charming. She had a hunch this man could charm anything he wanted from a person, male or female. For a flash, Christina wondered how it would feel to have a man as charismatic as Tony Callaway want her. Then reality came into focus and she reminded herself that her childhood had been left behind years ago. She'd learned not to waste her energy on fairy-tale wishes and fanciful dreams.

A man like Tony Callaway would never become a permanent part of her life.

Three

"Does Clem have breakfast with you?" she asked, ready to serve the second omelet.

Tony hadn't said much since sitting down to breakfast, but he'd shown his appreciation for her efforts by steadily eating his way through the plate-size omelet and half a pan of biscuits.

"Sometimes, but not this morning. He takes off early on Sundays and spends the day with friends. Sometimes he visits his brother over in Bandera. I won't see him until tomorrow morning."

"Oh." She looked at the omelet, then put it on another plate and sat down across from him. "Would you help me eat this?" she asked. "I could eat maybe half of it. I thought Clem would be here."

He looked at her plate, then at her. "You sure you can't eat it all?"

She grinned at the eager expression on his face and handed him the plate. ''Positive.''

He carefully cut the omelet in half and gave the plate back to her. She took a bite. Umm. It *was* good, particularly after the time it had taken to prepare it. She ate until she was full before returning her attention to the man seated across from her.

''What do you do on Sundays when you don't have uninvited company drop in on you?''

He grinned. ''Uninvited, maybe, but definitely not unwanted. You certainly know your way around a kitchen, lady. You cook like a professional.''

''Actually, I *have* cooked for a living. I've done alot of things to make a living.''

He leaned back in his chair, tilting it back on two legs and sipping his coffee. ''Yeah? Like what?''

She did a quick mental review of her life before saying, ''I left Birmingham as soon as I graduated from high school. I'd just turned seventeen.''

''That's a little young to graduate, isn't it?''

''I skipped the third grade.''

''Ah. Go ahead.''

''I went to Nashville and started busing tables until I graduated to waitressing. I made pretty good money at that, but one night one of the kitchen help got sick and they asked me to fill in. I found I liked working in the kitchen, creating things. It was a nice change from waiting tables, even if it didn't pay as well.''

''How long did you do that?''

''Until I saved up the money for business school.''

''Good for you. So you went back to school and…?''

"Learned about computers and accounting and took some other business courses, got a two-year certificate and hired out as a temp."

"A temp?"

"A temporary employee. You know, where businesses call to have someone fill in for vacation and sick leave of permanent employees."

"Why didn't you find a permanent position yourself?"

"Because I wasn't sure what I wanted to do. I decided to learn as many skills as possible and try as many different jobs as I could qualify for before settling down somewhere. Once I could afford transportation, I was no longer stuck in one place. That's when I started following my dream."

Tony leaned forward, watching her with interest. "Tell me about your dream."

She realized that she'd been talking to this man as though she'd known him for years. It was true she was naturally outgoing, but because of her interest in people, she was usually the one to draw *them* out.

A sudden shyness swept over her and she looked down at her empty plate. "It sounds silly, really."

"So what? If it's your dream, why do you care how it sounds to others?"

Her gaze flew to his. He still had his dark eyes focused on her, with a slight smile curving that sensuous mouth.

Oh, my. Nobody should look that good this early in the day.

She'd already blabbed this long, so she might as well go on, she decided. And he really did appear to be interested. She played with her water glass without looking at him before saying, ''I really didn't mind living in an orphanage. It could have been so much worse after my parents died. The authorities looked for relatives, but both my mother and father were only children of only children.''

''My mom was an only child, too, but she made up for it this generation,'' he said.

That's when she remembered what Clem had told her about Tony and how he'd grown up. Maybe he *would* understand a little of what she'd felt as a child.

''I was treated very well and I received a good education. There were a couple of times when there was talk about my being adopted, but nothing ever came of it. The thing is, we were always closely supervised everywhere we went. Everything had to be planned out well in advance. We were taken on outings on a regular basis, but nothing was done spontaneously or impulsively...and we never went much farther than the surrounding countryside.'' She could still remember her frustration with the careful routine of her daily life. ''I used to dream about someday being old enough to be able to be on my own, where I didn't have to meet a planned schedule, live an orderly life, dress a certain way, behave in a prescribed manner. I wanted to be free to roam whenever I decided to leave a place.'' She smiled at him. ''I wanted to enjoy my primitive pleasures, as you called them last night, without having to pretend to be civilized.''

''I was having a little fun with you last night,'' he admitted sheepishly.

''Maybe, but I think there're a lot of us in this

world who feel just as you said—we only pretend to be civilized when we have to be. I admired you for being so honest about it.''

Hercules ambled in from the hallway and headed for the door to the porch. Christina jumped up from her chair. ''You've got to go outside, don't you, precious?'' she said, opening the door for him.

The dog glanced around at Tony for a long moment, then walked past her.

''What was that look for?'' Tony asked.

''Making sure you're all right.''

''He's a regular Florence Nightingale.'' He picked up his plate and cup and headed toward the sink.

''Oh, leave those. I'll get them,'' she said, returning to the table for her dishes.

''No way. If you cook, I wash up. That's the rule in this house.''

She looked at him, surprised. ''Really?''

''Well, actually, since I live alone, I generally do both, but I cheat on the cooking part. A friend comes out from town every week to clean for me. She prepares several dishes and puts them in the freezer, so all I have to do is heat them up. I'm not going to know how to act, being able to eat some freshly cooked meals around here.''

Christina set her dishes on the counter next to the sink, which Tony was already filling with soapy water.

''Have you always lived on a ranch?'' she asked, wanting to change the subject.

''Nope. I lived in town until the middle of my fifteenth year. I spent my summers after that on the family ranch, but the rest of the time I went to school in Austin.''

''How long have you had this place?''

''About three years. I want to start raising and training rodeo livestock. I've always been fascinated with rodeo skills. Over the years I've learned what they look for to stock the shows.'' He gave her a lopsided smile as he glanced at her. ''I'm obviously getting too old to be out there myself much longer.''

''You said you were riding a bull yesterday?'' She wiped down the stove and counter while he was working at the sink. ''Are they wild bulls?''

''Supposed to be—the meaner the better.''

''How do you know if you're doing it right...if you stay on?''

''Partly. At the very least, you have to stay on the bull's back for eight seconds, which can be the longest eight seconds in a person's life, let me tell you. But there are other rules. You've got to keep one hand high over your head so the judge can see you're holding on with only one hand. You've got to work those spurs to make sure you get the best ride and, of course, you've got to keep from getting yourself killed. Sometimes it's the luck of the draw. Some bulls make you look better than others.''

''So you're competing against time and not the other contestants?''

''Yeah. I mean, we compete, but everybody involved with the rodeo is a buddy. It's the cowboy against the animal, not each other.''

''So when you go to the rodeo, that's what you do—ride bulls?''

"That's what I really work on during the season, to build points. Occasionally, if the rodeo's near enough that I can take my own horse, I do team roping."

She leaned against the counter, watching him. "Fascinating. I had no idea about any of this."

"You've never seen a rodeo?"

She shook her head.

"If you hang around for a while, I'll take you to one."

A sudden rush of giddiness made her want to shout and throw her arms around his neck with glee, but she reminded herself that she had to at least act like an adult. "I'd like that," she said softly.

There was a scratching at the door and she went to let in Hercules. When she turned back to Tony, he was at the door to the hallway.

"I'm ready to get off this ankle for a while. Let's go into the living room."

Hercules bounded past her and disappeared around the corner, following his newfound friend. She knew exactly how the dog felt. Oh, to be able to express her feelings so freely.

The tantalizing aroma of Tony's after-shave still clung to the kitchen. She followed it into the other room.

Tony was amazed to discover that he was actually enjoying himself. Christina was different from other women he'd met. She didn't do any of the things that the women he knew did to gain his attention.

She didn't stutter and stammer around him, blushing and giggling every time she said something to him.

She didn't flutter her eyelashes and give him seductive looks from the corner of her eyes.

She didn't give him soft little pats or accidentally brush against him.

In short, she didn't flirt with him at all. She looked him in the eye when she spoke to him. She did nothing to indicate that she was attracted to him.

He sank down into his easy chair and propped his foot up on the stool. Hercules sank down beside him with a loud sigh and closed his eyes. Tony watched Christina enter the room and sit on the couch across from him.

"You mentioned last night that you'd lived in Atlanta for five years. You must like it there."

She slipped off her shoes and tucked her feet beneath her before answering him. "Actually, I thought I'd found a career there, but as it turned out, I was wrong." She sounded sad.

"What happened?"

"I took a temporary job in the accounting department at one of the large banks in Atlanta. I really enjoyed that job and decided to apply for a permanent position when one opened." She sighed. "I thought I was doing okay. I mean, I got a couple of raises, I set up some new systems and streamlined the reporting techniques. I felt like I finally had a handle on my life and career." She fiddled with one of her bracelets. "Then they fired me," she said in a low voice.

He straightened. "Fired you! Why?" He felt almost as incensed as she must have been.

"The reasons they gave didn't make much sense. I suppose I could have fought the dismissal, but what good would that have done? I decided that I didn't want to be there if they didn't want me." She rested her head on the back of the couch and looked at him, her smile wistful. "That's when I decided to visit Texas. Who knows? If I like it, maybe I'll look for a job here."

"You're quite a woman, Christina O'Reilly."

"Not really."

"I'd say you're definitely one of a kind. I would like to know, though—why are your toenails each a different color?"

She blinked once, obviously not expecting the abrupt change of subject. "My toes? Oh. I did that to remind myself about the rainbow." She straightened one of her legs and looked at her foot. "The rainbow is a reminder that we should never give up hope. Whenever I forget to look ahead, and look down instead, I remember that I need to keep on with my journey, no matter what happens."

"'Let not your heart be troubled,'" the voice of a kindly old woman said.

Tony jumped and Christina chuckled. "Sorry. That's Minerva doing Mrs. Bledsoe. She's really amazing. She can sound like anyone. I've had to be very careful not to allow her to listen to television. She picks up remarks very quickly."

"'Ye are the salt of the earth.'"

"So what's got her started this morning?"

"Who knows? Maybe she just wants to be part of the conversation."

He looked around the room. "I haven't seen your cat this morning."

"He's asleep on my bed. He had a busy night, checking the house out for scurrilous creatures. He dragged himself in and threw himself at my feet this morning, convinced that he now has the place properly secured against all invaders."

"Your animals have been company for you, haven't they?"

She nodded. "I had to move out of my apartment and rent a small house when Hercules joined us. He's only been with me a few months. I found Prometheus three years ago."

"And Minerva?"

"I've known her since I first moved to Atlanta and lived next door to Mrs. Bledsoe, but I've only had her a few weeks. Whenever I can, I take Mrs. Bledsoe out for lunch, then home to visit with Minerva. I know they miss each other. I'm gone for a large part of the day. I hate to make judgments, but I think Minerva sulks."

Tony tried not to laugh. "Really?"

"I know she talks much more around Mrs. Bledsoe than she does around me. That's why she's surprised me here." She cocked her head speculatively. "She must like you. I bet children and animals love you, don't they?"

He thought of his brothers and sister, the horde of cousins, and said, "I guess. I never thought about it."

She was quiet for several moments before she said,

"Is my staying here with you going to cause you any trouble?"

"Trouble? What kind of trouble?"

"You said you live alone, so I know you aren't married. I figured you must be seeing someone and that she might not understand my being here."

"I'm not *seeing* anyone, as you so delicately put it, but even if I were, there's no reason why you can't stay here."

"Oh, I know I'm not the sort of person who causes jealousy, but if she only heard about me, she might—"

"Whoa, wait a minute. What do you mean, you're not the sort of person to cause jealousy? Explain that remark."

Her cheeks pinkened. "I shouldn't have to. It's obvious."

"Not to me."

"I'm nobody's idea of a femme fatale," she muttered, obviously embarrassed.

"So? Why would you want to be? You're a very attractive, intelligent, original-thinking woman who needs to make no apologies to anyone about anything."

Her face had now turned a bright red. "Oh, please. I'm sorry. I wasn't trying to get you to pay me any compliments. That's beyond the call of duty of a conscientious host."

He sat up in his chair and stared at her. She was serious. She thought he'd made up everything he'd just said to make her feel better. The shock of it all was that until he started listing what he'd noticed about her, he hadn't realized just how true his comments were. She *was* intelligent and damned attractive. It took courage to have left the only home she remembered to strike out on her own at the young age of seventeen. She'd made the best of what life had offered to her. Surely she could see...

He got out of his chair and limped the few steps to the couch, where he sat down beside her. Her eyes grew larger as he moved closer.

And that was another thing. She had beautifully expressive, vulnerable eyes. He felt as though he could see through them to her soul.

Tony picked up her hand. She stiffened at his touch.

"Hey, relax. I'm not going to bite you, you know."

"Sorry," she muttered, leaving her hand on his palm.

"Don't you ever look in the mirror?" he asked softly.

"What?" Now she really seemed confused. "What are you talking about?"

"Don't you see how lovely you are?" He touched her cheek with his forefinger and discovered it felt every bit as soft as it looked, but the satiny smoothness surprised him. This close to her he could see golden flecks of color in her emerald eyes. Thick lashes framed them. He could count the smattering of freckles across her nose.

He smiled into her eyes. "You really are a beautiful woman," he said softly.

The poignant expression on her face almost unmanned him, causing a lump in his throat. He wasn't used to the surge of strong emotion that suddenly swept over him. Tenderly he slid his hand to the nape of her neck and gently eased her closer to him until their lips met.

Her lips were warm and quivering. This close, he was aware of her quick breathing. She was as still as a deer caught in the sudden headlights of a car.

Tony had a strong need to hold her in his arms, to keep her safe from a sometimes uncaring, thoughtless world.

He increased the pressure on her mouth ever so slightly. She didn't draw away, but she didn't relax her lips, either. A startling realization hit him; that she had never experienced a kiss.

She wasn't fighting him or trying to pull away. She seemed to be waiting to see what he would do next.

Tony drew away from her slightly, shifted his body and lifted her onto his lap, so that she was leaning against his shoulder with both of his arms securely around her.

He liked that much better. When he looked down at her, he discovered her eyes were closed. Her chest was quivering from the rapid beat of her heart. Come to think of it, his own heart had started pounding just as fast, despite the fact that they had done nothing more than press their lips together.

"Christina?"

Her thick lashes fluttered open and she gazed up at him. "I want to kiss you very much, but if you'd rather I didn't, I'd be content to just sit here and hold you, if you don't mind."

She licked her lips, a movement to which he reacted strongly. ''I'm not very good at it,'' she admitted honestly.

That's when a crack appeared in the wall around his heart.

He stroked his tongue gently across her lips, enjoying the taste of her. ''I could teach you,'' he offered lightly while he gauged her reaction to his touch.

''Okay,'' she whispered, so softly he wasn't certain whether he heard the words or just saw her lips move.

''I promise not to take advantage of you in any way. I'll stop whenever you want. Deal?''

She nodded, as though unable to verbally respond.

In his best instructor's tone, together with a teasing smile, he said, ''Open your mouth for me, okay?''

She blinked in surprise, then obligingly dropped her jaw.

''Not quite that much.'' He adjusted her chin. ''There.'' He took a deep breath. ''Oh, yes. You got that just right.'' He closed his eyes and found her waiting lips with his, feeling another strong surge of desire rush through him.

When he brushed past her lips with his tongue, she stiffened at first, then slowly relaxed. She returned the pressure of his mouth and shyly touched her tongue to his.

Oh, yes.

Tony forgot that this was supposed to be a lesson of sorts, which wasn't surprising, since he was the one learning the most. She felt fragile in his arms, small boned and lightweight. He was afraid he could crush her if he weren't careful.

His body was ravenously enthusiastic, hardening with such intensity that he stiffened and pulled away from her, hissing through his teeth.

"Did you hurt your ankle?" she whispered, turning her head.

"Uh, no. Just got a cramp for a second. It's okay," he improvised.

Her face was flushed now, but not with embarrassment. Her eyes sparkled, looking like multifaceted gems glinting in sunlight. This woman was absolutely adorable. How could it have taken him so long to have recognized it?

He kissed her again. She immediately put what she'd just learned to use and kissed him back with unfeigned enthusiasm. She was so honest, hiding nothing of what she was feeling, and what she was feeling at the moment was strong sexual desire. He recognized it, since he was experiencing the same thing.

The difference was he knew where this was leading and she didn't. He had to cool it quickly or the situation was going to get out of hand.

When he attempted to pull away, she tightened her hold around his neck.

Another kiss wouldn't hurt, he convinced himself. Just one. The third kiss felt so natural he was certain that he'd been kissing this woman all of his adult life. Her mouth molded to his, her tongue dueled with his, her heart beat in the same rhythm as his.

He placed his hand just below her breast and she immediately arched toward him. He eased his hand upward until it cupped her small breast.

He'd been correct. She wore no bra, an incendiary discovery he could easily have done without. He brushed his thumb restlessly across the tip and felt it become pebble hard.

He heard her moan and knew that he had to stop...now...or his control would be gone.

Tony raised his mouth from hers and began to kiss her face, soothing her and him as well with a contact that didn't add fuel to their already overheated state.

He brushed his fingers through her hair, loving the springy wiriness that gave it a life of its own.

She clung to him, her face buried in his shoulder. He sat there holding her without any thought of time passing. He wondered about this woman-child in his arms. Who had held her like this when she was hurt, or scared or ill? Who had kissed her bruises, chased the bad dreams away, nurtured her?

Was that why she had provided a haven for her menagerie of strays, the discards of society? Because she knew what it was like to be alone in the world, unloved, unwanted?

His arms tightened for a brief hug, to let her know that he cared. He felt different, somehow, as though something had shifted in his view of life. He was at peace, even tolerant of the pets newly introduced to his usually well-ordered existence.

Which was just as well, since Minerva chose that moment to add her opinion. "'I will try to walk a blameless path, but how I need thy help!'"

He grinned, his chin resting on Christina's head. He felt her quiver, then heard her snicker. He threw his head back and laughed. She raised hers, caught his eye and burst into melodious laughter.

With his arms still around her, Tony basked in the moment, enjoying holding her and sharing her infectious laughter as much as he'd enjoyed making love to her.

With a brief flash of insight, he realized he was glad that Christina O'Reilly had set out to explore her genealogy. Otherwise, they might never have met.

Four

After lunch Tony suggested they ride into town. The house had become a provocative setting in his mind, a fact that dismayed him. He'd only met Christina the day before, hadn't even liked her when they met, and now he had to fight to keep his hands off her.

It should have made him feel a little better that she seemed as affected by what had happened to them that morning as he did. He felt like he'd been innocently crossing an empty railroad track when a train suddenly barreled out of nowhere and pulverized him.

He found himself gazing at her whenever she wasn't looking, then averting his eyes when she happened to glance at him...which she seemed to be doing with unnerving frequency. He kept finding excuses to be near her, to touch her or to accidentally brush against her, and was thoroughly ashamed of himself for his behavior.

The trip to town was a desperate measure.

"You didn't go through Mason when you came here yesterday, did you?"

"No, why?"

"No reason. Sometimes I drive into town on Sunday, maybe get a bite to eat, check to see what's playing at the one movie house in town. I thought you might like to see the town where I grew up and went to school."

What a stupid thing to say. What made him think she'd care anything about where he went to school?

Her face lit up. "That sounds like fun." Then her smile faded. "But I don't think you should be trying to drive, do you?"

"My car's an automatic. I don't use it as much as the truck, but it will do it good to take it out on the road, blow some of the carbon out of the exhaust."

She glanced down at her clothing. "Should I change?"

"You wear whatever you want, honey-chile. You look just fine to me." And she did. My oh my, she looked good enough to snack on, and he could think of several places he'd like to—

Enough! Tony shoved his hand through his hair.

"Are you okay?" she asked. "Is your ankle bothering you?"

His ankle had been the last thing on his mind for the past several hours. Christina was certainly a great distraction for pain. Unfortunately, she'd created a new kind of discomfort, one so out of character for him that he was at a loss how to deal with it.

He felt like a bull pawing the ground to get into the pasture of a prime heifer. Boy, if his uncle Cody could see him now, he'd laugh his head off. He'd been telling Tony for years that he just hadn't met the right woman to ring his chimes for him, but that when he did, he'd be just like all the rest of them, following her around on a leash.

He wasn't *that* bad, of course. She'd just stirred him up a little, that's all. A drive would do him good.

"Is it all right to leave the animals inside?" she asked.

He eyed that walking demolition derby, Hercules, a little doubtfully. He hated to think about the possible damage the dog could do without trying.

As for Prometheus... "I dunno," he admitted. "What do you think?"

"Well, Minerva will be fine, of course. Prometheus has already checked out everything in the house and seems to have accepted it, but sometimes when they're left alone, he likes to tease Hercules. At least I think that's what happens, because I saw him tease Hercules into chasing him once, which explained why the house looked like a tornado had gone through it when I got home."

"We'll take Hercules with us," Tony decided recklessly. "He can sit in the back."

"You're sure?"

"Oh, yes."

"Or I could put him on a leash and tie him to the front porch."

"I have a hunch that if he decided to chase something, he'd take pillar, porch and all with him. No. He'll come with us."

Which was how Tony happened to spend the twenty-mile trip into town having the back of his neck licked by a grateful canine.

They stopped for coffee at the local Mexican restaurant and saw Clem visiting with a couple of his friends. The shocked look on the man's face alerted Tony to the very real possibility that Clem would accidentally reveal to Christina that this was the first Sunday Tony had been to Mason since he was in high school. He seated Christina in one of the booths and excused himself for a moment. He stopped by Clem's table and said hello to the others. To Clem he said, "I thought I'd show her around a little. I'm supposed to entertain her until the folks get back, which will be another week."

Clem's brows rose. "A week? You're going to have her and all them crazy animals around that long?"

"They aren't that bad once you get used to them. It was all new to them at first, but they're settling in."

If possible, Clem's brows rose even higher. "You feeling okay, Tony? Did you double up on your pain pills or something?"

"No. The ankle's much better today."

"It ain't your ankle I'm a worryin' about. It's your head. Do you think you got a concussion that we don't know about?"

"Of course not."

"Well, you're shore actin' strange."

"The hell I am. I'm just entertaining my guest, which means I've got to get back over there. Uh, in case she says anything to you, I told her I often spend my Sundays here in town. I didn't want her to think I was making some special trip out of it. You understand?"

"Hell, no. I don't understand none of this, but if you're telling me to keep my mouth shut, that I can do with no problem."

Tony straightened, slapped him on the back and said, "Good. See you tomorrow." He rejoined Christina in the booth. Her eyes were shining.

"Would it be possible to look in the window of some of the shops along the square? This place reminds me of several of the small county towns scattered throughout the South. I'd love to go in some of the stores and look at things, but I noticed they're closed today."

"I have to come to town in the morning on business. If you want to ride in with me, you can look around while I'm at my meeting."

"Great idea. I love craft stores. They give me some great decorating ideas."

"Sure. No problem. We can—"

"Hey, Callaway! How come you brought one of your horses into town in the back of your car? Your truck-and-trailer rig broke down?"

Two of the locals had just walked through the door. Tony had grown up with both of them. He closed his eyes and gave a brief shake to his head. He knew without a doubt that he wasn't going to live this one down, no matter how long he tried.

He nodded when they walked up to the table. "Howdy, Jim...Pete. I'd like you to meet Christina O'Reilly. She's visiting with the family for a while. Christina, these two yahoos are the poorest excuse for linemen in all of Mason's illustrious football history."

"Yeah, right. If you had ever learned to get the ball off in decent time, we could have held 'em with no problem," Jim said.

Christina looked at Tony. "You played football?"

Pete whistled. "You mean ya haven't pulled out all your trophies and done a little bragging? You're slipping, boy."

"What position did you play?"

Before he could answer, Jim jumped right in. "Quarterback. He made quite a name for hisself when he was playing with the Aggies."

"Aggies?" she repeated.

"Texas A & M."

"So where'd you get the hoss in your car?"

"He belongs to me," Christina said with quiet dignity.

Immediately the joking around stopped, the men grew very polite and began to pay increasingly outlandish compliments with regard to Hercules's looks, size and heredity.

"You ready?" Tony asked Christina, knowing that these two characters weren't about to leave them in peace. They were having too much fun...at his expense.

"Sure. Whenever you are."

He knew everybody in the restaurant and they, of course, knew him. By the time Christina walked out of there, every one of them would have been able to describe her well enough for an artist to do a full-body composite of her.

The joys of living in a small town.

Instead of being irritated, he was amused. Part of the reason was that if he needed any kind of help at any time, he knew there wasn't a person in the place who wouldn't have leapt to his aid without hesitation.

The joys of living in a small town.

"So? Now what?" Tony asked when they got back to the car. Hercules was so excited to see them that the vehicle rocked with his enthusiasm.

"I think we're going to have to take him home, don't you?" she asked. "We'd better not risk seeing a movie."

"I think you're right. Clem will be at the ranch tomorrow and can keep an eye on him for us. For now, we'd do better to head on back."

By the time he could reasonably be expected to be tired enough to excuse himself for the night, Tony's body was humming with sexual tension.

They'd watched a couple of hours of television, interspersed with Minerva's singing psalms of thanksgiving and praise. Surprisingly enough, she sounded good. Christina explained, "Mrs. Bledsoe has a beautiful voice and used to sing around the house. I think that's how Minerva learned so much. She certainly didn't get it from me. As much as I love music, I can't carry a tune.''

They were both working on keeping a casual conversation going, but the undercurrent in the room was twanging with tension. Tony knew that she must be as aware of him as he was of her. There wasn't a damn thing he could do about his reaction to her, either. He felt like he'd suddenly been fine-tuned to her frequency, and he kept picking up all kinds of messages that were driving him crazy.

She wasn't doing a thing to cause him to react this way. She wasn't flirting, fluttering her eyes, touching him, giggling or blushing. She was just being herself, and his body was going wild.

''I think I'm going to turn in. You go ahead and stay up if you'd like. The house is locked up. You'll be fine.''

She got up and turned off the television. ''That's all right. I'm a little tired myself. I'll go to bed, too.''

There. He'd deliberately refrained from using the word *bed.* It provoked too many responses in him at the moment. Didn't she have any idea what he was going through? He was acting like some crazed animal.

''I'll keep Hercules with me,'' she said, starting down the hallway toward the guest room.

''You don't have to. As long as I know where he is, there won't be a problem.''

She leaned against her door. ''Okay. Sleep well. I hope your ankle's better by morning.''

''Oh, it's practically well,'' he lied. ''Good— Uh, would you mind if I gave you a good-night kiss?''

She flushed but she was smiling. "Sure. As you've probably guessed, I need the practice."

He wrapped his arms around her and pulled her up snug against his body. "Oh, I don't know," he murmured, nuzzling her throat and ear, "you're a real fast learner."

"Am I?" she whispered into his ear. "Is there more you want to teach me?"

His body jolted like he'd just been jabbed with an electric cattle prod. "Damn right there is," he muttered, nibbling on her earlobe.

"I'm always intrigued by the possibility of additional education," she murmured demurely.

He raised his head and eyed her. "You making fun of me?"

She chuckled. "Not at all! Rather, of myself. I'm woefully ignorant when it comes to men."

With his arms still around her, he leaned his back against the wall of the hallway, his legs braced apart. He pulled her into his body, knowing he was playing with fire but not caring. In that position he could feel every part of her pressing against every part of him. She was getting a post-graduate anatomy lesson standing right there in the hall.

"Haven't you ever had a boyfriend?"

Her head lay against his shoulder while her arms were looped around his chest. "Yes and no."

"What does that mean?" He rotated his hips and felt the soft material of her skirt rub against his hard and sensitive denim-clad flesh.

She mimicked his movement, causing such a riot of sensation that his knees quivered. She was learning much too fast for him to keep teasing both of them like this.

"That, uh, means that I've dated a few men, considered them friends, so in that respect I've had boyfriends."

"But no one serious?"

"Of course not."

"Why do you say it like that?"

"I'm not the type men get serious about," she explained patiently, as though to a slow-learning child.

"You're doing it again," he warned.

She pulled away from him and looked down into the narrow space between them. "Doing what?" she asked, puzzled.

He laughed and pulled her back to him by sliding his hands over her rump and lifting her into him. "Putting yourself down."

She looked at him in surprise, her expression even more puzzled. "No, I'm not. I'm just telling you the truth. I become every guy's pal, his buddy, his sister. He tells me his troubles with the woman in his life, or grouses about his ex or moans about his boss, but I certainly don't arouse him into seeing me as a romantic object."

"Oh, no?" he murmured, rubbing suggestively against her.

"But this isn't about you and me," she astounded him by saying, perfectly serious. "You just offered to teach me some things I don't know anything about." She stroked his cheek fondly. "And I appreciate it very much." She nuzzled her face into his chest. "This is wonderful."

Tony pushed her away from him so that he could see her face. "Do you mean to stand there and tell me you think this is some kind of advanced sex education we're doing here?"

She studied his face carefully before she asked, "Are you angry with me for some reason?"

Tony had an urgent desire to howl like one of the coyotes in the surrounding hills. "Angry? Me? Why should I be angry that you might think I would brutally and callously treat you like some sex object, a plaything to fondle and caress out of some insane need to drive myself out of my ever-lovin' mind?"

"This bothers you, what we've been doing?"

"You're damn right it 'bothers' me, or hadn't you noticed the steam shooting out of my ears?"

She cupped her hands over his ears and smiled up at him so warmly, so openly that the cracks splintered and shattered and the walls fell away from around his formerly guarded heart. "You're so sweet, Tony. I'm glad I got to meet you."

Sweet? Nobody had had the nerve to call him sweet since he was out of diapers.

The bottom line was that she didn't believe him. His kisses earlier today had awakened her, there'd been no doubt about that, and their sexual play here in the hallway had aroused her, still no doubt there. But she didn't understand that it wasn't just because she was female that he was breathing like a runaway steam engine. It was because of her, Christina O'Reilly of Atlanta, Georgia.

His frustration caused him to grab her and kiss her without pretense or apology. He put all of his own longing and formerly banked passion into it, telling her without words how much he wanted her, how he wasn't sure he could get through the night without taking her, that she was the sexiest, most seductive woman he'd ever come across.

By the time he eased away from her, she was limp and would have fallen if he hadn't held on to her. So he used that excuse to continue to hold her until she could slow her breathing and her heart rate.

"What am I going to do about you?" he murmured, more to himself than to her.

She lifted her face until he could look into her brilliantly gleaming eyes. "I'll only be here for a few days," she said, as though consoling him.

He straightened from where he'd been leaning against the wall once again, opened the guest-bedroom door and gently pushed her inside.

"That's what scares me," he said, closing the door.

He opened his own door and said, "Hercules? You coming to bed?" He heard a scrambling of feet, an ominous thud as though something had hit the floor, and the dog appeared in the hallway, looking delighted and eager. Tony pointed and the dog dashed past him, slid to an ungainly halt beside the bed and collapsed in a heap, his tongue lolling.

Tony shook his head and closed the door behind him. He must be out of his mind. He was actually becoming attached to this ridiculous animal.

He lay in bed for a long time before falling asleep, trying to come to some understanding of why he was becoming even more attached to Hercules's owner.

* * *

Christina floated over to the bed and sat down, staring into space. Today had been the most astonishing, wonderful, unbelievable day of her life.

She'd been kissed by Tony Callaway. She was still having trouble taking it in. Why had he spent so much time with her? Of course, he'd told his mother he'd look after her, which was kind of him. But he was being more than kind. He was being…ardent.

And that last kiss. Wow! It had turned her bones to water. She'd heard that expression before, but she wasn't sure she actually believed it could happen…until tonight.

If he hadn't been there to catch her, she would have melted into a puddle at his feet.

Her body was behaving so strangely. Parts of her that she'd never given much thought to were ultra-sensitive and throbbing. She felt restless and languid at the same time. Most of all she hadn't wanted Tony to stop holding her and kissing her. She wanted to discover whatever came next, and next, and next. She wanted to experience the whole spectrum of what all of these sensations meant and how they played a part in a person's life. She knew that once she left here, she'd never have the opportunity to experience them again.

Tony didn't treat her like a buddy, a sister, a pal. No. He treated her like some movie-screen siren that drove him mad with desire. She hugged herself and laughed quietly with excitement at the thought. He wasn't faking his reactions. A man couldn't fake those kinds of physical responses.

The strangest part about the entire day was the surprising discovery that she didn't mind being touched and held by a man. Or was it only Tony? She didn't know and at the moment it didn't matter. She'd grown up knowing that there was something wrong with her. People were nice to her, they spoke to her, listened to her, complimented her. They just didn't touch her.

By the time she was a teenager she wasn't comfortable being touched. Once she started to date, her personal boundaries were obvious to any man who came around. If he ignored her wishes, she didn't see him again.

Tony was different and she didn't know why. She'd felt safe when he held her in his lap. Safe and seductive. Warm and wanton.

She could have done without Minerva's comment, but it had freed the tension between them. She'd been hiding her face, wondering how she was going to be able to look him in the eye. And then he had laughed, something she wouldn't have expected from this tough, hard man.

She loved his laugh. It was full of life. She wondered if he laughed often. Somehow she doubted it. The photographs sitting on the fireplace mantel revealed him to be a solemn child. Later snapshots taken with various family members invariably captured him staring into the camera without a hint of his so-attractive smile.

She hoped that her visit would add a little humor to his life. It would be nice to know that she'd made a difference to him. She knew that she would never be the same after meeting him. She wouldn't have missed it for the world.

Her mind calmed as her body eased into repose. Christina took a shower and changed into her thigh-length nightshirt. She stretched, then slipped into bed, smiling.

Tomorrow she would go to town with Tony. She wanted to repay his hospitality by doing something special for him, something he wouldn't do for himself.

She knew she had come up with a great idea that would remind him of her once she was gone. She drifted off to sleep, her head filled once again with wishes and dreams.

Five

Tony was jolted awake the next morning by a rough tongue being slapped across his face. He sprang into a sitting position, blinking in the pale dawn light.

Hercules sat and watched him expectantly.

"What? What do you want? Don't do that again, all right? Whatever you want, find another way to get my attention." He wiped the side of his face in disgust.

Hercules whined.

"You want out?" Tony guessed.

The dog stood up and whined.

All right. He could handle that. It was time to get up anyway. He fumbled for his jeans and slid them over his legs and hips. He padded barefoot to the bedroom door, eased it open and motioned Hercules through. He let him out the kitchen door and watched the dog bound across the ranch yard to investigate the row of cedars planted as a windbreak.

It was a shame to have a dog that size cooped up in a house in the city. No wonder Hercules sometimes expended some of his energy chasing the cat. Tony winced at a sudden vision of what the house would look like as a result.

Something soft brushed against his bare ankle. He glanced down and saw Prometheus. He didn't know where the cat had been or how he'd gotten outside. Maybe he could escape through closed doors, for all Tony knew.

The cat stalked past him, turned and rubbed against his leg once again.

"What is this? Are you trying to make friends with me?" Tony gingerly knelt, noting that his ankle felt much better this morning, even though it was now turning a vivid yellow and blue.

Prometheus stopped moving and watched him without blinking. "I don't know anything about cats," he said. The feline continued to stare at him. "You hungry?" No response. Tony held out his hand. Prometheus leaned forward and daintily sniffed, then regally lowered his head. Tony scratched tentatively behind his ear. A loud rumble emanated from the cat's chest.

Hercules came dashing back to the house, slinging legs and paws in all directions. With dignity, the cat leapt up on the porch railing and stared down at the large animal. They eyed each other thoughtfully, as though agreeing to meet on the field of combat at some future date.

Tony shook his head and ushered the dog back into the house. He put some coffee on and went to take a shower. He had a big day planned. The meeting at the bank would decide his immediate future. If he got the loan, he would be attending cattle auctions and buying stock. Without it, he would continue following the rodeo circuit this year, hoping for big-enough winnings to eventually buy the stock he needed.

One way or the other, he was going to get what he wanted without asking for help from the Callaway empire.

When Tony came out of his room dressed for his meeting, he heard voices in the kitchen. Christina's light, melodious tones interwove themselves with Clem's deeper ones.

Tony paused in the doorway. Christina had also dressed for town. She wore a demure shirtwaist dress in a soft yellow. Her shoes hid her colorful toenails. She'd pulled her hair back from her face into a French braid, although wiry tendrils resisted being subdued. She looked peaceful and composed, nothing like the seductive temptress that had filled his dreams.

"'Who can find a virtuous woman? For her price is far above rubies,'" Minerva announced from her new position in front of the kitchen window.

Clem grinned. "Mornin'," he said with a nod.

Christina jumped up. "How do you want your eggs?" she asked, gliding to the stove.

"Over easy." Tony sat down at the table and poured himself a cup of coffee.

"You made quite a stir in town yesterday," Clem said.

Tony glared at him over his cup.

"Oh, really?" Christina asked, glancing over her shoulder. "Why is that?"

Tony continued to watch Clem without blinking.

Clem drank from his cup before answering. "Not too many folks seen a dog that size before. Them that saw him had to describe him to them who didn't."

Tony allowed himself a small smile. Clem winked at him.

Christina returned to the table with Tony's plate. The eggs looked perfect—not lacy around the edges, not broken, not too hard. "Thanks," he said.

"You look very nice this morning," she said softly.

He almost choked on the bite of food he'd just placed in his mouth. He chewed carefully before saying, "Thank you."

Clem couldn't leave it alone. "I should say so," he added expansively, leaning back into his chair. "You look like you're going to a weddin', all suited up like that."

"When do we have to leave?" Christina asked in all innocence, catching Clem off guard.

"Wha—!" The front legs of his chair thumped as they hit the floor. "Are you—?"

Tony hastily interrupted. "Christina wants to look at some of the stores while I'm talking with Lin Schulz." He turned to her. "We need to leave in about half an hour." Once again he focused on Clem. "I'd like you to keep an eye on Hercules for us. He should be all right in the yard. If you go check on any of the pastures, take him along."

"Me?"

Tony looked at him coolly. "That's right."

Clem glanced at Christina. "Sure thing, Boss."

Nothing more was said through breakfast.

By the time they left Mason it was almost two o'clock. They'd stayed in town for lunch, indulging in sinfully delicious hamburgers from the local bakery-restaurant.

When Tony had come out of the bank, he'd found Christina near the car, peering into one of the art galleries on the square.

"Been waiting long?" he asked, coming up to her.

She spun around at the sound of his voice, smiling. "No. I just brought some of my purchases to the car and decided to wait here for you." She watched him expectantly. "Well?"

He shrugged. "I got my loan, but not as much as I wanted. He said he'd wait to see how things go this next year for me. If I can prove this will be a viable operation, he'll agree to loan me the rest."

"You should feel good about that."

He helped her into the car before he responded. "I guess. This is the first time I've ever asked for a loan. I don't like the feeling."

She looked at him in surprise. "Didn't you have to borrow for the ranch?"

He shook his head. "I used the earnings I'd saved up from the rodeo."

"Rodeoing must pay well."

"I was able to save most of what I got."

"Clem mentioned that you've won World Champion Bullrider three times."

"Clem has a big mouth."

"He's just proud of you."

"He can be proud and still have a big mouth."

She'd chuckled, and Tony had allowed himself a small smile.

He was glad to be heading home now so he could get out of his suit. He'd worn his dress shoes, the only pair he had, because his dress boots would have been too much for his ankle. He intended to spend the afternoon checking fences. He'd have Clem drive the truck for him.

He was surprised to see Clem coming from the barn as soon as they drove up. He wondered what Hercules had done this time. He hated to think about the possibilities.

Clem met them at the front door as Tony helped Christina carry in several packages.

"You had company this morning 'bout an hour after you left."

Tony heard a different tone in Clem's voice. When he glanced around, he saw that Clem's comment hadn't been addressed to him, but to Christina. She, too, paused and looked at Clem with a puzzled expression.

"Are you saying that *I* had company?" she asked. "How could that be? Nobody knows I'm here."

He shrugged. "I heard a car and thought you must've forgot something. I came out of the barn in time to see this green sedan pull up in front of the house and two men in suits get out. Of course, the great guard dog had to be pulled off 'em before I could find out what they wanted."

"Hercules attacked them?" She looked around. "Where is he, anyway?"

"Ah, he's plumb tuckered out after his strenuous morning greeting those guys. He 'bout licked 'em both to death with that giant tongue of his before I could get him inside the house."

"Did they say who they were and why they wanted Christina?" Tony asked. He followed her into the house and dumped his packages on the couch in the living room. Hercules dozed through their arrival, barely twitching his ear in acknowledgment of their presence.

Clem was right behind them. "Wouldn't say. Just asked if Christina O'Reilly was here and wanted to know when she would return. When I told them, they said they'd be back later."

"What did they look like?" she asked.

Clem shrugged. "Dark suits, red ties, short haircuts, polished shoes. I'd say government men."

"Why would they want to see me?" Christina asked.

"Since they weren't telling, if you don't know, I wouldn't either," Clem pointed out with a grin.

"How strange," she murmured.

"'Happy is the man that findeth wisdom and the man that getteth understanding.'"

"Thank you for that bit of enlightenment, Minerva," Tony said, shaking his head.

"'The Lord will not suffer the soul of the righteous to famish,'" she added.

"That's good to know," Tony replied. "But at the moment it doesn't give us much in the way of answers."

"If you'll excuse me," Christina said, "I'm going to change clothes. The only thing we can do is wait for them to come back and find out what they want."

Tony didn't like it. He had an uneasy feeling about the whole thing. Suppose it was somebody connected with the government. Why would they want to talk to Christina? It must be important or they wouldn't have taken the time and trouble to track her down in Texas.

After all, how many people knew she'd come here?

Clem had gone back outside, and Tony decided to ask Christina. He tapped on her door. When she opened it, he realized that he'd caught her in the midst of changing. She held her robe in front of her, which was modest enough unless he looked beyond to where her backside was revealed in the full-length mirror across the room.

She wore a tiny pair of bikini panties that highlighted the smallness of her waist, the rounded flare of her hips and the delectable shape of her legs.

She wore no bra.

"Yes?" she asked, looking up at him.

He forgot why he'd knocked. He shut his eyes for a moment in an effort to erase the image he'd just witnessed. "I, uh—oh! I was wondering who knows where you are?"

"I've been thinking the same thing. I can't remember telling anyone, well, except for my next-door neighbor, who promised to water my garden while I was gone."

"Did you tell her specifically where you were going?"

"No, although I mentioned a few names—Allison Callaway in Austin, Trudi Flaherty in Corpus Christi, Jerome Kelly in Houston. They were just names I intended to look up."

"Jerome Kelly?" he repeated. "Who is he?"

"Another line from my great-grandmother. She had several brothers and sisters, and I've been—"

"Okay. But you haven't met him, have you?"

"I don't know if I can even find him...or Trudi. I wasn't certain I'd find Allison, either, for that matter."

"So whoever these men are, they've had to follow up on those names."

"I guess so."

He'd been conscientiously focusing on her face during their conversation. His concentration wandered, however, and he darted a glance into the mirror once more. Slender and sleek, like a race horse. He wanted to... "Uh, I'll let you get dressed then," he said, and watched in the mirror as she carefully adjusted the robe she clutched to her chest.

He felt like a damn Peeping Tom. He turned on his heel and said over his shoulder, "I think I'll check with Mom's housekeeper, Carlita, and find out if anyone showed up there asking about you."

Carlita quickly confirmed that two men had indeed arrived at his parents' home early that morning, asking for Christina. She had given them the same directions to his ranch as she'd given Christina.

"That's fine, Carlita, but do me a favor. If anyone else asks for her, tell them you don't know anything. Then call me immediately. Something's going on. I'm not sure what it is, but I don't like it."

"Oh, Mr. Tony, I'm so sorry. I didn't know what I should do. They were very serious, these men. I was afraid not to answer their questions."

"Don't worry about it. Whoever they are, I'll take care of them."

When he hung up, he decided not to check fences this afternoon. Instead, he and Clem would work around the ranch buildings, doing some needed repairs. There was always something breaking down.

After she closed the door on Tony, Christina quickly put on her oldest pair of jeans and a paint-spattered T-shirt. She could tell that Tony was worried about her visitors, but she wasn't. Whatever they wanted, it could have nothing to do with her. She lived a very quiet, uneventful life. She carefully obeyed all the rules and laws of the country.

She gathered up some of the items she had bought and headed for the kitchen. Actually, she was a very dull and boring person.

Once in the kitchen, she decided there was no reason why this room needed to be so dull and boring, however. What it needed was some color, and a little more light.

She looked around the utilitarian room. It spoke plainly of a man's lack of interest in decorating. Very little light came through the curtains at the window. Dingy walls looked neglected.

She smiled with anticipation. She could hardly wait to see Tony's face once he witnessed the results of her plans to transform this room.

Tony worked until almost dark before deciding to call it a day. There had been no sign of visitors. Had they decided not to return? Somehow he doubted it. They had gone to a great deal of trouble to find Christina. Now that they had, he felt certain they'd be back.

The question was when. He didn't like this waiting around and wanted to be there with her when they came. At the same time, he refused to examine this new protectiveness he was feeling toward her.

"I'm going into town for supper," Clem said, stripping off his work gloves, "as soon as I get cleaned up. That is, unless you think I should hang around, just in case."

"Nah, go ahead. I can handle whatever it is."

They looked at each other for a long moment before Clem nodded. "See ya later, then."

Tony was looking forward to a hot shower and a hot meal, not necessarily in that order. He took the back steps two at a time, strode across the porch and opened the screen door.

Only then did he come to a sudden halt and stare in stupification at the sight in front of him. His kitchen was gone. He gave his head a brief shake, deciding his mind was deceiving him.

"What do you think?" Christina asked brightly.

Slowly he turned his gaze to hers. "It's... I can't tell you how... It's, uh, different. Real different."

"I wanted to brighten everything up."

"You managed to do that, all right."

The truth of the matter was that Tony didn't remember the original color of his walls. They just sort of blended in with the rest of the kitchen.

Now they were a sparkling white, except for one that was covered in a colorful wallpaper print featuring blue-and-white ducks. The cabinets had also been painted bright white, with blue-and-white ducks appliquéd on the doors.

Ruffled curtains hung on either side of each window. The ducks were in evidence on the curtains as well.

"I had to make a choice between cows, pigs and ducks. I thought the ducks would look nice."

He swallowed. Ruffles at the windows? He didn't want to think about Clem's reaction when he saw his bachelor kitchen done up in blue-and-white ducks... and ruffles.

"It, uh, looks a lot brighter," Tony offered lamely. Damn, but he didn't want to hurt her feelings. She looked like a little girl in her spattered shirt and jeans, barefoot, with rainbow-colored toenails. She was so blasted pleased with herself.

"I wanted to surprise you," she said shyly.

"Oh! Well, you certainly did that!" he quickly agreed, finding a way to show his enthusiastic response to her efforts. He looked around the kitchen once again. The room was much lighter, he had to admit. Of course, the tile floor looked old and worn in comparison. It had all blended together before.

"I'm afraid dinner's going to be a little late tonight. I lost track of the time. I wanted to be finished before you returned to the house."

"Don't worry about it. I'll get washed up while you're heating up something. There's probably something in the freezer already made up from last week."

She followed him into the hallway. He paused in the living room to toss down his hat and work gloves. She came up behind him and said, "You don't mind that I decided to change your kitchen without asking you, do you?"

He turned and met her green eyes, which were filled with worry.

He didn't care about his blasted kitchen, one way or the other. It served its purpose, as far as he was concerned. But if she wanted to change it, she could change it.

He looped his arms around her waist and drew her to him, pleased at how well their bodies aligned to each other. "I'm touched that you went to so much work for me. I want to pay you for all your supplies. I want to show you how much I appreciate your efforts."

Her face lit up in a mischievous smile. She slipped her arms around his shoulders and went up on tiptoe. "I'm ready for my next lesson," she whispered, brushing her lips against his. "That is, if you're up to it."

"Honey-chile," he drawled, "I always seem up to it whenever you're around." He touched her eager lips with his, his tongue invading, teasing her, teasing them both with its suggested rhythm and primitive possession.

"'Mercy and truth have met together. Grim justice and peace have kissed!'"

Tony released his tight hold on her and allowed Christina to lean against him while they both worked to catch their breath. He waited until he could speak without panting, then said, "I have only one question. Am I grim justice or peace?"

Her answering laugh reassured him as he made his escape down the hall to his room.

All the while he was in the shower, Tony lectured himself on his behavior. Christina was a guest in his house. As her host, he had a responsibility not to take advantage of her. She had no idea what she was asking as she teasingly requested lessons in lovemaking. The problem was that he knew exactly what such lessons would entail. If he had any doubts, his dreams graphically reminded him.

He liked Christina. How could anyone not like such a warm, openhearted, personable woman? She deserved better than to get her lessons from a battered cowboy whose focus remained on ranching and rodeoing.

Besides, he wouldn't be able to look his mother in the face when she returned if he took advantage of the situation they were in this week.

Six more days, that's all he had to get through. Six more days. Six more days...and nights. He could do it. Of course he could. However, he'd have to limit himself to an arm's-length relationship. Any closer and he promptly forgot all his good intentions.

They had finished dinner and were putting away the last of the dishes when he heard a knock at the front door.

"Wait here," Tony instructed Christina. He strode to the door and opened it.

The men looked much as Clem had described them, both of indeterminate age, nothing conspicuous or unusual about them.

"Yes?" he asked.

"We would like to speak to Ms. Christina O'Reilly," the blue-eyed one said.

"Why?" Tony asked bluntly.

"Is she here?" the brown-eyed one asked politely.

"It's all right, Tony," she said from behind him. She stepped around him. "I'm Christina."

Blue eyes nodded. "Hello, Ms. O'Reilly. My name is John Malone and this is Sam Johnson." He reached into his pocket, as did the other man. Both held out something toward her. She leaned closer, saw their names and faces and an official emblem stating Treasury Department.

Malone said, "We'd like to ask you some questions, if you don't mind."

"What about?" Tony asked.

Johnson said, "Would you mind if we come inside?"

Tony minded out of general principles. What did the Treasury Department want with Christina? However, they weren't here to see him and he grudgingly admitted to himself that this was none of his business.

However, he might very well decide at some point to make it his business. He glanced down at Christina and saw that she was waiting for him to invite them in, which he did rather begrudgingly.

She led the way to the couch and chairs. "Please be seated," she said, sounding like a gracious hostess. The men chose the matching armchairs facing the couch.

"We'd like to speak to you in private if we may," Malone said, causing Tony, who still stood near the door, to bristle.

"Please. I'd much rather have Tony with me, if you don't mind," she said quietly, giving him a beseeching look.

He immediately wanted to grab his armor and sword and charge into battle for her. He contented himself with walking over and taking her hand.

Johnson said, "You're Tony Callaway?" he asked, as though reading from some mental file.

"That's right."

Malone asked, "Cole Callaway's son?"

"Yes."

Malone allowed himself a brief smile. "I happen to know your father. He's a tough adversary, but a good man."

"Yes."

Malone and Johnson looked at each other. Johnson shrugged. Malone said, "I don't suppose it matters, if she wants him here."

"That's a relief," Tony muttered sarcastically. He

nudged Christina to sit down on the couch. He sat down beside her, still holding her hand.

"What is your connection with the Callaways?" Malone asked.

"None," she began, but Tony interrupted.

"What does it matter to you guys? She's visiting with me for the week until my parents return from vacation. Exactly why have you gone to the trouble of looking for Christina?"

Malone reached into his inside coat pocket and pulled out a small notebook. He flipped it open and cleared his throat.

"I understand you used to work at the Federal Commerce Bank in Atlanta. Is that correct?"

"Yes."

"We'd like to know the circumstances under which you left the bank."

"Why?" Tony demanded.

Christina squeezed his hand. "I don't mind telling you, even though I'm a little sensitive about the circumstances. I've never been fired before."

Tony watched the men make eye contact with each other once more.

"What reason were you given for being fired?"

"I was told my work wasn't up to the bank's standards," she said in a quiet voice.

"Who told you this?"

"The head of accounting."

Johnson looked at the notebook he'd pulled out of a pocket. "That would be Marvin Leroy Thomas?"

"That's correct."

"Why do you care about all of this?" Tony wanted to know.

"We have reason to believe that someone working in the Federal Commerce Bank in Atlanta was laundering money through the bank. From what we've been able to uncover, Christina O'Reilly might be the one person who could give us details we need to build a case against them."

Six

Tony turned and looked at Christina. Her face registered her shock. He turned back to the men, who were watching her response just as intently.

"Do you mean you didn't know?" Malone asked gently.

Her eyes looked huge in her pale face. Tony slipped his arm around her protectively. She shook her head. "I had no idea."

"It's our guess that your dismissal was tied up in some way with this matter. Were you given severance pay?"

"Only what the law stipulates."

"Did anyone else at the bank discuss your employment with you? Were you given any other warnings about your performance before you were asked to leave?"

She thought about his questions before answering. "No. I had no idea. In fact, I'd gotten a merit raise the month before. I arrived at work Monday morning, as usual. I was generally the first one in the office. I had a routine of turning on the machines, making coffee, that sort of thing, and—"

"You say you were early?"

"Yes, sir."

"According to your personnel file, one of the reasons cited for your dismissal was your habitual tardiness."

"But that's not possible. My working hours were eight to five. I caught the same bus each morning, which dropped me off in front of the bank at twenty minutes before eight. I was always on time."

"What about absenteeism?"

"I think I missed three days in the five years I worked there."

Johnson was making notes while Malone directed the questions. "I see."

"Did they say something about that as well?" she asked.

"They noted an excessive amount of absenteeism."

Christina rubbed her forehead. "I don't understand."

"I think we can build a strong case, but we'll need you to work with us. You are our key witness because you had access to the accounts in question. What we'd—"

Christina gasped, her hand flying to her mouth.

"Are you talking about the five accounts I found misidentified in the computer?"

"Five, did you say? We've only found two so far."

"There were five that had been erroneously catalogued. At least, that's what I thought."

"Did you check with anyone before changing them?"

"No. I generally just go ahead and do whatever I think needs to be done. Most employers have praised my initiative."

Tony recalled his new, brightly painted kitchen. Yep, initiative was definitely one of her strong suits.

Malone closed his notebook and leaned forward so that his elbows rested on his knees. "Ms. O'Reilly, I don't want to alarm you, but what you did affected a money-laundering scheme that seems to be working along the eastern seaboard. From what you've told us you inadvertently stumbled across a highly sophisticated system that has taken years to put into place. We have a large number of people working on this thing. It would be very helpful if you would be willing to come back to—"

"No."

Three pairs of eyes turned to Tony.

"She's staying right here."

"I'm afraid you don't understand," Malone said with the beginning of strained patience. "We need her help. If she can help us identify anything with regard to—"

"What you're suggesting could get her killed."

"Well, as to that, we're prepared to make certain that she remains safe."

"So am I, and I'm her best bet in this deal."

"I don't follow you," Malone replied, no longer hiding his impatience.

"The first thing we have to do is contact her friendly neighbor and tell her to just water the damn garden and keep her mouth shut. If anyone else comes looking for her, they won't have any idea where she is."

"How did you know—" Johnson began.

"Because she told me that her neighbor is the only person who knew where she was going. Mrs. Bledsoe only knew she'd be out of town for a few weeks. Since Christina isn't working, she has no reason to return to Atlanta any time soon, which is the safest course for her at the moment."

Johnson rubbed his jaw, thinking. "He's got a good point, John," he said, thoughtfully. "We had the dickens of a time finding her, remember?"

"It didn't take you all that long," Tony pointed out. "She's only been here for three days."

"Yes, but I left Atlanta two weeks ago," she said. "I took my time traveling along the coast and seeing new areas of interest."

"We started looking about ten days ago," Malone said. "To be honest, your disappearance was what alerted us that there might be something going on."

"What do you mean?" she asked.

"When the bank filed its quarterly reports with the government, we saw a couple of unusually large accounts that hadn't been reported in previous quarters. When we sent a routine inquiry, we were told that the reports filed had been wrong, that no such accounts existed, that the error was due to incompetent help in the accounting department, which had since been corrected. A few days later another report was filed that matched the previous ones."

"You didn't believe them?" she asked.

"Let's say we were a little curious, especially when you're talking about those kinds of numbers. We decided to do some independent checking. During a routine bank-examiners audit we went in and got the names of everyone who'd worked in the accounting department who'd left during the past twelve months and then looked them up to interview them. When we got to your name, we figured you were the one they'd been referring to. Then we discovered you'd gone, and your neighbor said you hadn't been sure when you'd be back."

"But I could still have been an incompetent employee who'd been terminated."

"That's true, except the bank examiners found a number of interesting discrepancies in the area they'd been told to carefully inspect. Although we gave the bank the impression everything was in order, we came away with bits of information that we've been piecing together. They're forming a very interesting picture."

Christina turned to Tony. "This is exciting. I want to go back and—"

"No," he said firmly. "The professionals are handling it now, leave it to them. You stay out of it."

"I suppose it would be possible to work with her here in Texas. I think you're right. It would be much safer. Once we start filing indictments, we'd need to place her in protective custody until time to testify.''

''When would that be?'' Tony asked.

''We can't be certain at this point, of course. We want to have a foolproof case before we go after these guys. With the kind of money involved, they can pull in some heavy artillery.''

''Your mother isn't going to want to be bothered with—'' Christina began.

''You'll stay here,'' Tony stated emphatically. ''You will be with me. From now until this thing is concluded, I'm going to be your shadow, understand?''

She didn't, he could tell, but that didn't matter, as long as she accepted what he was saying. ''But, Tony—''

''We can discuss it later.'' He turned to the men across from him. ''Is there anything else you need to discuss with her tonight?''

''A few things, yes. If you could tell us about the files you saw and anything at all that you remember about them. With you working with us, I think we'll be able to move ahead faster, knowing what to look for. So far no one at the bank is suspicious of the investigation, which makes our job easier.''

Tony stood and stretched. ''Why don't all of you go into the kitchen, where you can spread out your notes and things,'' he said expansively, now that he'd gotten his own way without argument. ''I'll make some coffee and leave you to discuss the details.''

Malone looked at him in surprise. He, too, stood.

"I appreciate that, Mr. Callaway. Your cooperation will make all of this a little easier."

"Glad to oblige. Just as long as you understand that Christina is my one-and-only concern in this matter."

Malone gave him a very masculine smile. "I would never have guessed."

Almost two hours later, Christina showed her visitors to the door and returned to where Tony was sprawled on the couch watching television, Prometheus on his chest.

He watched her walk toward him.

"You look comfortable."

"I am. So how did it go?"

She sat down in one of the chairs across from him. "Very well." She leaned back with a sigh. "Isn't all of this amazing? I wouldn't have dreamed that I would ever be mixed up in something so exciting."

"You sound almost pleased."

"Well, I am. I never expected to stumble across something like this in real life. This is the stuff of television movies."

Tony lifted the cat off his chest and sat up. Prometheus promptly stepped on his leg and stretched out the length of his thigh. Tony frowned at the animal but left him where he was. "The part to remember, Christina, is that this isn't a movie. There are some really dangerous people out there who are going to become more dangerous when this operation comes to light."

She shivered, knowing he was right. Mr. Malone

and Mr. Johnson had both warned her of the potential danger, but there was no question in her mind about what she had to do. What amazed her was how quickly she recalled the details of her job. She had been able to answer their questions with specific names as well as remember who had access to certain accounts, how she had stumbled across them and the system she had used to be able to correctly track them.

Mr. Malone had expressed his admiration for what she had done and said he'd certainly be glad to offer his recommendation when she looked for another job.

"Did they say when they might return?" Tony asked.

"No. Just that they would be in touch. Mr. Malone gave me his card. He said for me to call him when I leave here."

"You aren't going anywhere," Tony stated firmly.

She wondered if he had any idea just how gorgeous he was with his hair rumpled and his eyes so sleepy-looking. She had the strongest urge to wrap herself around the man and never let go.

"I can't stay here indefinitely," she pointed out.

"Why not?"

"If nothing else, I need to look for another job in a few weeks. I can't live off my savings forever."

"Do you miss working?"

"I never think about it. It's part of what I do to live."

"What I mean is, if you married, would you want to work?"

"I don't expect to marry, but if I did, I certainly wouldn't expect my husband to support me."

"What do you have against marriage?"

"Nothing. I'm just not the type of woman that causes a man to think about marriage."

"There you go again with your ridiculous assumptions. "'Not attractive enough,'" he mimicked. "'Not the type.' You've got to stop sticking labels on yourself like that."

"I just don't kid myself about who I am, that's all. I'm very happy with my life. I've created a home that's comfortable. I have my pets, my hobbies, a career.... Well, maybe career's too strong a word, but I'm qualified to hold a well-paying job. I'm healthy. I have everything I want."

"Haven't you ever wanted someone to love?"

She looked at him a little uncertainly. "What kind of question is that?"

"Someone who loves you, protects you, cares what happens to you. Haven't you ever dreamed about a time when you'd be the most important person in another person's life?"

"Have you?"

He straightened, as though unprepared for his questions to be tossed back at him.

He rubbed his chin. "Yeah...there are moments when I've given some thought to the idea. I don't have any particular time frame in mind, and I wanted to get the ranch built up a little more, but yeah, I want to get married someday."

Christina felt a sense of sadness seep through her. This man had so much to give someone. She bet there were dozens of women who were waiting to become that special someone in his life. She could almost see them in her mind's eye—beautiful women with luscious bodies all having the knowledge they needed to keep him dazzled with their allure.

She pushed up from her chair and said, "I'm sure it will happen when you're ready," she said wistfully. "I can't imagine any woman foolish enough to turn you down. I think I'm going to go to bed. I've had a rather exhausting day, all things considered. I'll see you tomorrow."

Tony watched her walk away, her slim back straight, her graceful stride reminding him of a dancer.

What had he said to make her look so sad? he wondered. Did she think he was becoming too personal, asking her so many pointed questions? As far as that went, he wasn't certain why he was so interested in her answers.

All he knew was that this woman had come into his life like a miniature tornado—her and her menagerie—and his life was still spinning.

Now he had T-men at his door, blue ducks with matching ruffles in his kitchen, a three-legged cat on his knee, a giant dog trailing him around and a bird that was doing her best to save his soul.

His previous life, from his present perspective, now appeared to him as a little dull. Absently he placed the cat on the couch beside him, stood and snapped his fingers at Hercules. It was time for a quick run around the yard and then bedtime. He'd had a fairly eventful day himself.

* * *

Hours later, his first thought was that he was in the middle of a horrendous earthquake. Not only was there booming, thunderlike noise and a keening wail nearby, but one of the heavy beams in the ceiling must have fallen, trapping him in the ruins of his bed.

One moment he'd been dreaming about Christina, about holding her in his arms, kissing and caressing her, then bam! The world had gone crazy.

He was trying to get his breath, wondering what could have caused such an event here in the Texas hill country, when his bedroom door flew open and Christina came dashing in, exclaiming, "Oh, no! I should have warned you. Oh, Hercules, look what you've done!"

The keening wail continued, almost drowning out her words.

She turned on the light, and Tony, in his dazed condition, thought it odd that the electricity was working. He could still hear her voice amidst the noise. "Get off him, do you hear? You're too heavy to lay on anybody. Haven't I explained all of this to you before?"

The beam across his middle shifted, then moved, and Tony took his first deep breath in what seemed like hours. He lay at a drunken angle, his feet higher than his head, and peered up at her.

She ran around the bed and knelt beside him. That's when he realized that part of the bed was now on the floor.

"What happened?" he asked.

Another crash of thunder sounded overhead and

Hercules frantically scrambled to burrow beneath him.

"I should have warned you," Christina explained, clearly upset. "I just wasn't expecting a storm. Do they always come up so quickly here in Texas? If I'd had any idea..."

Tony shoved the dog away. "Stop that, you idiot hound. What's gotten into you, anyway?"

"He's afraid of thunder," she said. "Whenever we have a storm he tries to get into my lap or under the table. I've tried to explain to him that it's just noise and perfectly harmless, but he won't listen."

Tony pushed himself awkwardly up off the mattress, which was a little difficult, since his feet were still tangled in the sheets at a forty-five-degree angle above his head. After he got them free, he rolled to the edge and got up, looking down at the ruins of his bed.

"He must have gotten frightened and tried to get in bed with you."

Tony lifted the mattress and spring and saw that one of the slats had fallen, another one had snapped in two. "How much does he weigh, anyway? This bed should have held both our weights."

Christina stood as well. "I think he must have gotten a running start and leaped. He did that once to one of my chairs and it collapsed beneath him."

Tony turned and looked at the dog, who currently had his head under the covers and was still emitting a shrill, keening noise.

"Enough, Hercules," he said sternly. "Now shut up!"

The noise stopped, but the violent trembling continued.

"He's really frightened, isn't he?" Tony said in amazement. He shook his head in disbelief. "A would-be guard dog who welcomes everyone he meets and has a phobic fear of storms." He turned to Christina, and for the first time since she'd rushed in, he noticed what she was wearing—a nightshirt that stopped at midthigh. There was a giant panda on the front with the words *Hug Me.*

He grinned and followed instructions.

"What are you doing?" she gasped as he picked her up in his arms.

"Taking advice from your panda." He paused in the doorway, and after a brief glance back at the whimpering dog still huddled in the remains of his bed, he turned off the light. Crossing the hall, he entered the guest room and closed the door. She hadn't bothered to turn on a light in her mad dash to save him from possible suffocation. Other than the sporadic flickering of lightning from the storm passing overhead, the room was dark.

Tony didn't care. He knew where the bed was. He made his way carefully to its side, then sat down before rolling them both onto its surface. He gathered up the sheet and covered them.

"Have you lost your mind?" she squeaked.

"Not at all. Since your dog just destroyed my bed, I think it only fair that you share yours with me."

"Oh!" She was quiet. He wished he could see her face. Since he still held her in his arms, he knew that she wasn't afraid of him. Her body felt relaxed and immensely pleasurable. He draped his leg over both of hers and sighed with satisfaction.

"I can sleep on the couch," she offered after a moment.

"That won't be necessary," he reassured her politely, glad she couldn't see the smug grin he couldn't seem to wipe off his face. "This is just fine."

She gave a little wiggle of adjustment, which brought her body more securely against him. Her head rested on his shoulder. He rubbed his chin against her cheek, still smiling.

"I've never attempted to sleep with anyone before," she said after a moment.

"Really? You have no idea what you've been missing."

She was silent for several minutes before she said, "You've probably slept with lots of people, haven't you?"

"Not lots, no. And not people as a class. A few...a very few...females."

He knew that to be a lie. He'd never slept with a female before. He might have been in bed with one, but he never fell asleep. He liked waking in his own bed, even if it was in a rented motel room. He liked waking up alone, but he didn't mind making an exception in this case.

In fact, he could get used to going to sleep wrapped around this particular female real easy. Almost addicting, it was.

Now that he was awake, though, he was wide awake. He must have had several hours of sleep before the storm blew into the area. Not only was he wide awake, but his body was stirring with anticipation.

"Tony?" she whispered.

"Mm?"

"Doesn't this bother you?"

"What?"

"Lying so close like this?"

"What do you mean, bother?"

"I just think that since this bed is so big, we could probably lie far enough apart that we wouldn't have to touch."

"That's true."

"Wouldn't you rest better that way?"

"No doubt."

She raised her head and tried to push away from him by placing her hands on his chest. Since his mother hadn't raised a fool, Tony left his arms around her. She was firmly anchored to his side by his leg across hers as well.

Christina brushed her hand across his chest in a smooth caress that made him want to purr. "Don't you want to rest?" she finally asked.

"Not particularly. Given the choice, I'd much rather hold you."

"Oh."

Minutes marched along in silence.

She stroked his chest again, as though exploring the contours. He trailed his hand down her spine, sliding it beneath the hem of her nightshirt and being rewarded by the feel of her satiny skin just above the waistband of her bikini panties. He caressed the slender indentation of her spine, tracing it slowly back to her neck.

She stirred restlessly and rubbed her cheek against his neck. He nipped her earlobe and was rewarded by a shiver. When she moved her head, he found her mouth, open and willing. He couldn't contain a groan of pleasure at her response. His mouth molded and shaped itself to hers and he nibbled her bottom lip, then soothed it with his tongue.

He moved his hand to her hip, then around to her stomach. She sucked in her breath when he trailed his fingers up to her breast.

"They're too small," she whispered sadly.

"No. They're perfect. See?" He wrapped his hand carefully around her. "They fit perfectly in my palm as though they belong there." He moved to the other one, rocking his hand back and forth over the tip until it stood erect.

Her breath made a whooshing sound as though she'd been holding it too long.

"Am I hurting you?"

"Oh, no."

"Do you want me to stop?"

"Oh, no!" She gave a breathless chuckle. "That feels so—so… I don't know how to describe it," she whispered, a little breathless.

"Me, either. I just know that I love holding you, touching you, kissing you. I can't seem to get enough of it." As if to prove his words, he began to kiss her again, as though he'd been deprived long enough of the taste of her lips.

He shifted his leg and rolled onto his back, pulling

her on top of him. He loved feeling her light frame resting against him. He was also giving her control of the situation.

As though freed by his unspoken invitation, she explored his shoulders and chest with her hands and lips, sliding down his body and stroking the taut muscles of his abdomen.

His briefs could no longer contain his arousal, the elastic band causing him some discomfort. He reached down to make an adjustment and her fingers followed him, brushing his away and soothing the distended flesh.

He couldn't control the involuntary spasm that her touch caused him. She tugged the briefs down his legs and eased them off before returning to her exploration of him. There wasn't a hint of self-consciousness in her movements, just one of wonderment and new discovery.

Her touch was so gentle that there were moments when he felt like he was experiencing the flutter of butterfly wings wafting across his skin. He shuddered and forced himself to lie quietly. It was almost as though he were seeing himself from a brand-new perspective as a result of her innocent and guilt-free exploration and discovery of his maleness.

Her hands cupped his hardness and she placed a kiss very tenderly on his heated flesh, as though in benediction and acknowledgment of the basic difference between them.

A sudden jolt of unexpected emotion caused tears to spring to his eyes. He'd never experienced such an honest expression of appreciation from one human being to another. He was at a loss as to what he could do or say, and so he continued to lie there, waiting and watching her shadowy figure move above him.

By the time she touched her fingers against his cheek once more, she had explored every inch of his body, as though she'd needed to learn his anatomy through touch. Her words, when she spoke, shattered him with their sweet simplicity.

"Will you make love to me?"

Seven

The shock went through his body, and if possible, he became more rigid. He rested his hand on her hip as she stretched over him once again.

"Are you sure that's what you want?" he asked hoarsely.

"More than anything in my entire life," she replied.

Another wave of undiluted emotion swept over him. This time the tears trickled down his cheeks. He didn't bother wiping them away.

"Ah, Christi, you're something else." His voice broke.

"What's wrong?"

"Nothin'. You've just knocked down all my walls and crept past my defenses until all I can think about, dream about, is you."

"Really?" She sounded delighted.

"You've got me going in fifteen directions at once."

"Is that a yes or a no?"

"I want you so bad I ache with it."

"That sounds like a yes."

"I can't take your innocence."

"That sounds like a no."

"Don't ask this of me."

"You won't be taking anything. You'll be giving to me. I want my first time to be with you. You are so beautiful."

Tony had a lot of trouble with that. Nobody had ever called him beautiful. In fact, he would have decked almost anyone who ever did. Worse than that, she had said she wanted her first time to be with him. Knowing he would be the first didn't come as any surprise. He already knew that, but the way she said it bothered him. He didn't mind being the first, but he wanted to be the last and all the in betweens as well. He didn't want this beautiful woman-child to ever share herself with anyone but him.

The realization of what that meant scared the holy hell out of him.

When he didn't answer her, she moved away from him so that they were no longer touching.

"Where do you think you're going?"

"I got my answer. I'm going to let you go to sleep."

"Christi—honey-chile, what you're witnessing is the toughest struggle a man ever had with himself. If I win I lose and if I lose I lose, so I'm in trouble whichever way I decide." He turned on his side so that he was facing her. "The thing is, I want to make love to you more than anything I know."

She slid over to him and hugged him. "Show me," she said softly.

"But if I do, I've got to go back to my room for protection. That's a rule I never break."

"Because of what happened with your mom and dad?"

"How did you know about that?"

"From Clem."

"I told you he talks too much."

"It helped me to understand you better, I think. To understand why you're so independent."

"I love my dad. Don't ever doubt it. But I've got to live my own life and live it my way, not his. I also don't want to make the mistakes he made."

"You consider yourself a mistake?"

That stopped him. "Not exactly, but it sure made things tough on my mom."

"I don't know why your dad didn't learn about you for all those years, but if your mom had to lose him, at least she had you."

"That's what she told me."

"That's the way I would feel in her place. You couldn't be anybody's mistake, Tony Callaway. You're a very special gift."

Tony rolled away from her, off the bed, and strode into the other room. He found Hercules curled up in his bed, snoring slightly. Shaking his head, he fumbled in the drawer of his bedside table, grabbed the packets and went back to the guest room.

"You're the special gift, Christi," he whispered as he lay down beside her once more and pulled her into his arms. "I don't deserve you, but I want you so much, more than I've ever wanted anyone."

The talking was over, the decision made. Tony had done what he could to resist the temptation of her candid request, but he succumbed to his humanness and his burning desire to show this woman what love-making could be.

This time it was his turn to discover all the lush curves and planes of her body. His silent instruction was followed by her equally silent response as he lifted her nightshirt and she pulled it over her head. With a flick of his wrist he removed her panties so that he was free to memorize every quivering inch of her.

By the time he was kneeling between her knees, she was reaching for him, silently commanding him to take her—now!

He took his time, forcing himself to prepare her for his possession. When he'd finally broken through her barrier and buried himself within her, they were both shaking.

She placed frantic little kisses over his face, almost sobbing with the need for relief. In his concern to make certain she was ready, perhaps he'd pushed her too close to the edge without her understanding what was happening.

When he started moving within her, she quickly met him with eager thrusts of her own. Then, as though she suddenly understood, she gasped and clung to him, panting and pressing kisses on his chin and neck.

Her spontaneous contractions triggered his already overtaxed system and he felt as though he'd exploded into pieces of pure pleasure. He clung to her in dazed wonder, unable to comprehend what had just happened to him. He didn't want to let her go. Not now, not ever. She had become a part of him. In claiming her, he had claimed a part of himself he'd never known existed.

Her blissful sigh as she fell asleep snuggled in his arms brought a smile to his lips. Her wholehearted acceptance of him humbled him and made him feel unworthy.

He lay there listening to her soft, even breathing, attempting to cope with the rush of feelings he'd experienced. It was as though he now understood many things about life that had puzzled him in the past.

For the first time, he could understand what had happened between his parents so many years ago. He finally understood how they must have felt about each other, and with this new awareness, he was able to forgive.

Christina moved and Tony reflexively tightened his hold on her so that she continued to lie closely against his side. He didn't want to move from this wonderfully relaxing place. He couldn't remember a time when he'd slept so peacefully.

"Tony?"

"Mmm?"

"I've got to get up."

"Why?"

"Because Clem will be looking for his breakfast."

He opened one eye and peered at the clock. "Let him make his own."

"We can't just stay in bed all day," she pointed out.

"Sure we can."

"Don't you have things to do?"

"Oh, yes," he agreed, turning so that she was facing him. "This—" he said, giving her a leisurely, very thorough kiss "— and this—" he pulled her hips against his arousal "—and especially this." He stroked her inner thighs and moved upward to test her readiness for him. His actions made her sigh with unfeigned pleasure and she opened eagerly to him.

He joined them, careful not to rush her, but he needn't have worried. She was eagerly clutching him, moving with him with soft little moans that drove him wild.

He rolled to his back and arranged her legs on either side of his hips, then guided her into a rhythm they could both enjoy without ending their pleasure too soon.

He touched her breast with his tongue, then slipped his lips around the tip and tugged gently. "Oh, Tony," she whispered between panting breaths, "Oh...oh," she crooned in rhythm with him.

He couldn't control his responses much longer. He placed his hands on her hips and guided her with shorter, faster strokes until she let out a whimpering cry and stiffened, her body pulling him deeper, higher into her depths before he lost what little control he had.

Only then did he remember he'd forgotten to protect her from his early morning possession.

As soon as he thought his legs could hold his weight, he scooped her in his arms and strode from her bedroom into his, past the broken bed and into the bathroom. He switched on the shower, adjusted the water temperature, then allowed her to slowly slide down his body as the water washed over them.

He kept one arm around her waist while he industriously lathered first her back, then her front, taking special care to cover her breasts and to softly stroke between her legs. She leaned against the wall and smiled, holding out her hand. "My turn," she said.

Reluctantly he handed her the soap, knowing what the feel of her did to him. She carefully scrubbed his back, then his chest and downward, holding him gently as she soaped him all over.

"Christi?"

"Mmm."

"I forgot to protect you this morning."

Her long lashes veiled her eyes. "Oh."

"I'm sorry. I was more than half-asleep and I wasn't thinking about anything but—"

"It's okay."

"No. It's not okay."

"What I mean is that it's the wrong time for me to get pregnant."

"You're sure?"

She didn't look at him. She just nodded her head.

He lifted her chin so that those big green eyes had to meet his gaze. "Would you lie to me?"

Her gaze was shy but very steady. "No. You really have nothing to worry about. I promise."

Then she ducked her head under the water, dousing her curls. He grabbed the shampoo and began to run his hands through her hair, watching the foam and making little peaks on top of her head and over each ear before helping her rinse.

Once out of the shower, he helped her dry her hair and body before hastily finishing his own.

"I'll go start breakfast," she said.

"I'll be there shortly."

He watched her leave the bathroom, a towel wrapped around her, before he went about the business of shaving and dressing for his day.

They were both at the breakfast table when Clem came through the door.

"What in blazes happened?"

Tony stiffened, wondering how Clem could possibly know that he and Christina had... Then he remembered that Clem hadn't seen the kitchen since Christina added her touch to the room.

He grinned at the older man. "Livens the place up a bit, wouldn't you say?"

"Ducks?" Clem said, dazed.

"It was a choice between ducks, pigs and cows," he explained with a straight face.

"You mean you—"

"Christina decided to surprise me. She did all of this yesterday afternoon while I was working with you."

Clem looked around at the cabinets, the walls and the gaily patterned wallpaper.

"Do you like it?" she asked.

He poured himself some coffee and sat down before attempting to answer. He shifted his gaze to Tony, who smiled blandly.

"Looks real good," he said, nodding slowly. "Nice and bright." His quick glance took in the ruffled curtains before he buried his nose in his coffee cup.

They said very little over breakfast. Tony's thoughts kept returning to the hours he'd just spent with Christina, replaying in his mind how she'd felt and tasted.

"'He goeth after her straightway as an ox goeth to the slaughter.'"

Tony could feel his ears burning. He didn't look at either Christina or Clem.

"Where does that blasted bird git some of them silly sayings?" Clem asked, looking over at Minerva, who was preening her feathers in a wide arc.

"Mrs. Bledsoe taught her different Bible verses," Christina explained.

"I never heard anything about going like an ox to slaughter before."

"'Lust not after her beauty in thine heart,'" Minerva warned, causing Tony to squirm. He decided to change the subject.

"Do we have any lumber out in the barn to replace a broken bed slat?" he asked.

Clem's brows shot up in surprise as he glanced from Christina to Tony.

Oh, hell, Tony thought. He'd just made Clem think that... He closed his eyes in frustration at his predicament. It was then that Christina, bless her pure and innocent heart, blithely explained.

"It's my fault," she said, causing Clem's brows to climb almost to his hairline. "I forgot to tell Tony that Hercules is deathly afraid of thunderstorms."

"Thunderstorms?" the older man repeated, his puzzlement obvious.

"He's been that way since I first got him," she went on. "He's been sleeping in Tony's room since we arrived. Last night when the thunder started, he leaped up in the middle of the bed on top of Tony. The force of the jump caused the bed to collapse."

"Not to mention almost suffocating me with his weight," Tony added for good measure.

"Where's the dog now?" Clem asked, obviously convinced Tony had taken suitable measures, such as skinning him and hanging his hide on the barn door.

"Still asleep in the remains of my bed, obviously exhausted from the strain of his traumatic experience."

Clem coughed in a poor attempt to hide his amusement. "So where did you..." He realized that line of questioning was none of his business and quickly changed it to, "When do you want to fix the bed?"

Tony leaned back in his chair and stretched. "The sooner the better. I didn't get much sleep last night," he said with perfect truthfulness.

"I'll go look in the loft first thing," Clem replied, finishing his coffee. "Great breakfast, ma'am. If you keep this up, I'm going to be getting pretty hefty."

Christina waited until Clem had left before she looked at Tony and grinned. "You should be ashamed of yourself. 'I didn't get much sleep,'" she repeated, lowering her voice in imitation.

"Well, I didn't," he protested innocently.

"Maybe not. But how can you blame that on an innocent dog who's terrified of storms is beyond me."

He sighed. "I know. I'm past redemption," he admitted. "Which reminds me, Minerva's choice of quotes can be downright eerie at times. Do you coach her, by any chance?"

She laughed and shook her head. "Don't tell me you've been 'lusting after my beauty,'" she teased.

"You mean you haven't noticed? I've been wasting my time?"

She stacked the breakfast dishes, stood, leaned over and placed a hard kiss on his mouth. "On the contrary, you've been very instructive, and I want you to know I appreciate the lessons."

"Lessons?" He felt as though a cold hand had brushed down his spine.

"You know—lovemaking lessons. I had no idea that sex felt so good. No wonder people talk about it so much. It's really powerful. I'll never forget it." She picked up the dishes and walked over to the sink.

He stared at her back, feeling his anger grow. "Is that what you think's been happening here? A little sex education?"

She looked around with a surprised expression. "What is it? What did I say to upset you?"

He got to his feet and strode over to her. "You don't know? Do you think I just hop into bed with any woman who takes my fancy? You think I just sleep around, like some kind of cheap, some kind of...'' Words failed him.

She was the picture of dismay. ''Oh, no, Tony. I mean, well, yes, I do think you probably can have any woman who attracts you. I can't imagine a woman silly enough to turn you down. But that doesn't mean I think you're cheap, or promiscuous or...'' She paused for a moment. ''Is that what this is all about? You're afraid I won't respect you in the morning kind of thing?''

''Dammit!'' He spun on his heel and headed for the bedroom. ''I must be out of my mind!''

''Tony?'' she called, but he kept on going until he reached his room. He slammed the door. Hercules lifted his head and blinked sleepily at his intrusion.

''Get out of my bed, you lazy excuse for a dog. Haven't you caused enough trouble?''

Hercules scrambled off the bed, trying to get his footing on the sloping surface, then lumbered over to where Tony stood with his hands on his hips. He licked one hand.

''And that's another thing,'' he shouted. ''Don't you have enough sense not to be friendly with someone who's yelling at you, for Pete's sake? Get out of here!''

He jerked the door open and watched Hercules amble out of the room.

Tony slammed the door once again.

My God, I'm having a tantrum! he thought in disgust. *A door-slamming, yelling tantrum. If Prome-*

theus was handy, I'd probably kick the cat...and roast the bird on a spit!

He wrested the mattress and springs off the bed, propping them against the wall. He replaced the slat that had fallen and picked up the pieces of the other one.

What was the matter with him this morning? He was going from satiated pleasure to rip-roaring anger. His emotions were bouncing around like yo-yos gone berserk.

He'd always taken pride in having control over his emotions. He'd never let anything or anyone get too close to him, much preferring a solitary life-style devoid of complications.

Well, he certainly had more than his share of complications now. For all he knew, Christina could be pregnant! If she were, he would be at fault.

If she were, would she let him know?

If she were, would she raise his child without a father rather than ask for his help? Would he be perpetuating yet another generation of Callaways who caused pain for those they loved?

He didn't want to hurt Christina. He loved her.

The truth of his feelings caused his knees to buckle, and he sat down on a nearby chair with a thump. Why had he just realized how he felt about her? Hadn't his behavior toward her been a signal that something unusual was going on?

He wasn't a womanizer by any stretch of the imagination. In all honesty, he was shy with women. The more aggressive the woman, the more he withdrew. He wasn't comfortable with the obvious come-ons that he saw around the rodeo scene. He wasn't good at innuendos or flirting or coaxing a woman into the sack.

Was that why Christina's remarks had touched a nerve? Why he felt used and taken advantage of? He hadn't the experience necessary to take what had happened between them lightly. They had shared something so special, so right to him that he felt totally committed to her, while she casually offered him her thanks for the sex education.

He rubbed his furrowed brow, feeling helplessly confused.

The phone rang. He picked up the extension there in his bedroom. "H'lo?"

"Mr. Callaway?"

"Yes."

"John Malone. I'm afraid I have some bad news for you."

Tony stiffened. "What is it?"

"Someone in the bank got wind of our investigation and alerted our quarry. Two bank employees didn't show up to work this morning and at the present time can't be located. We aren't certain whether they were part of the operation or whether they discovered too much and have been taken out. Either way, we've got serious problems on our hands. My people want to bring Christina in now, today, to make certain she can't be touched. She is proving to be an invaluable source of information for us. If we know that, so does the other side. There's going to be an all-out effort on their part to make sure she doesn't talk."

"I'll take care of her," Tony said.

"I'm convinced you'll do your best," Malone agreed in a soothing voice. "I'm just not certain that—"

"Mr. Malone, you told me that you know my father."

"Well, yes, but I don't see—"

"My father is one of the most powerful men in this state, wouldn't you agree?"

"Probably, but—"

"He knows how to protect himself and his family."

"No doubt about that, but—"

"Christina's family, Mr. Malone. For all intents and purposes, she's a Callaway. They won't find her. I promise you that."

"Well..." Malone paused. When Tony said no more, Malone added, "You won't take any unnecessary risks, will you?"

"I'll do whatever I need to do to ensure her safety."

"Well, we'll be in touch. I'll have to check with the head of the department."

"You do that," Tony said and hung up.

He picked up a piece of paper on which he'd scribbled a phone number what felt like a lifetime ago, but which in linear time had only been two days. He punched out the numbers and waited, giving an extension number.

"Mom, sorry to keep bothering you like this," he said, when Allison answered.

"Tony, I don't care what you say, we are not cutting our vacation short to save you from an unexpected guest.'' She sounded very firm.

He laughed. ''Glad to hear it. What I'm calling for is to speak with Dad. Is he around?''

''You want to speak to your father?''

She made no effort to hide her surprise at his request. He couldn't blame her for her reaction. So much had changed for him in such a short time that he was having difficulty recalling why his stiff-necked pride had kept him from appreciating the positive role his father had played in his life during these past fifteen years.

''Yeah, if he's there.''

He heard her call to his father and felt a measure of relief that the man was available.

''Tony?'' Cole said, sounding puzzled.

Tony's throat tightened as his father's voice came on the line. ''Hi, Dad,'' he said hoarsely. ''Good to hear you. How's the vacation going?''

There was a brief pause. In a cautious tone, Cole said, ''About what you'd expect. The kids are running our legs off. I keep telling them I'm too old for all this hoopla, but they won't listen.''

''You aren't old, Dad. You'll never be old.''

''Hah. Tell my feet that. We must have walked fifteen miles yesterday.''

Tony could hear his mother's voice in the background and his dad's amused but muffled response. ''Your mother said to tell you that she's making certain I bear up under all this strain by joining me in the hot tub each night and giving me a full-body massage.''

Tony laughed. "No wonder you're feeling old. That kind of help can kill a man!"

Cole repeated his remarks to Allison, and he could hear them both laughing, the intimate sound of two happily married people. Tony felt a jolt of envy and a yearning to experience a similar relationship.

"Uh, Dad, I don't want to keep you, but—"

"No, problem, Son. I'm delighted you called."

"Dad, I need your help," Tony blurted out, knowing this was the first time in his life he'd spoken those words.

Eight

Cole Callaway looked ten years younger than his fifty-one years, despite the gray hair that only emphasized his dark good looks. He'd been the head of Callaway Enterprises for thirty-one years. The weight of his responsibilities may have bent him, but he'd never broken.

Tony should have known his dad would waste no time in dealing with the present situation.

Within hours of their conversation, Cole had arrived at the ranch to discuss what needed to be done.

He walked into the house through the kitchen and stopped cold, looking at the transformation. Damn, was everybody going to react that way? Tony wondered.

"Just sprucing the place up a bit," Tony explained nonchalantly. "How about some coffee?"

"Sounds good," Cole absently replied, looking all around the room. "This your idea?"

"Not exactly."

"Didn't think so."

"But I like it."

"Uh-huh."

"I want you to meet Christina."

Cole gave another quick look around. "So do I."

Tony stepped into the hallway. "Christina? My dad's here." He watched as she came out of her bedroom.

"I don't want to disturb the two of you," she explained, coming toward him. She wore jeans, a sleeveless top that showed her slim midriff, and sandals.

"He wants to meet you. This meeting is about you, remember."

She touched her hair in a nervous gesture. It had dried in its natural state after their shared shower that morning. "You look fine," he offered reassuringly.

The look she gave him was unreadable. "He's not here to see what I look like."

That's what you think, he thought.

He took her hand and led her back into the kitchen just in time to hear Minerva announce in an excited voice, "'O Lord, save me! Protect thy turtledove from the hawk!'"

Cole spun around and looked toward the source of the sound, then glanced at his son in disbelief. "Did that black bird just say what it sounded like it said?"

Tony grinned and spoke to the bird. "You're not any turtledove, loudmouth, so cool it."

"'Who will protect me from the wicked? Who will be my shield?'"

Cole walked over to the cage and peered inside. "How did you teach it to talk?"

Christina released Tony's hand and approached Minerva's cage in turn. "I'm afraid I can't take credit. She belonged to a neighbor of mine who thought talking birds should be taught more than sailors' oaths."

"Amazing," Cole replied, shaking his head.

"We also have a very friendly Great Dane and a bashful three-legged cat lurking around here somewhere."

Cole straightened and cocked an eye at Tony. *"We?"* he repeated softly.

Tony could feel his ears burn.

"They're mine, actually," Christina said with a smile. She stuck out her hand. "I'm Christina O'Reilly. You must be Allison's husband."

Cole grasped her hand and stared intently at her. "That I am. I'm very pleased to meet you, Ms. O'Reilly. I understand you and Allison are related."

"Not really," Tony insisted. "It's a very distant connection."

"I see," Cole said, obviously amused. Tony had no doubt that his dad *did* understand. He knew he wasn't being subtle about his feelings for Christina.

Tony poured Cole some coffee and the three of them sat down at the table.

"I thought about what you told me on the flight over here," Cole began, "and I think the simplest solution is for Christina to stay at the Circle C until she's needed to testify. The place is built like a fortress. There's no way anyone could sneak up on the place without being spotted. With that in mind, I called Cody as soon as we landed to see what he thought about the plan. He agreed with me."

"I can take care of her," Tony began. "I just thought that—"

"Of course you can," Cole agreed. "That's what I told Cody. That you would be there to make sure she's all right."

He eyed his dad thoughtfully. "You think I should go with her?"

"Absolutely. She'll need you there," Cole promptly replied.

"Oh, but I don't want to take you away from the ranch and your rodeo commitments," Christina said. "I appreciate your concern—everybody's concern," she added, including Cole. "I'm just sorry that you had to get mixed up in all of this. I had no idea that my job in Atlanta would have such far-reaching consequences."

"You're more important than the ranch or my rodeo schedule," Tony said, not caring that he had given his feelings for Christina away to his dad. Cole's eyes narrowed slightly, but he didn't comment. Tony reached for Christina's hand. "Besides, you'll enjoy getting to know Cody and his wife Carina. They've got a houseful of kids that will love our menagerie, although Minerva may learn some phrases that have never been heard in church."

"Is this what you want to do?" Cole asked Tony. There was no doubt in either man's mind what he was asking.

"Absolutely." Tony held his father's gaze. "I'll have Clem move into the house and take care of things here, maybe hire a couple of men to help him in case the search for Christina actually gets this far."

"I've got the men, don't worry. They're already on the payroll. I intend to have a few of them stay at the Circle C to watch for any unusual traffic around there as well."

"Mr. Malone didn't know exactly when I'd be needed to testify," Christina said worriedly. "I can't take advantage of your hospitality indefinitely."

Cole patted her hand. "Of course you can. You're family now," he said with a welcoming smile. "Isn't that right, Tony?"

"Absolutely."

The back door opened and Clem walked in carrying a long board. "Hello, Cole. Didn't know you were in these parts," he said, grinning. He stuck out his hand. "Good to see you."

Cole stood and grabbed the proffered hand. "Thanks, Clem. You're looking fit."

"Yep, but this danged boy of yours keeps me hoppin', that's for sure." He turned to Tony. "Here's that new slat for your bed. Next time don't be so rough with it. It wasn't made for all that leapin' around."

Tony jumped up and grabbed the slat from Clem. "You're a real help, Clem," he said through gritted teeth. "I'll go put it in place right now." He spun around and headed out of the kitchen.

He heard a chair scrape behind him and Cole said, "You may want some help."

Just what I need, Tony thought, stifling an audible groan.

He was replacing the slat in the frame when he heard the bedroom door close behind him. When he straightened, he saw Cole leaning against the door, watching him.

"It was the dog, Dad," he explained. "The damn dog is afraid of thunder and we had a storm here last night. He leaped up on the bed and the slat broke. It's no big deal. Really."

Cole crossed his arms and leaned against the door, crossing his ankles as well.

"You're saying you haven't slept with her?" His gaze was steady, his tone mild.

"Well," he motioned toward the bed, "the collapsed bed is all perfectly innocent—"

"I understand that. That wasn't my question."

"Dad, I'm thirty years old, not some teenager sowing wild oats. It's really none of your business what I'm doing or not doing."

Cole leaned his head against the door and sighed. "I know that. Hell, you were grown by the time I first laid eyes on you. I'm just concerned about you, that's all. According to your mother, you only met this woman a few days ago and from what I recall, you weren't all that pleased to have her here."

"A lot has happened since then," Tony said.

"For example?"

"I mean, I've gotten to know her better. I understand her...and admire her. She's got a lot of courage. She's been on her own most of her life, but she hasn't let it stop her from enjoying life."

"In this day and age, a person can't be too discriminating," Cole said, picking his words with care. "You don't know enough about her to know whether—"

"She was a virgin," Tony blurted out.

"Was?"

"All right, so maybe I did rush things along, but I know how I feel." He paused, gathering his thoughts. "What I mean is, I know how you must have felt ... about Mom. It's like I found the other half of myself that I didn't know was missing until I met her. She's got my emotions going in all directions. I don't want to think about not having a life with her."

"Does she know how you feel?"

"I don't think so."

"Do you know how she feels?"

"About me?"

"About any of this."

He remembered her casual comments, which had stabbed him to his soul. "I don't think she has a clue. She's got some weird idea that men don't find her attractive, that she'll be single all her life, which doesn't seem to bother her."

"I don't know how to break the news to you, Son," Cole drawled, "but today's women have discovered that they can have perfectly comfortable, productive, well-rounded lives without having a man about."

Tony frowned. "Are you making fun of me?"

"Not at all. I'm just saying that it isn't a foregone conclusion a woman will automatically decide that marriage is her destiny. You should hear your sister go on about the subject. It's highly enlightening."

"I love her, Dad."

Cole straightened away from the door and walked over to his son. He hugged him, then slapped him on the back. "I'd say that's a good first step. Why don't you gather what you need for a few weeks and take her down to the Circle C? Spend some time with her, get to know her a little more. Once you're certain that your feelings haven't changed, then tell her what's in your heart."

"What if she doesn't care?" Tony had a tough time getting the words out.

"You'll have to accept whatever happens. We don't really have much control over how another person feels. I learned that lesson fairly fast where you're concerned."

"What do you mean?"

"I mean that I know you've wrestled with how you relate to me and to the Callaway clan. I was proud that you were willing to take my name, but that's about all you've ever accepted from me. I'm here to tell you that when I hung up that phone from talking with you this morning, I bawled like a baby. I've been waiting for you to ask for something from me for a long, long time."

Tony's eyes filled. "I love you, Dad."

"I know. That's what got me through all of this."

"And I really appreciate your dropping everything and coming over like you have."

Cole smiled. "Having a private plane at my disposal eases things along. Tom's waiting in Austin to get me back over there by the time the family's finished their day's exploration. Your mom thinks I put you up to calling just to give me a day's rest."

"You can show her how much you benefited from the rest by giving *her* one of those full-body massages."

Cole laughed. "Yep, those massages have got quite a family history."

Tony had a sudden flash of the night before, with Christina kneeling beside him, her hands and lips kissing and exploring him. He flushed. "I'll have to try one sometime," he managed to say.

"Here, let me help you with this box spring and mattress. I suppose Clem will be staying in here while you're gone."

"Yeah. I want him close to the phone. I'll have him notify me if anything happens around here that's in the least suspicious."

Four hands and two strong backs made short work of the bed. When the two men left the room, more than a bed had been restored to a better condition.

When Christina decided to visit Texas and look up the names on her family tree, she'd had no idea that Allison Alvarez had married into one of the richest, most powerful families in Texas.

Granted, she'd been impressed with the home she'd visited in Austin and had decided that Cole Callaway must be a successful businessman. Tony's ranch had shown signs of care and industry, and the buildings were in good repair, but there was nothing fancy about the place. He'd mentioned going to the bank for a possible loan, like everyone else she knew.

Only now was she beginning to understand the wealth of the Callaways. Cole had flown from Florida to Texas in a private jet. The Callaway companies owned several planes. The house she had seen in Austin was only one of several. The ranch they were presently heading to had been in the family for four generations. Earlier, Tony had explained that his uncle Cody lived there and the other two brothers—Cole and Cameron—visited whenever they had the time. Their visits never inconvenienced anyone because each brother had his own wing in the hacienda-style Big House, as Tony called it.

His own wing? She'd heard about the state that liked to brag about everything being bigger and better, but she'd never expected to witness the phenomena with her own eyes.

One thing she knew without doubt, though—the Callaways were much too rich for her orphan blood. Of course, she'd always known that at most she could have only a casual sort of relationship with Tony. She'd never considered for a moment having anything else. Wishes and dreams could only stretch so far, and Tony was way beyond her wildest dream.

But, oh! She would never forget him, not for as long as she lived. She had learned years ago to live in the moment, to accept what happened each day as though she were being given a gift to enjoy. She refused to make herself miserable by creating unrealistic expectations that could never materialize.

She wondered if there was a possibility that she

might be pregnant. She hadn't wanted to let herself think about it for fear of disappointment. A baby...Tony's baby. To have something that was a part of him would be the greatest gift life could offer her.

What she'd told him was the truth. She wasn't supposed to get pregnant at this stage of her cycle. Hoping she was wrong was one more expectation that was counterproductive.

"Do you want to stop somewhere to eat?"

Tony's question pulled her attention back to the van and their trip south. Because of the animals, they had decided to travel in her vehicle, where there was more room. She glanced at Hercules stretched out on his special blanket, Prometheus curled up on his pillow and Minerva's covered cage.

"That would be nice," she said, smiling at the man driving.

"We need gas, anyway."

They hadn't had much to say to each other since Cole left the ranch. Tony had explained their plans to Clem, she had packed her things, Tony had thrown some clothes in a suitcase, they had gathered the pets into the van and left the T Bar C Ranch behind them.

Tony had appeared preoccupied, which wasn't surprising. She had come for a quick visit and ended up completely rearranging his life. They hadn't said much to each other since he'd stormed out of the kitchen right after breakfast. She'd had time to replay their conversation several times in her mind during the day and she was still confused over his reaction.

Tony turned off the interstate on the outskirts of

San Antonio and pulled into a gas station. After filling the tank, he drove into the parking lot of a chain restaurant next door.

"Will they be all right?" he asked, locking the van and peering through the window.

"Yes. That's why I have bars on the back windows—so I can leave them open when I have to stop. They're used to traveling by now. I spent my weekends exploring the southeastern part of the country when I worked. I just packed them up and took them with me."

They went inside and sat down. After giving the waitress their order, Christina said, "I was wondering if I could ask you something."

Tony leaned back in his chair. He didn't like the serious tone of her voice. "Ask away."

"I recognize that I'm naive about male-female relationships, and that I'm showing my ignorance, but I really want to know something."

"I'll be happy to answer any question you have."

"Why were you so angry this morning?"

She watched him closely, trying to read his expression, but he was good at hiding what he was thinking.

"Lack of sleep, maybe?" he replied with a lopsided smile.

"You acted as if I'd insulted you. I certainly didn't mean to, and I'm sorry if I said something to make you think that."

He sighed. "I'm sorry for blowing up like that," he admitted. "It was stupid to throw a tantrum because I felt misunderstood. I guess I'm not handling this situation very well.''

''What situation?''

''The way I feel about you.''

Christina's heart began to pound in her chest. What was he saying? She stared at him, nonplussed. He reached over and took her hand.

''I don't want to rush you,'' he went on. ''The last thing I want is to scare you off. I want to give us some time together, to get to know each other. That's why I'm coming to the ranch with you. Dad was teasing me about your needing me there. You'd do just fine. Carina's wonderful. She'd make you feel at home right away. Cody will make certain the place is safe. He's tough, with a lot of experience. I just didn't like the idea of not seeing you.''

She didn't want to start believing in something that wasn't there, that wouldn't happen. That way lay pain and heartache.

''Is it because we made love?''

His brows drew together in confusion. ''What do you mean?''

''Do you think you're obligated to look after me because we went to bed together?''

''No, of course not.''

''Then I guess I still don't understand why you're saying this, why you're taking time away from your ranch to be with me.''

He closed his eyes for a moment, showing frustration. ''You don't have a clue, do you?'' he said after a moment. When she didn't answer, he took a deep breath.

"Christina, have you ever loved anybody?"

"No." She didn't have to think about that one.

"Not anyone at all?"

"I have warm feelings for Mrs. Bledsoe...and of course, my pets."

"Not anyone else, like someone you've dated?"

She laughed. "No."

He hesitated, as though wanting to say more, then shook his head. "Let's just take this one step at a time, okay? Let's go to the ranch, hang out for whatever length of time we need to keep you safe before you have to testify, and get to know each other. I want to be your friend, Christina. I want you to learn to trust me, to come to rely on me."

"I do trust you, and what is this trip if it isn't an example of my relying on you?"

"But you don't need me."

"Well, no, that's true."

"You could have gone with John Malone, to be kept in protective custody somewhere."

"Yes, although I may have had some difficulty because of my pets."

"Oh, I'm quite sure of that!"

"You've accepted them all right," she pointed out.

"Yeah, well, I must admit that surprises me, but you're right. I've gotten used to having them around...even self-righteous Minerva."

The meals arrived and they spoke little until they were back in the van, heading south once more.

"Have you ever wanted to need someone?" Tony asked several miles down the road.

What a strange question, she thought. Maybe he

was trying to make conversation to keep her from getting bored. "I don't think so," she replied. "I've never pictured myself as a helpless person."

"You don't have to be helpless in order to need other people in your life to make it complete. As a matter of fact, I just recently learned that lesson myself. I thought I had to stay totally independent of my family to prove I could make it without them. I learned I was wrong. It's not a sign of weakness to admit I need other people."

"Is that why you told your dad before he left that you'd like his help buying rodeo stock?"

Tony grinned. "Yeah. You would have thought I'd given him a priceless gift, when I was actually hitting him up for a loan."

"I'm sure he can afford it."

"I guess that's one of the reasons I've been so prickly about wanting to take anything from him. Sounds a little silly, now that I'm talking about it."

"You love your family very much. It shows whenever you talk about them."

"They could become your family, too, if you wanted them to be."

She rested her head on the seat, considering his remarks. "What a lovely idea. I could be an honorary member of the Callaway clan, a part of the family." She looked at him as he concentrated on the road. "I wonder what the rest of the family would think?"

"They'd accept you with open arms, believe me."

"It's certainly something to think about, I must admit."

Once again they lapsed into silence. Christina was

glad that Tony was driving, so that she could watch the ever-changing landscape. When he began to slow down, she saw a pair of adobe pillars supporting an arched wrought-iron sign with a large *C* in a circle.

"We're here!" she said, feeling a sense of anticipation.

"Close, but not there."

"Isn't that the gate?" she asked, pointing over her shoulder. It was fancier than the one at Tony's, but it gave the same sense of being on ranch property.

"Oh, yes. But we still have a ways to go."

So she found out. After several miles they reached the top of an incline, and Tony stopped the van so she could see this first view of the Circle C Ranch.

She caught her breath in amazement. It looked like a village. Nestled in the hills was a rambling, multistoried stucco building with a Spanish-tiled roof. A wall encircled the cluster of buildings, with an arched opening in it for the road.

"Oh, Tony, it's beautiful! I had no idea. It looks as though we've traveled back in time a hundred years."

"Be thankful we haven't. The family keeps the place up-to-date. There's running water, indoor toilets, all the comforts of modern-day life."

She turned to him, unable to contain her excitement. "This is where I'll be staying?"

"Where *we'll* be staying!" he corrected.

"How do you keep from getting lost in a place that size?"

"The main part of the house is laid out very simply around a courtyard. Most of the rooms on the first floor open onto the courtyard, so you can't get too confused.

"Upstairs the hallway splits off in three directions. We'll be using dad's wing. He and Mom seldom come down. Even if they do, there're several bedrooms in each wing."

"Do you have any idea how lucky you are to be a part of all of this?"

"Yeah. Finally, I think I'm beginning to understand how fortunate I am. You see, until I was fifteen, I thought my mother was the only relative I had in the world. I remember what that felt like. I can relate to what you've gone through. Now I want to share my family with you. We'll learn to appreciate them together."

Nine

"So you're flying to Washington tomorrow, are you?" Cody said to Tony. They'd decided to escape the hacienda for a few hours and ride into the hills.

"That's right. Dad and I are escorting Christina in the jet. We'll be staying with her for however long it takes for her to testify."

"I'm going to miss having y'all here. Christina's been great company for Carina. She's got my girls with rainbow-colored toenails, taught Carina how to make some unusual crafts. Hell, I'm even going to miss that damn bird preaching at me."

"It was your idea to put Minerva in the solarium. I would have kept her upstairs, you know."

Cody grinned. "Yeah, but then I couldn't have taught her a few phrases of my own without Christina catching me '

"I warned her that you'd corrupt that bird."

"Who, me?"

"You don't mind looking after Hercules?"

Cody adjusted his hat and shook his head. "I've never known a dog like him. He lets the kids ride on his back or sprawl all over him, lets the baby pull his ears without a whimper...yet sets the place on edge with his howls when it storms."

"I'll admit he's not your run-of-the-mill canine."

"How about you? What are your plans after all this is over?"

"That depends."

"On what?"

"If Christina agrees to marry me."

Cody lifted his brow slightly. "You mean there's a chance she won't?"

"I don't know. I keep putting off asking her."

"No lie! Afraid of what she'll say?"

"Something like that."

"Well, don't look to me for advice. I fell into marriage backwards and upside down. It took me a few years to get it all straightened out to my satisfaction."

"You have a great marriage, Cody."

"'Course I do. That's because of Carina. That woman managed to whip me into shape, cured me of my wild and woolly ways, keeps me home and makes me love it."

"I never gave marriage a thought until I met Christina. It took me less than forty-eight hours to realize that she was the only woman I'd ever love."

"You've known her how long?"

"We'd just met a few days before we came here.

We've been here—'' he thought for a moment ''—almost three months. At least she has. I've had to go back to my place every week or so.''

''Has she made any plans for when the trial is over?''

''She's still paying rent on a place in Atlanta. Seems she thinks she's supposed to go back there and find a job. I keep telling her she's not going to be able to do anything like that after testifying in this case.''

''So you're going to offer an alternative?''

Tony nodded, a slight smile hovering on his lips. ''I guess I can't accuse her of burying her head in the sand, since that's what I've been doing all these years.''

''What are you talking about?''

''Dad finally told me that, like every other member of this family, I draw a percentage of the profits of Callaway Enterprises on a quarterly basis. But when I got touchy about his paying for my college fees, he decided not to mention that he'd set up an account for me as soon as he knew I existed. It's just been sitting there for all these years, untouched, adding interest and compounding interest. He took a certain amount of it and invested it in a few stocks and other things.'' Tony rubbed his neck. ''Here I've been watching my pennies, determined to make it on my own, while I had all that money waiting for me.''

''Cole's no fool, Tony. He knew what you were going through.''

''Well, I guess meeting Christina opened my eyes to lots of things. I'm here to tell you that it makes my life much simpler to offer to place her in my own witness-protection program. She'll become Christina Callaway of the Texas Callaways. The Feds are fairly certain no one on the other side knows where she is. They think she went into hiding, and they don't know the government agents found her. Once she's testified, we're going to whisk her out of there without a trace and quietly erase all sign of her in Atlanta. Dad has the contacts to do it without anyone knowing how it was done. We'll come back here until she and I decide, together, where we'll live and what we'll do."

"You still want to ranch?"

"Oh, yeah. If she wants to stay where I am, we can do that. I want to build us another place. We'll let Clem have the house. I want Christina to create the kind of home she wants."

"Doesn't that scare you a little? I mean, that woman does get carried away with color schemes from time to time."

"I can live with it."

"So. Everything's set with just one minor detail. You don't have Christina's agreement to the whole idea."

"I don't want her to feel that she has to marry me in order to be safe. Dad made me promise not to try to force her into marriage. He said that, if she truly prefers to remain single, he'll have a long talk with her, explain the government's concern, maybe even convince her the government is footing the bill—which they would do, by the way—and help her start over somewhere else. At least I've got her becoming comfortable with the idea she's part of the Callaway clan."

"You just want to make it legal, is that it?"

"You got it."

"I don't envy you your selling job. She strikes me as a woman who's comfortable with her independence."

"That's why I've spent the past three months letting her see that having me in her life wouldn't take away from her independence. I just want to be a part of her life."

"My, how the mighty have fallen. I can't believe I'm hearing this from Tony Mr. Independence Himself Callaway. Anyway, I wish you the best of luck. If I can help in any way, I hope you'll let me know."

"You've already helped tremendously by letting her see a happy marriage, a contented family circle and the normal workings of a household. It's amazing what she didn't have in the way of social and family interaction when she was growing up. I've noticed in the last few weeks that she's stopped watching from the sidelines and begun to take part in the family gatherings."

Cody glanced at the sun, which was hovering over the western hills. "Guess it's time we head back. Thanks for keeping me company this afternoon. Riding out like this soothes me, somehow. It helps me keep my perspective on life. When I was kid I could hardly wait to leave home. I knew I was an adult when I could hardly wait to come back."

"I know the feeling exactly," Tony said as they turned their horses back toward home.

* * *

Christina watched the two riders in the hills, silhouetted by the setting sun, draw closer to the house. Tony would soon be home.

She felt so silly, getting excited every time she saw him, as though they'd been separated for days. Since they'd moved to the Circle C, he'd never been gone longer than a day and a night, when he went to check on his place.

She'd never admitted to him how much she wished she could go with him on his trips, because she knew she had to stay hidden here until after the trial.

She had such mixed feelings about the upcoming ordeal. On one hand she was eager to have it behind her, feeling as though there were a sword dangling over her neck while she waited. On the other hand she knew that once the trial was over there would be no more need for her to hide, and therefore no more need to stay with Tony.

Need was such a strange sensation. She remembered a conversation she's had with Tony a few months ago. He'd asked something to the effect of whether she ever wanted to need someone. She'd thought the question strange at the time. She didn't know about *wanting* to experience such a thing, but she had certainly discovered all about *needing* someone.

If she wanted to get fanciful, she'd discovered a whole list of needs she'd never thought of before, like the need to wake up and find Tony asleep beside her, his hair rumpled, his face unshaven…the need to reach out and touch him at night to make certain she hadn't dreamed up his existence…the need to hold him and feel his desire for her pressing against her, making her feel seductive and desirable and wanted...the need to look up from whatever she was doing and see him watching her with a soft smile...the need to fall asleep every night with his arms around her, knowing she was safe from the world.

Yes, she had come to understand about need. It had made her feel more vulnerable than she'd ever felt before. It made her want more than she could have, yearn for the glitter of a far-off star. It made her want to believe in the magic of a special world where all her dreams would come true.

She had to keep reminding herself to just enjoy the moment. She had today. If she enjoyed each minute, appreciated every happening, no matter how small, she would have a wonderful collection of memories that no one could take away from her.

The riders reached the barn. She watched them climb off the horses and turn them over to trainers who would see to their needs. The men walked toward the house, talking intently, their heads close together.

She'd been surprised at how much Tony and Cody resembled each other. They could easily have passed for brothers. Tony rubbed his rump and laughed, pretended to take a couple of limping steps before continuing toward the side door in his normal gait.

She spun away from the window and hurried to the bathroom, one of her favorite places in the house. The walls were lined with mirrors and there was a large hot tub where she and Tony had spent some highly charged moments.

She really was without shame where he was concerned. She had learned so much about lovemaking in general and how to please him in particular. He'd taught her about her own sensual nature.

She quickly adjusted the taps and dumped in a few ingredients to scent the water and soften it. Then she pulled her blouse over her head and unfastened her jeans.

"Christina? Where are you?" Tony called, coming down the hallway.

Her first day here, he had shown her to a bedroom that opened onto this bathroom. With a wicked grin, he'd opened another door and shown her the master bedroom. If she went to bed in her own room at night, he joined her. Other times he coaxed her into sharing his. No one knew that they slept together in the privacy of the suite, and if one of the maids may have mentioned it, nothing was ever said.

Cody and Carina accepted her so completely that she felt as though she warmed herself with their friendly openness much like she might warm her hands near a friendly fire.

She heard the door to the master bedroom open. "Christina? You in here?"

She grabbed a towel and wrapped it around her. "I'm here," she said a little shyly, stepping out of the bathroom.

He spun toward her at the sound of her voice, then did a slow and penetrating visual inspection from her bare toes to her hair pinned on top of her head.

"Am I interrupting something?" he drawled, reaching for the snaps of his western shirt.

"Not at all. I'm just getting ready to go into the hot tub and was hoping you'd join me."

"You saw me coming?"

"Uh-huh. I saw you and Cody ride in. I thought a relaxing soak might ease some of those weary muscles before dinner."

He tossed the shirt to the side, hopped a couple of steps jerking off his boots, unzipped his jeans and stepped out of them and ended up in front of her, a trail of clothes marking his route.

He casually took her towel and flipped it over his shoulder, then picked her up by crossing his arms beneath her rump and lifting her so that her breasts were pressed against his face. "I've missed you," he mumbled, nuzzling and nipping her, teasing the tips with his tongue, then giving a sharp, erotic pull on them.

There must be a direct connection between her breasts and her lower body, Christina decided, because every time he touched her, she became moist and eager for him.

He ambled into the bathroom without looking, still kissing and caressing her, making her tremble with anticipation. By the time he allowed her to slide down his body, he was pulsatingly hard.

She made no effort to stiffen her knees, but allowed herself to kneel and take him into her mouth, teasing him in the same way he had teased her, with the nibbling, sucking bites that made her wild.

Funny how he seemed to have the same reaction.

She loved to hear him groan with helpless pleasure. She loved the way he gripped her head, running his long fingers through her hair.

"Enough," he finally said, stepping back from her, making no attempt to hide his trembling. "You're going to unman me!"

"Oh, I don't think so," she replied, rubbing her hands up, down and all around his solid length. She moved away and stepped into the tub, turning off the tap. Sinking down into the water, she looked up at him impishly and said, "Care to join me?"

She barely got the words out of her mouth when he was climbing in beside her, sliding down and reaching for her at the same time. He tugged her to him, urgently pulling her knees wide and around his hips. With a feverishness she'd rarely seen in him since she'd known him, he adjusted their positions and slid his length deep inside, clutching her to him and holding her tightly as he began a furious rhythm that swept her away.

The water quickly became choppy with waves as she hooked her feet behind him and held on, giving him long, moist kisses and teasing him with her thrusting tongue.

He stiffened, dropped his head back and let out a shout. She felt the same convulsive surges from her core and could only hang on to him, helpless to combat the wave after wave of intense pleasure that swept through her.

She lost track of how long they stayed in that same position. It didn't matter. Tony had never been like this before—so out of control. They had made love in the tub before, but only the preliminaries. They had always ended in bed, where he…

Where he always carefully used protection.

But not this evening.

This time she wasn't in the safe part of her cycle. This time she could very easily become pregnant.

She rested her head on his shoulder. There was little she could do at this point. She would just have to deal with the consequences of their behavior when and if it became necessary.

Dinnertime at the Callaways was always a laughing, noisy affair. All four of Cody's children ate with their parents, including the baby, ten-month-old Denise.

Christina spent her time helping Carina feed Denise, who sat in her high chair between Carina on the end and Christina to her right.

The men talked about cattle and raising horses, while answering the hundred-and-one questions asked by Clay, Sherry and Kerry.

Once in a while Tony would casually place his hand on Christina's thigh and stroke it lightly from her knee to her hip. When she'd look at him, he would give her the innocent smile of a choirboy.

After dinner Carina took Denise upstairs to get her ready for bed. Cody suggested that once the kids were down, the four of them could play spades. Christina was surprised to hear Tony say, "Not tonight, Cody. Christina and I have some things to discuss before our trip tomorrow."

Cody winked and said, "Sure, I understand. I guess we'll see you tomorrow before you leave, then."

Tony slipped his fingers between hers and led her up the stairs and down the long hallway to his bedroom. Once inside, he adjusted the light before leading her over to the love seat in front of the TV.

He sat down and pulled her into his lap. She laughed. "Do you realize that you never let me sit on a piece of furniture? I always end up in your lap. I'm surprised you don't sit that way in the dining room."

"The thought has crossed my mind a few times, I must admit."

"And what was this stroking-my-thigh business tonight? You would have been awfully shocked if I'd reached over and grabbed you in a sensitive area."

"Not at all," he replied with dignity. "I would have politely excused us from the table and brought you upstairs to finish what you'd started."

"You're insatiable, you know that?"

"It's your fault. You've trained me very well. This is a perfect example of the student surpassing the teacher."

She kissed him on the nose. "You're so silly."

"Not tonight. Tonight I'm serious. I need to talk to you. It's very difficult for me to talk to you because I get distracted and forget what I was trying to say. I keep touching you and one thing leads to another, and before I know it I'm completely inert, immobilized and brain dead. Therefore, I refuse to allow you to have your way with me...at least not until I've said what I mean to say."

She folded her hands together in a demure pose. "What is it you have to say?"

She waited for him to begin. He cleared his throat, made a couple of sounds that faintly resembled words though she wouldn't swear to it, then said, "About tomorrow." His voice sounded hoarse.

"What about tomorrow?"

"We're going to DC."

"We discussed that three weeks ago. Have the plans changed?"

"Uh, no. You're to testify, then we fly back here."

She nodded. "Okay."

"What we haven't discussed is the fact that once you testify, you will be marked by the people who are on trial."

"According to the prosecutor, my testimony will guarantee them very long prison sentences."

"That doesn't mean they can't see to it that you pay for putting them there."

"Well, the first night they interviewed me, Mr. Malone did discuss the possibility that I might have to go into a witness-protection program."

"He did?"

"Yes."

"You never mentioned it to me."

"I didn't think it had anything to do with you."

"Do you still feel that way?"

Puzzled by his line of questioning, she asked, "Well, since we're talking about my job at the bank, my discovery of the accounts, my testimony regarding them and my possible danger as a result, I'd say yes. This is about me, not you."

"Do you always have to be so blasted logical?"

She drew back. "My logic makes you angry?"

"Frustrated. Very frustrated."

"That happens a lot when you talk with me. Do you suppose we have a problem communicating?"

"Only in some areas," he said, slipping his hand into the collar of her shirt and cupping her bare breast. "Other times I notice you get my message just fine."

"I always get your messages, Tony."

"Are you sure?"

She watched him for a moment, trying to figure out his mood. "I think so."

"All right. Let's test your little theory. Are you aware that I'm in love with you?"

She caught her breath. "In love?" she repeated faintly.

"Yes. Not to be confused with in like or fond of or merely interested in, but the whole nine yards. I am besotted with you, dream about you, can't stop thinking about you, in love with you. There. Did that get my message across plainly enough?"

She was shaking inside. She couldn't help it. She was hearing Tony say things she'd never thought to hear, never expected to hear. She wanted to laugh and cry at the same time. Instead, she laid her forehead on his shoulder and said, "Oh, Tony."

"That wasn't the response I was hoping to hear." He sounded rueful.

"Wh-what do you want to hear?"

"How you feel about me."

"Oh." She smiled. "That's easy. I love you."

"Just like that?"

"Uh-huh."

"You told me you'd never loved anybody before."

"I never have."

"But you just said—"

"Except you."

He seemed to relax a little. "So. You really do love me," he mused. "That gives me hope."

"For what?"

"That you'll marry me."

She felt like he'd slapped her. She scrambled off his lap and backed away from him, arms outstretched as though to ward him off. "I've never known you to be cruel before, Tony. Please don't joke about something like that."

"My God, woman, you think I'm joking?" He, too, leaped off the couch and glared at her. "What did you think I was doing, living here with you for the past three months, just killing time until the trial?"

"No, of course not. You obviously enjoy my company. We have fun, but we've neither one talked about the possibility of a future together."

"Only because I thought you'd take off running at the mention of the idea."

"Tony, let's be sensible about this. I can't tell you how wonderful it is to know that you love me. It explains so much—your patience with me...your kindness and understanding. I couldn't get over how—"

"Just call me Saint Tony," he offered sarcastically.

"All I'm saying is that it makes sense to me that you've acted out of loving feelings for me. I know

I've loved you for a long time. At first I didn't understand what it was I was feeling. I mean, how could I? I thought love was what I felt for Mrs. Bledsoe!"

"I know!"

"Well, I certainly feel differently toward you than I do her."

"Glad to hear it," he said dryly.

"But marriage is something else again."

"Oh, I don't know. Generally it's all part of the whole. You fall in love with someone, then you court them—or in my case, try to get you to fall in love with me. Then you marry them. It's really a relatively simple process."

"But I've never thought about getting married!" she wailed.

"Oh, I can believe that easily enough. Why do you think we're having this particular conversation tonight?"

"Why?"

"So you can think about it."

"You mean, actually think about the possibility of you and me getting married?"

"Does the concept totally boggle your mind? It sounds really natural to me."

She stood on one side of the room while he stood on the other. She didn't want him to come any closer. She didn't want her reason to be compromised by the feelings he always evoked every time he came close to her.

"It's because you think I might be pregnant, isn't it?"

"What? When? How could—?"

"Tonight when we were in the hot tub."

He smacked his palm against his forehead. "I can't believe I never gave it a thought." He lowered his hand slowly. "Yes, I can. I've been thinking of you as my wife for so long that I don't really care if you get pregnant or not. I want a family. I want to look just like Cody and Carina in a few years, with a dining table lined up with our little ones."

"You're shouting," she said quietly.

"Then it's a good thing Minerva's downstairs, or she'd be lecturing me right now!"

Christina grabbed her mouth but the giggle escaped. He gave her a ferocious frown.

"You're yelling at me because you want to marry me and have a family," she pointed out.

"No, I'm not. I'm yelling because you can't believe that I want to marry you."

"But if I go into the witness-protection program—"

"Why do you think I'm discussing this with you now? If you agree to marry me, you won't need to go into their program. We have one already going for you here in Texas. Nobody knows who you are. We can make up a different past for you. Dad will erase all sign of you in Atlanta—retrieve your things, close up the house, that kind of thing. He knows what needs to be done."

His dad, she thought. Cole Callaway, of the Texas Callaways.

"I can't marry you, Tony," she said steadily. "I wish you hadn't asked me."

He looked as though he'd been struck by lightning.

He stiffened and stared at her, his eyes wide with shock. "You can't?" he whispered hoarsely. "Why not?"

She had to swallow twice before she could answer. Why was he forcing her to put it into words? Why should she have to spell it out? "Because you're a Callaway, that's why," she said with dignity. Then she turned and walked through the bathroom to the other bedroom.

Ten

Tony sank back into the seat beside his father and strapped himself in. Christina had chosen to spend the flight in the small bedroom at the back of the plane, which was just fine with him. He had no more desire to see her than she did to see him.

He stared blindly out of the window as the runway raced by, then fell below them in a stomach-grabbing drop.

"Trouble in paradise?" Cole asked.

He fought a strong desire to lie. He didn't want to talk about what had happened to him. However, they had a long flight ahead of them. Tony knew his dad well enough to know he wouldn't ignore his silence for much longer. He shrugged after a long pause and muttered, "Something like that."

"Want to talk about it?"

"There's nothing to talk about."

"Meaning?"

"That when we get through in Washington, Christina O'Reilly intends to get on with her life and I intend to get on with mine."

"She turned you down, huh?"

"Flat."

"I see."

Tony continued to stare out the window.

"You're pretty angry about it, I take it."

"Yeah, I guess you could say that."

Tony thought his dad had decided to drop the subject, because nothing more was said for several minutes. Then Cole spoke again. "You know, the thing about anger is that it can create a smoke screen so we don't have to look at what we're *really* feeling."

Tony didn't reply. Instead, he closed his eyes and dropped his head on the back of the seat, feeling very vulnerable and exposed.

"I have a hunch you're hurting pretty badly about now."

"Yeah," Tony whispered.

"I remember like it was yesterday finding your mother after losing touch with her for over fifteen years." His dad's voice was low and Tony could hear the pain in it. "God, I had never stopped loving that woman. I felt like my heart had been ripped out of my chest when she disappeared."

Tony certainly knew that feeling. He'd had a gaping wound in his chest since the night before.

"Finding her...and you...again was the best thing

that had happened to me. I immediately began to make plans. I was convinced that our lives would be worked out in a new and better way.''

Tony straightened, shifting in his chair. ''I remember. You asked her to marry you and she said no.'' He'd forgotten about that.

''That's right.''

He thought about that time in his own history, trying to put himself in his father's place. ''Is this how you felt?''

Cole nodded. ''I bet it's pretty damn close.''

Tony looked at him, recognizing a fellow sufferer. ''How did you survive the pain?'' he asked quietly.

Cole shook his head slowly, as though reliving that time in his life. ''I took a real nosedive. Wished I could die. Prayed for it. But then I remembered that I now had a son and that I could at least get to know him.''

Tony nodded. ''I remember how you used to call and talk with me.'' He smiled at the memory. ''It felt good to have a real father. I was so proud of you. You were famous and everything.''

''That's why your mother didn't want to marry me.''

Startled, Tony asked, ''Why? Because you were famous?''

''Because I was a Callaway.''

Tony jerked forward in his seat. ''That's exactly what Christina said! Can you believe it? What does that mean? Why would they both... It doesn't make sense. It just doesn't...make...sense!''

He leaned over and rested his head on the heels of his hands, his elbows propped on his knees.

Cole reached out and rubbed his son's back. He loved the man beside him so much, more than he could find words to express. He'd been deprived of so much with this child of his. Katie and the twins had given him another chance to enjoy a family, but they couldn't give him his firstborn's childhood. He'd grown to accept what he couldn't change because he had no choice.

To see Tony in so much pain almost brought him to his knees. Tony could get to him like none of the others. He was so proud. So independent. So aloof. Cole had been loving him from afar for a long time now. He blessed the young woman who'd come into his son's life because she had triggered so many things in him. She'd caused him to open up, to share his heart's desire with his father.

If there was any way on God's green earth he could, Cole wanted to provide his son with that heart's desire.

He continued to rub Tony's back and felt his shoulders heave, but there were no sounds.

"I was really puzzled by your mother's decision," he went on, as though there'd been no interruption. "It didn't make any sense to me. I guess that's why they say men are so different from women. I figured that I loved her and she loved me, so we'd naturally want to get married. Seemed simple enough."

Tony nodded, but kept his head in his hands.

He was listening.

"So I decided to give her some time to think about

it. I insisted on keeping the lines of communication open between us. I remember getting pretty corny at times, telling her that I would wait for her forever if need be. Just because it was the truth didn't make it any less corny, you understand. I tried to draw her out, get her to explain her feelings. Of course, the Callaways had hurt her and her dad pretty bad, and she had reason to hold a grudge. The funny thing was she'd forgiven us for that. What she was having so much trouble with was the family name, the legends, the money, the power. Most people might think those things would make life a hell of a lot easier—and I'll admit that at times it does. At least it's damn convenient. But when it comes to matters of the heart, well, that seems to be a different story. It can also be seen as control. If there's one thing Allison didn't want, it was to lose control over her own life."

Tony straightened and leaned back against the chair once again. His eyes, when he looked at Cole, were red but dry.

"Do you think that's the way Christina feels?"

"Could be. She's made her own way in the world for a while. As far as I can see, she's done a fine job of taking care of herself. It seems to me that you'd be able to understand that need. I remember you made it real clear to me that I couldn't buy you, that you didn't want or need my help, that just because I was your father didn't mean I could control your life."

Tony felt a wave of embarrassment sweep over him as he remembered that conversation from several years ago. Had he really sounded so arrogant and self-righteous?

"I can't believe I could have been so sanctimonious about everything," he muttered.

"Don't be too hard on yourself, Son. I had to admire the fact that you stood up to me, refused to be intimidated by anyone, even your father. That's why I've stayed out of your life unless you asked for my advice or help. I respect you, Tony, and respect your choices. You've done a good job making your life work for you."

Tony just shook his head, feeling more than a little sheepish. "It's a wonder you haven't lost patience with my belligerent attitude these past few years. I certainly haven't been the easiest person to be around, I know."

"All I'm saying is that there's nothing wrong with being independent, wanting to be on your own and enjoying a sense of your own accomplishments. You've got a considerable amount to be proud of, particularly because you did it on your own." Cole was quiet for several minutes before he asked, "Tell me, was Christina surprised when you asked her to marry her?"

"Flabbergasted. Acted like she'd never heard of the word. Especially where I'm concerned."

"Somehow, that doesn't surprise me. From everything I've heard you say about her, she's never considered the idea of marriage."

"Yeah. She can't imagine anyone wanting to marry her. Isn't that crazy?"

"At least you've given her something to think about."

"I doubt that. She couldn't say no fast enough."

"Because you caught her by surprise. Let's suppose that you allow her to leave, allow her to get on with whatever life she envisions without you. Meanwhile, you stay in touch with her, let her know that you still want to be friends, if nothing else. Give her some space, but don't drop out of her life entirely."

"Like you did with me?"

Cole grinned. "I didn't think you'd noticed."

Tony returned his father's grin with a lighter heart than he'd had since his painful conversation with Christina. Then he remembered something that caused his grin to fade.

"But once she testifies, she's going to have to go into some kind of a protection program. I won't know where she is or how to find her—"

"Do you recall our conversation awhile back—when I told you that if she decided not to marry you. I would make certain she got the help she needs?"

Tony nodded.

"Then we'll put that plan into action as soon as she's finished giving testimony at the trial. We'll let her decide where she wants to live. I'll help her get a place to stay and a job. Most important, she'll always know how to contact you. If she wants to get in touch with you, there won't be anything to stop her. You aren't a part of her old life."

"What if she doesn't want anything more to do with me?"

"Then you have to love her enough to respect her wishes. She hasn't had an easy life. She's struggled hard to get her education and make something of herself. She's used to taking her time to think things through and to decide what's best for her."

"You don't think I'm any good for her, do you?"

"I didn't say that. My thinking on the matter is this. Her life has been in total disruption for the past few months. She's had to live with strangers. I think she wants to get back to her home and belongings, even if they're located somewhere else. What I think is that she needs time. In this case, I would say time is on your side."

"How can you say that? Once she's gone, she'll forget all about me!"

"Just like you'll forget about her?"

"I love her!"

"How does she feel about you?"

"She said she loves me," he mumbled.

"So, she's going to set up her own life once again, find a routine and remember what life was like with you. She's going to remember going to sleep in your arms, waking up in your arms—"

"How did you know about..." Tony stopped, flushing.

"Because I know all about the connecting doors between those two bedrooms. That's my part of the house, remember?"

Tony dropped his chin on his chest. "Christina may be pregnant," he muttered.

Cole tensed. "She told you that?"

"No. But I got carried away in that hot tub last night and lost control."

A faint smile crossed Cole's lips. "Your sister

Katie was conceived in that hot tub. It's amazing how history tends to repeat itself."

"But what if she is pregnant?"

"Give her the chance to tell you."

"If she doesn't?"

Cole's jaw hardened. "If she doesn't, then I will. I'll have her watched so closely that she won't be able to hide it."

"You'd do that for me, Dad?"

"I'd do it for the three of you. Like I said, there's some history that doesn't need to repeat itself. I've kept out of your affairs. But I find that I have to draw the line at the thought of not protecting a grandchild." He grinned at Tony. "The possibility of a grandbaby. Hot damn! Wouldn't that be something? Wait 'til I tell Allison."

Tony stiffened. "Dad! You can't tell Mom. She'll know that—"

"Tony, has it ever occurred to you that your mother might assume a thirty-year-old man has a normal sex life, particularly when he walked away from his prized ranch and rodeoing life-style to stay with a woman for three months?"

"But she never acted like—"

"Of course not. She was delighted to meet Christina, liked her immediately, but more important to both of us, liked to see the changes in you the young woman has caused. What you do in the privacy of your bedroom—or hers, or in that hot tub—is none of our business."

"I don't know what I would do without you, Dad," Tony said.

"Don't worry about it. You won't ever have to find out. I intend to stick around for a long, long time."

Six weeks later, Tony wearily mounted his porch steps and let himself into the dark house. The days were growing shorter, just when light was at a premium for him.

Hercules followed him into the house, his tail dragging. He was one tired hoss of a dog. He'd spent the day chasing rabbits and in general being a complete nuisance to the men who were building the heavily enforced corrals for the bulls they intended to bring in.

In the weeks since the trial and telling Christina goodbye, Tony had buried himself in his routine of hard work on the ranch, trying to put her out of his mind. He knew that his dad had been right. He didn't want Christina to stay in Texas and marry him if she felt that was her only choice. He only wanted her if she wanted him and his life-style.

He'd been impressed with the lengths to which the government people had gone to protect Christina. After meeting her in Washington, DC, the two men who had first interviewed her at the ranch accompanied her to Atlanta, where the federal case was tried.

Meanwhile, Cole began the careful process of having all of Christina's belongings packed up and moved, creating false paper trails and names that would confuse any would-be tracker.

Once her part in the trial was over, Christina met with government representatives as well as Cole to decide what she wanted to do and where she wanted to live. After taking a few days to consider, she chose to move to Portland, Oregon.

According to Cole, she'd taken a job as bookkeeper of a car dealership. The Treasury Department had suggested that she stay away from banks, just in case anyone attempted to trace her through her line of employment.

Cole, Christina and Tony had returned to Texas first to decide what she should do with the van and her animals. Cole had convinced her that she would be wise to leave the van and buy something new once she reached Portland. It was Cole who had suggested she interview with a man he knew who had a car dealership. He was certain she could get a good deal on a new car or van, as well.

Tony had watched her as she listened to the older man and considered his advice. She appeared calm throughout the discussion of her options, as though giving up her old life and friends was an accepted part of her existence.

The only time Tony saw her break down was when he offered to keep Hercules. It made sense to him that a dog that size should live in the country. She'd agreed that Hercules would be much better off on the ranch than in a small apartment, even if she could find an apartment complex that would accept an animal that big, which was doubtful.

She also understood the necessity of accepting Cole's offer to fly her to Portland in the company jet and help her get settled. At the moment, none of her identification could be used. The government had promised to prepare the necessary paperwork, giving her a new name and background as quickly as possible. In the meantime, Cole would ease her way into a new life.

Tony had gone to the airport to see them off.

Christina had kept any conversation between them very light. He hadn't pressed. Despite her outward appearance, he knew that she was shaken by recent events. It saddened him to think that his love for her had come as such a surprise, creating more stress in her life.

Cole went up to the front of the plane to speak to the pilot while Tony placed the cages holding Minerva and Prometheus in a place where they could see Christina.

He took her hand in his. "Let me hear from you, okay?" he said, clearing his throat of its sudden huskiness.

"Thank you for everything," she whispered. "You've treated me much more kindly than I deserve."

"You deserve much more than you seem to believe."

"I'll never forget our time together."

He forced himself to smile and say lightly, "I hope not."

"You deserve the very best that life has to offer."

"I found the best."

"Oh, Tony. Don't. You'll forget me soon enough."

He leaned down and gave her a very gentle kiss. When he lifted his head, he stared into her eyes. "Somehow I doubt it." Rather than make a complete fool of himself, he turned on his heel and left the plane.

In the six weeks she'd been gone, he hadn't heard anything from her. His father had kept him up-to-date on her life, which was how he knew about the apartment and the job. Cole told him that he and Allison had gotten into the habit of calling her on a weekly basis so that they could visit with her.

Tony knew that he could call her, but he hadn't. If she wanted to talk to him, she knew how to contact him. Besides, he couldn't think of anything casual to say to her. The gaping hole in his chest where his heart used to be had never healed. He wondered if it ever would.

On the brighter side of life, he'd had some fun calling Lin Schulz at the bank, thanking him for the offer of a loan and explaining that he didn't need it after all. He didn't bother to tell him that he'd discovered the interest he'd received on some of the lesser investments his dad had made for him was more than the original loan he'd requested.

It had been a strange feeling to realize that he'd been the one to let money stand between him and his father. He better understood what Cole had been trying to say about wealth. Having enough was fine; it made life comfortable. But having more than enough? It was just there, to be invested or worked or donated— whatever he chose to do with it. But it didn't change who he was.

Tony still loved the ranch. It felt good after a full day of hard physical labor to come home, knowing he'd accomplished something worthwhile. He looked forward to filling the giant tub he'd installed in his bathroom with hot water and lying there, soaking his weary bones.

Since Christina had come into his life, he'd learned to appreciate the small pleasures in his daily routine. She'd opened his eyes to so much that he'd been too busy to notice before.

Now, as he let himself into the house, he turned on the light, steeling himself to the sight of the brightly decorated kitchen. He certainly didn't need a reminder of Christina. She was never far from his thoughts.

It was funny what kept a person going. He looked after Hercules, knowing how much Christina loved the crazy mutt. It took only the first crack of thunder anymore and Tony prepared himself to help his poor, scared buddy through another traumatic experience.

Hercules was there for him, as well. We all have traumatic experiences to face from time to time, Tony thought to himself.

He checked Hercules's water bowl, refilled it, dumped dry food into another dish and opened a can of the moist stuff.

When he bent over to place the dish in front of Hercules, Tony groaned and rubbed his back. Boy, he was dragging tonight. They were really pushing him to get the corrals finished. He was eager to drive up to Fort Worth and pick up his new stock. Setting goals to work toward helped him to keep going.

He dug some leftovers out of the refrigerator and heated them up. Food didn't hold much interest to him these days. Consequently, he'd had to tighten his belt a couple of notches, and his jeans were beginning to hang on him.

The food had no taste, but he ate it anyway, then cleaned up the kitchen, turned off the light and headed for the bedroom. He was glad that he had never shared this bed with Christina, otherwise he couldn't have forced himself to sleep there at night.

Except to pick up Hercules, since she'd left he hadn't been back to the Circle C, but no one in the family found that unusual. Not with the self-imposed schedule he was keeping to.

He didn't wait for the tub to fill completely before he climbed in, groaning with the feel of the warm water on his tired body. He'd had to knock a bathroom wall out to install the thing, but it had been worth it.

He still toyed with the idea of building another home on the property. This house had been built in the twenties. The plumbing and wiring had been updated a couple of times, but there was a lot that needed to be done for real comfort. He might get around to building another place one of these days...or months...or years. Maybe, someday, when he was ready to look ahead at life rather than delving back into his past with a series of "what if's."

He'd been in the tub only a few minutes when the phone rang. Damn. He listened to it for a moment, debating whether to climb out and go answer it. Now he understood why his dad had a phone in every bathroom. Tony used to tease him about being decadent, but it would certainly make life a little easier.

He halfheartedly stirred, considering the need to

answer, but then the phone stopped ringing. He relaxed back in the water. If it was important, they'd call back.

He didn't get many phone calls. He talked to his folks every week, but generally he called them. The steamy moisture began to work on his aching muscles. He leaned back in the tub and closed his eyes, letting his mind drift.

The ringing phone awakened him. Startled by the noisy intrusion, he flung himself out of the tub, splashing water onto the floor, and dashed to the phone before whoever was calling could hang up. He glanced at the clock, startled to see that he must have been asleep for almost an hour. Damn thing to do. He could have drowned.

He grabbed the phone and barked, "H'lo!"

"Tony?"

Dripping wet and without a towel, Tony sank down on the side of the bed, trying to draw some air into his lungs. The sound of Christina's voice had knocked all the wind out of him.

"Christina?" he asked, thinking he must be wrong.

"Did I call at a bad time?"

He glanced down at the rivulets of water trickling down his body. "Not really," he said, feeling himself start to smile like a fool. God, it was good to hear her voice! With a chuckle he said, "I was in the tub when the phone rang." A thought crossed his mind. "Is this the first time you've called?"

She hesitated before answering. "No. I called about an hour ago. I thought I'd try again. If you didn't answer this time, I'd know you'd gone somewhere for the evening.''

''No, I'd just gotten into the tub and decided to ignore the phone. Then I ended up falling asleep. If you hadn't called, I might have spent the night in there!''

There was a long pause. Tony tried to think of something to say, but he was afraid of saying the wrong thing. So he remained silent, waiting to see why she had called.

Finally, Christina asked, ''How have you been?''

He took a deep breath, concentrating on refilling his lungs before he attempted to answer. In a wry voice, he replied, ''You want the truth or shall I be polite?''

''I always want the truth from you, Tony,'' she replied softly.

''You always get it.'' His mind was whirling with a jumble of feelings. There was so much he wanted to say, so much he was afraid to say. She wanted the truth. ''Okay.'' He swallowed hard. ''For whatever it's worth, I've been missing you like hell.'' He felt better just having said it out loud. With a little more confidence, he added, ''There are times when I feel like all my insides have been ripped out and I'm dragging myself around half-dead.'' Was that honest enough for her? He brightened his voice very deliberately. ''So. How have *you* been?''

''Oh, Tony,'' she whispered, her own voice breaking.

''Hey. I'm not trying to get sympathy.... Well, maybe a little. So tell me how you're doing. Do you like where you are...your job and apartment and everything?"

"I don't know who I'm most frustrated with at the moment, Minerva or your uncle Cody."

"Cody? What's he got to do with your life these days?"

"One thing he probably didn't know when he was playing his little joke was that a mynah bird mimics the voice as well as the saying. I recognized him immediately."

"Uh oh. I remember Cody mentioning something about teaching Minerva new phrases. What does she say?"

"A truly revolting singsong rendition, of 'Tony's in love with Christina, Tony's in love with Christina,' just like a little boy razzing another on the school grounds."

"I'm surprised it wasn't worse."

"It gets worse. There's also a very piercing, drawn-out wolf whistle and a comment about a pair of legs. Also a social comment about the color of my toenails...."

"You see what happens? The Callaways can easily corrupt the purest mind."

There was another long pause before she said, "I miss you, too, Tony."

He couldn't wipe the grin off his face. "I can't say I'm sorry to hear that."

"It's been so strange. I thought this move would be like all my other ones. I assumed that once I got settled and established a routine, my life would be like it has always been in the past. This time it's different. I keep thinking about you...and Hercules...and Texas...and wondering what's going on at the ranches. I think what I've been feeling is homesickness, or something similar. Isn't that ridiculous?"

"Not at all. I told you—we're your family now."

He heard a faint sound, as though she might be crying. He hated to think she was upset and all alone.

"Christina?"

"Yes?"

"How would you feel about my coming out to visit you?"

"Tony? Are you serious? Aren't you too busy to—"

He immediately dismissed the tight schedule he'd been keeping in order to get the stock moved to his ranch and said, "I could spare a couple of days. That is, if you wouldn't mind my coming out."

She laughed, but her voice trembled slightly. "I'd like very much to have you visit."

"Good! I mean, that's better than good. I'll call Dad and make arrangements to fly out. Is there anything I can bring?"

"I'd love to see Hercules, but the flight would scare him to death."

"Well, maybe you'll have to come to the ranch sometime to visit him."

There was another long pause before she said, "I'd like that, Tony. Very much."

Eleven

Tony hung up the phone and realized his jaw hurt from the wide smile that had been on his face since he'd discovered who was calling. He went back to the bathroom, grabbed a towel and finished drying himself off.

When he returned to the bedroom, he nudged Hercules with his foot. "Did you hear that, you lazy, good-for-nothing hound? She's misses us both. With your looks and my charm, we're going to coax her around to our way of thinking, just see if we don't."

Hercules lifted his head, sleepily blinked at Tony a couple of times, then sighed and returned to his exhausted slumber. He hid his excitement well.

Tony picked up the phone and called his dad to share the news and make plans to fly to the Pacific Northwest.

* * *

He recognized her by her untidy mop of reddish corkscrew curls. He'd caught a ride to the main terminal from the hangar where the plane would be waiting for his return flight. The crowded lobby didn't distract him in the least. He saw her right away.

"Christina?"

She whirled around at the sound of his voice. "Tony! There you are! I should have met you at the hangar, you know. There was no reason to have you come all this way just to—"

"It s good to see you," he said, interrupting her nervous chatter.

She burst out laughing and launched herself into his arms. He clutched her to him, silently vowing not to ever let her go so far from him again.

"Oh, Tony!" She pulled back and looked up at him, her hands cupping his jaws. "You've lost weight," she said accusingly.

"Probably." Who cared? He dipped his head and found her mouth. Oh, yes. This was the woman who had haunted him in memories and in dreams. His body responded as enthusiastically as his heart.

She pulled away from him. "Uh, Tony..." Her cheeks were flushed.

"Yeah, I know. You do seem to have that kind of an effect on me."

She glanced around at the milling people, most of whom were too busy with their own business to notice anyone else. "Are you ready to go home?"

His mouth twitched. "You could say that."

Her blush deepened and he laughed. The last few

weeks were forgotten in the joy of being with her again. "C'mon and show me this new van you're driving these days." He wrapped his arm around her shoulders and they headed toward the parking area.

"Did you find a buyer for my old one?"

"Nope. Been driving it myself. Hercules is more comfortable in it."

"You take him with you?"

He brushed a kiss along her cheek. "Sure. He likes to go into town. He's got a regular following, you know. He's become the star of the county."

When they reached the new silver van, she handed him the keys. "I don't live far from here. I'm in northeast Portland."

Tony concentrated on following her directions. They got on the freeway and headed south and eventually took one of the exits east. She guided him to the apartment complex and her parking space, then took his hand and led him up the stairs.

He followed her into the apartment and stopped. The room was bright with color—yellows and greens, splashes of orange and gold—so that he felt he was on some South Seas island with all its tropical lushness.

White wicker furniture abounded, as did a multitude of plants. A familiar voice erupted from the bay window.

"'Praise the Lord!'"

"Well, hello, Minerva. It's good to see you, too."

A blur of yellow fur came flying across the floor and wrapped itself around his ankles. Tony knelt on one knee and scooped up the cat. "I'd swear that you recognize me," he said in amazement.

"Of course he recognizes you. He's very intelligent. I think he's missed you and Hercules."

Tony stood and walked over to one of the chairs. He sat down with the cat still in his arms. "I don't think my ego could handle discovering which of us you and Prometheus missed the most. I'll just be grateful I'm included."

"Are you hungry? I have something ready to pop into the oven."

"Sounds good. My appetite seems to be returning." He eyed her in her yellow ruffled blouse and gray slacks. "All of them," he muttered, still a little uncomfortable from his earlier reaction to her. "You're looking good, honey." What an understatement.

She walked over to the small kitchen area off the living room. "You look exhausted. You've been working too hard, haven't you?"

He shrugged and allowed Prometheus to stretch out along the length of his thigh. "Just trying to beat the bad weather."

After placing something in the oven and tossing a previously prepared salad, Christina brought him a glass of iced tea. "I'm surprised that you'd take any time off," she said, handing him the drink.

He took it, wrapping his fingers around hers so that she couldn't move away from him. "Seeing you was more important."

She sat down beside him. He released her hand so that he could drape his arm around her. He needed to touch her. He would always need to touch her; he'd learned that lesson very well these past few weeks.

"One of the things I need to do up front," she said, nervously twisting her fingers, "is to apologize for the way I behaved that last night at Cody's place."

"What do you mean?"

"The way I acted when you asked me to marry you. I didn't mean to be so insulting, as though being a Callaway was something bad. It's just that the Callaways are out of my league."

"We're just like anybody else, you know."

"Not really. Although, since I had time to think about everything, I realized that you yourself aren't wealthy. I mean, you went to the bank for a loan, just like most of us have to do. I was being silly, objecting to something over which you have no control. My only excuse was that I was so shocked you asked me to marry you that I wasn't thinking clearly. The whole idea really frightened me."

"So I gathered," he drawled.

"I think it was really good for me to move here. It gave me a chance to look at my life...and what I want from it."

He reached over, took one of her hands and placed it on his thigh. "There. I thought I'd give you something to do with your hand."

Hesitantly, she smoothed her fingers over the taut denim fabric that clung to his leg.

"I guess what I'm trying to say is..."

Tony tensed. He knew what he hoped she was trying to say. He was afraid to second-guess her. "Yes?"

She buried her head in his shoulder. "Oh, Tony. I love you so much it frightens me. I don't know what to do. I don't know how to be a wife. I've never thought I would want to be married. Once I left Texas, I tried to put the idea out of my head...but I couldn't."

He slipped Prometheus off his leg and gathered Christina onto his lap. She curled against him like a frightened child. He held her tightly, silently conveying that she was safe with him, there was no reason to be afraid.

"I, uh, know what you mean," he said after a few minutes. "I never figured on getting married myself. You think you don't know anything about being a wife? Well, look at me. I'm certainly not husband material, you know."

She raised her head until she could meet his gaze. "I think you could do anything you set your mind to."

"Funny. That's how I've always felt about you."

She gave him a kiss that he felt was reward enough for the emptiness of the last few weeks. When one kiss led to another, then one more, Tony felt his control slipping away.

He stood, still holding her, then placed her on the chair and walked across the room. He peered out the window, concentrated on his multiplication tables and recited the names of the presidents until his body calmed down enough for him to face her once more.

"Christina, I need to know something."

She watched him with a puzzled look on her face. "All right."

"Are you pregnant?"

Whatever she was expecting him to ask, that certainly wasn't it. She looked jolted and he mentally cursed his blunt approach. When she didn't respond immediately, he said, "It doesn't matter if you are, you know. I mean, I want to marry you. You know that. A baby would be a bonus."

"Is that why you think I called you?"

He shrugged. "I hadn't given it much thought. From the time you phoned and said you missed me, all I've been able to think about was the possibility that you'd changed your mind about marrying me."

She sighed. "The answer to your question is, I don't know."

He crossed the room in a few strides and knelt beside her chair. "You mean there's a possibility you could be?"

She wouldn't meet his eyes. "I bought one of those home pregnancy tests a week ago, just to rule out the possibility. I haven't used it yet."

"Why not?"

"Because I'm not ready to know, one way or the other. My life seems so out of control already. Each day I kept hoping that I would... Then each evening I'd think about taking the test, but—"

He scooped her out of the chair and swung her around in a tight circle, laughing. "I'm glad you waited! I'm also glad I'm here. Christina, don't you understand? You aren't alone anymore. You've got me in your life, whether you like it or not. Plus, you've got the entire Callaway clan considering you as one of the family. If I could take away your lonely childhood, I would. The next best thing I can do is to provide you with a home and loved ones, and hopefully a family of our own."

She had slipped her arms around his neck when he'd grabbed her. Now she studied him from a few inches away. "You really wouldn't care, would you? I mean, if I happened to be pregnant."

The grin he gave her was definitely wicked. "If you aren't at the moment and I have any say in the matter, you will be shortly!"

"You really want to marry me, don't you?" she said with wonder in her voice.

"I believe I've pointed that out to you once or twice. Yeah. I want to marry you."

The oven buzzer went off, making them both jump.

Tony reluctantly allowed Christina to leave him long enough to turn off the oven. As soon as she turned around, he said, "For some reason, I'm not as hungry as I was awhile ago. I'd much prefer to rest for a while."

"Rest?" She eyed him doubtfully.

He nodded, full of innocence. "Before we rest, though, how about let's take that little test and see if we're going to be parents right away, okay?"

"Oh, Tony, I'm not sure that—"

"Don't worry. I'm sure enough for both of us. Fate wouldn't be so unkind as to have you walk into my life, let me fall in love with you, then have you walk away. I hope you are pregnant. I want you to learn to depend on me, to trust me, to let me love you."

She grinned and hugged him. "You Texans sure know how to woo a gal, I must say."

Then she took his hand and led him down the hallway to her bedroom.

Epilogue

Tony's back was sore from all the hard slaps he'd received recently from Cole, Cameron and Cody, but it didn't matter. All he could do was stand there grinning like a fool and loving every minute of it.

"Well, Grandpa," Cody said to Cole. "How's it feel to have a strapping eight pounder for a grandson?"

Cole angled the cigar between his teeth to point to the ceiling and smiled around it. "Nothing like it, bro. Nothing like it."

The four men were seated in Cole's den at his Austin home. They'd just left the hospital, after making certain that mother and son were resting comfortably for the night.

Tony was still feeling the strain of long hours in the labor and delivery rooms with Christina, entertaining her, coaching her, wiping the tears and perspiration away, promising never to do anything like this to her again and, finally, witnessing the arrival of his red-faced and angry young son.

He wouldn't have missed a second of it for the world.

His mother, Cameron's wife, Janine, and Carina had driven to San Antonio to check on their children, who had been left with Janine's housekeeper for the day. Tony had a hunch the woman would never be the same after that tribe got through with her.

Now he had a son to join in the confusion.

"I wonder when he's going to wipe that fool grin off his face?" Cameron asked no one in particular.

"Aw, leave him alone," Cole said with a suspiciously similar grin. "He deserves to gloat for a little while."

"It's funny how we take so much credit for something that we had so little to do with," Cody said, taking a puff on his cigar and blowing smoke rings.

"Our part may not take long, but it's a crucial part of the process," Tony pointed out.

"Not take long?" Cody repeated in a drawl. "Hell, Son. We're going to have to teach you a few things."

"He seems to have gotten the hang of things fine without your help," Cam said with a smile.

"You did fine, Son. Just fine."

"Thanks."

Tony rested his head on the back of his chair and closed his eyes. Lordy, he was tired. He hadn't been getting much sleep lately. Christina had been so uncomfortable these past few weeks. He'd gotten in the habit of sitting up with her, massaging her back or reading to her—whatever it took to get her mind off her condition.

She'd gotten upset when she could no longer see her feet, so he'd made quite a production one evening of placing her on the bed and carefully painting each of her toenails a different color so she would know her rainbow was still there.

The last months had been hectic, to say the least. He'd convinced Christina to fly back to Texas with him. When she'd called to explain to her boss, he'd been understanding. Tony found out later that Cole had already lined up another bookkeeper to take Christina's place in the event she decided to return to Texas.

Tony had hired movers to come in and pack everything for her, so that they were able to fly back right after she gathered some personal belongings together.

When they got home, Allison had been brimming with ideas for a quiet family wedding. Christina seemed relieved not to be expected to come up with plans. Allison had insisted that Christina stay in Austin until the big day, so Tony had returned to the ranch alone. However, he'd insisted on getting married almost immediately, despite all the plans his mother was suggesting. He smiled at the memory. He'd gotten his way, because Christina was eager to return to the ranch. Allison had laughingly agreed to having the wedding within a week.

The toughest part for him took place the morning

after they returned to the ranch, after a short honeymoon on the Texas coast.

They were finishing breakfast. Tony took a sip of his coffee before he said, "I've been thinking about building another home here on the ranch."

"But why?" Christina looked around the kitchen. "What's wrong with this place?"

"Well, it's a little small for a family, don't you think? Having you decorate the kitchen made me realize how shabby the rest of the house has become. To be honest, I never paid much attention to the place. It was just somewhere to hang my hat and sleep. But now—now I want a place that you've helped to plan."

She eyed him uncertainly. "But, Tony, with a baby on the way, won't we have to be more careful with money? I won't be able to go back to work right away. With your loan at the bank and wanting to prove you can make the place work, maybe we should wait on building for a few years."

He reached for her hand, needing to touch her, praying that he would know how to explain what needed to be said.

"I know what you said about the Callaways—how you felt the income generated by the family businesses puts us in a different league. But that isn't true, not really. I mean, I will always want to work, Christina. That's part of who I am. The thing is, you need to know that I don't have to work. In fact, I ended up not taking that loan after all."

"I don't understand."

"Well, it seems that my dad, in all his wisdom, set

aside my share of the company profits for several years without telling me. I can understand your distrust of wealth, because I felt that way myself for a long time. The thing that helped me to understand Dad's point of view was when I realized I didn't have to allow the money to come between me and the people I love. Money is a by-product, not the goal in life.''

''It is to some people.''

''But not to us, to you and me. Or to my family, for that matter. It's just there.''

''So what you're saying is you have the money to build a house if you want.''

''If *we* want. Any decisions will be made by both of us. I mean that. Whatever I have is yours. If you want to work once the baby's born, then we can make arrangements to have someone stay with him or her.''

''Oh, no! I don't want someone else raising my baby, not if it isn't necessary.''

''Then you can stay home and care for our child, and any others we might be fortunate enough to have.''

''You really want to build a new place?''

He nodded. ''I have some ideas that I'd like to show you. If we start building right away, we should have the place ready by the time the baby gets here.''

Building the house had kept them busy. The completion date had become a race with the stork. However, they'd made it. He would be taking his wife and son to their new home.

Tony vaguely heard his dad and uncles joking with each other, swapping tales about their experiences as fathers. Their voices were fading away and he knew he was almost asleep, but it didn't matter.

Letting Christina walk out of his life had been the hardest thing he'd ever faced, but his dad had been right. He'd had to respect her need to look at her life and make the best choices for herself. However, he hoped he never had to go through such a traumatic experience again. He could only thank God that Christina had wanted to marry him.

The baby was a bonus to help persuade her.

They brought the baby to her early in the morning. The doctor had suggested she attempt to nurse him. Now she was experiencing the tingling sensation of an eager little mouth tugging at her breast.

"Your milk won't come in for another day or so," the nurse who'd brought him explained. "But he'll still be getting nourishment from you."

Christina studied the tiny infant with awe. His hair was thick and dark, but she'd been told the color could change. His eyes were also dark and subject to change. He looked so much like Tony. Her heart melted every time she saw the resemblance.

Her son. She still had trouble at times believing that she, Christina O'Reilly Callaway, was a mother and a wife. She'd been too afraid of disappointment to dream of a future like this one. She'd been content with the life she'd made for herself without help from others. However, the Callaways had shown her what a little help and a lot of love could do to make her life complete.

She could hardly wait to get back to the ranch.

They'd moved into the new house last week. She woke up each morning with a sense of surprise at her good fortune.

The rooms were open and airy, with lots of light coming in from the wide windows and skylights. The house sat on a knoll overlooking the rest of the ranch. It was farther from the highway than the original house, so that the noise from the stock pens didn't disturb them.

She glanced down and saw that the baby had fallen asleep. She lifted him to her shoulder as the nurse had shown her and gently rubbed his little back. He smelled so sweet. She understood much more about love and its many aspects now than she had a year ago. Her heart had stretched and expanded to encompass all these new feelings that she'd never known existed.

The nurse had returned the baby to the nursery when there was a soft tap on her open door. She glanced around and saw Cole Callaway standing there, hat in hand, wearing a huge grin. In his other hand was a giant flower arrangement, which he set down on the table beside the bed.

"I could have had these delivered," he said softly, as he leaned over and kissed her cheek, "but I wanted to have the chance to see you and let you know how proud I am of you. You've shown real grit…and courage. I couldn't love you more if you were my own daughter."

She squeezed his hand and blinked away the tears his words evoked. "That means a lot to me. Tony has always told me that the Callaways are my family. I thought I understood what he meant, but having a family means more to me with every day that passes.''

''I peeked in on Jason Cole just now,'' he said, obviously pleased with his namesake. ''He's sacked out, dead to the world.'' His eyes misted. ''Tony's so proud of him. I have to laugh at his strutting.''

''I've never gotten the chance to thank you for all your help when I was so confused about everything,'' she said. ''Not only the financial part, which was considerable, but your emotional support, as well. You and Allison. You never made me feel that you judged me in any way. That meant so much to me at a time when my whole life was up in the air.''

''I knew you'd come around sooner or later. You're a smart woman. It was easy for me to see that you were in love with my son, even if you weren't as certain. It's a little easier to understand when you're watching from a distance. It gives a person some perspective.''

''Hey! What is this, sneaking in to see my woman when my back's turned?''

Cole straightened and looked over at his son. ''You were as sound asleep when I peeked in on you this morning as that son of yours is right now. A real family resemblance there. So I decided to sneak away early and congratulate Christina on what a fine job she did.''

Tony leaned over and kissed his wife. ''I agree,'' he whispered, pushing a wisp of hair away from her face. He didn't notice when Cole left the room.

"Can you believe this?" he said. "You and me, parents? It boggles the mind."

"We may have started off in life with not much in the way of families, but we've certainly made up for it since, wouldn't you say?"

The kiss he gave her was all the answer she needed.

* * * * *

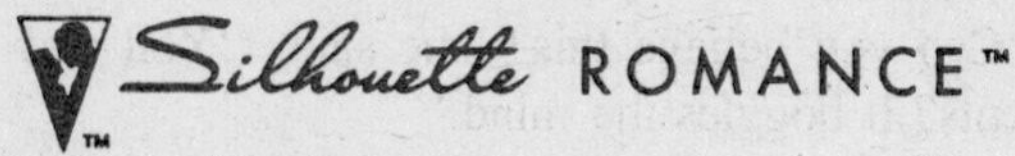

What's a single dad to do when he needs a wife by next Thursday?

Who's a confirmed bachelor to call when he finds a baby on his doorstep?

How does a plain Jane in love with her gorgeous boss get him to notice her?

From classic love stories to romantic comedies to emotional heart tuggers, **Silhouette Romance** offers six irresistible novels every month by some of your favorite authors! Such as...beloved bestsellers **Diana Palmer, Annette Broadrick, Suzanne Carey, Elizabeth August** and **Marie Ferrarella,** to name just a few—and some sure to become favorites!

Fabulous Fathers...Bundles of Joy...Miniseries... Months of blushing brides and convenient weddings... Holiday celebrations... You'll find all this and much more in **Silhouette Romance**—always emotional, always enjoyable, always about love!